"Fresh Off the Boat"

Diary of a F-O-B

Yukti Singh

ISBN-10: 146991137X
ISBN-13: 978-1469911373

DEDICATION

To My "Bittu"

&

To My Sonia and Maya……..

With Love.

Thanks to Wendy C.

Diary of a F-O-B

Yukti Singh

DISCLAIMER

This book is a work of fiction. Names, characters, places, and incidents either are products of the author's imagination or are used fictitiously. Any resemblance to actual events, locales or persons, living or dead, is entirely coincidental.

Definition of words in this Novel

- Kurta: long loose garment like a shirt without a collar worn by women
- Saree: several yards of light material that is draped around the body
- Salwar Kameez: a long tunic worn over a pair of baggy trousers
- Chaat: plate of savory snacks
- Idli and Dosa: Common South Indian food made with rice
- Bhajan: any type of Indian devotional song
- Yaar: Slang for good friend
- Thujhe dekha tho yeah jaana sunum: famous Hindi movie romantic song
- Subji: cooked vegetable dish
- Paapu, bhohot sona hai: he is gorgeous
- Mera naam Rich hai: my name is Rich
- Bhohot acha laga apse milke: nice to meet you
- DDLJ: famous Hindi movie
- Desi: slang for Indian
- Channa: chick peas
- Bunvas: exile
- Dada Khondke: Actor, producer whose plays and lyrics were often full of double entendres
- Andheri raat mein, diya tere haath mein: read as 'In the dark of the night, there is a lamp in your hand' or 'In the dark of the night, I put my junk on your hand'
- Diya: oil lamp
- Madhuri Dixit: famous Bollywood actress
- Chanay Ke Khet mein: sexy dance number in Hindi movie
- Dimple Kapadia: famous Bollywood actress
- Shiva Linga: representation of Lord Shiva
- Duniya mein hum aye hai: sad Hindi movie song representing despair
- Bhagat Singh: Indian freedom fighter
- Swades: Hindi movie
- SRK: famous Bollywood actor Shahrukh Khan

1

Looking through the clouds from so many miles above ground, I felt free. Free to be myself, to explore the entire world that awaited me and to finally be the chosen one. It was a moment I had been waiting for and yet there was also some sadness in my journey to another world. I had after all left behind my youth, my home, and family and was venturing into the unknown. The more I wanted to reach my destination, the more I was getting further from my past.

British Airlines Flight 4873 to Chicago O'Hare International Airport was a long seventeen hour flight from Lusaka, Zambia. Long enough to send many rushing for their throw up bag, but for some reason, I loved to travel on airplanes. I could eat more, sleep more and watch movies non-stop without feeling anything. Most of the people around me looked like they were in a torture chamber, their faces pale, unable to even look at their meals and constantly drinking ginger ale to keep everything down. I looked over and a lady sitting next to me had not touched anything from her meal. It was really delicious salad, cheesecake and the rice with chicken curry was to die for. I wondered if it would be rude to ask her for her tray. But since she wasn't going to eat anything, it would be a waste to let it go. So, after I had engulfed my entire meal, I mustered the courage to ask her.

'Excuse me, hello?,' I politely asked, at this point her pale face, dried lips and yellow eyes made an attempt to look at me but the motion of turning her head must have started something. The African woman with the puffy hair went rushing for her puke bag and for the next two minutes made every follicle of hair on my body stand at full attention. At that point, I lost my appetite to eat anything else. For the remainder of the flight, I figured I shouldn't disturb the lady and let her be in peace.

After our dinner and drinks, the lights were dimmed and I became comfortable in my chair to finally rest my eyes. It was going to be long journey and I needed the rest. I wanted to think of what tomorrow would bring, but had to start with what yesterday had been for me. I had lived in Zambia all my life. Even though I was born in Delhi, my life had been in Zambia. I had lived the perfect life; there were servants who did the cleaning, cooking and pretty much everything. It was a really comfortable life and I was going to miss it.

Drifting away into my past, I remembered all my friends, Preety, Sneha and Arjun, my buddies from school who had already left Zambia for Universities in the US. My home was in a city called Lusaka, the capital of Zambia where most of the economy was based on the Copper Mines and my father was an Exports Manager. I always went to the public schools in Lusaka from Preschool, to Primary then to Secondary school. Being of a lighter complexion compared to the natives, I got a lot of attention in school. In most of the schools I attended, there would be perhaps four Indian students in the entire school of four hundred. Everyone would know who you were and on day one of school you would have perpetual admirers. Being so different had its advantages and disadvantages. You could get away with a lot of things like breaking recess rules, getting help with homework from seniors, always being offered a chair during school events just for smiling at someone and giving him a little attention. While in tenth grade, the twelfth grade students were made Prefects and were given the task of monitoring the lower grades. This setup was perfect. The Prefects were older and some of the guys with their dark skin and strong shoulders made afternoon homework labs extremely attractive. I really enjoyed afternoon sessions with the Prefects who always ventured towards me and asked if I needed any help with my homework. There was Ian, a tall, dark and really handsome guy who had very cute curly hair; I referred to him as Chocolate Chip to my friends. He was muscular, which it seemed most of the African people usually were, was smart and was a top student in the twelfth grade. Being a Prefect, he had a different uniform from the rest of the school. While we all had to wear coffee brown pants or skirts with white shirts and brown tie, all Prefects wore black uniforms with white shirts. He looked like a darker Tom Cruise minus the goofy attitude. I loved it when he would walk along the aisles and eventually bend down to my table, look into my eyes and ask me;

' Rushmi,' you need any help?' Looking into his deep black eyes and smooth lips, his top button undone and loose tie stirred very dirty thoughts in me. I'd imagine myself being in his arms and while sitting in his lap, we would do calculus all day. Okay, so my dreams were also focused on studying, big deal!

'I'm good, but if I need any help I'll let you know, thanks,' I would smile and try to avoid eye contact so that he wouldn't notice my mouth salivating like a puppy. God! I wanted him. Ian was so adorable and he knew I liked him too. Brenda and Mary were my classmates who had told me that Ian's friends Muzambe and Brian had told them that Ian liked me too. I know, it's a lot of he said, she said but life in school is a lot of that. Hearing from others that Ian was interested in me, a tenth grader, was flattering, especially because he was so mature and smart and a Prefect. I don't know, I have this thing about men in power.

In any case, it was so delicious to get attention without even trying. But then there were cons of all this attention too. If everything was noticed then EVERY thing got noticed. Now, I am not a biased person but there are facts that you cannot get away from, like no matter how much you control your diet, a desi girl will always be fatter than the average Zambian. I was not overweight at all but for some reason, was the chubbiest in school. It seemed like I was more developed, which just added to the attention I received. Then there was the athletics part. For some reason, black people are just born runners with great athletic skills. The brown folks, as we were referred to, just were never the fit type. I really hated PE and with all the running and jogging I did, it was a given fact that I was going to be the last one at the finish line. During PE, which included classes from tenth through twelfth grade, the usual bet was how much after the last runner would I take to finish the run.

The worst was fifteen minutes and over the years I had that down to five minutes. Usually the entire week of admiration and attention from the hottest guys on campus, ego boosting and attitude went down the hell hole when we had PE on Fridays. The weekend was used to recoup from complete and utter humiliation. I would start the race by pacing myself, telling myself to breathe and not rush into it, telling myself "just keep pace with the worst runner" and counting step after step knowing that three miles would be over in almost forty minutes. But then, I would watch the faces of those perfect guys looking at me, smiling as they watched my body parts swing up and down, my flushed face turn red and panting furiously like I had run ten miles. They then turn to each other, exchange smiles, then laugh out loud. Suddenly, I was no longer the coolest girl in school, more like the only fat ass who if in the wild would have been attacked by the lions and eaten away. Yeah, for some reason, National Geographic was a common thing to watch on Saturdays and whenever I saw a buffalo eaten by wild animals, it reminded me of my humiliation. I could feel the buffalo's pain. The torturous moments were when out of breath, sweating, I would look around to see all the girls at the finish line and I was the only one still running, by now dragging, hoping for this nightmare to be over. The crowd would get up on their feet and I would find it hard to breathe, then I would look around myself and find myself alone while the rest of the group was ahead. That's when the timer would go off and now the game was to see after how many minutes after the last runner would I reach the finish line.

I hated Fridays. The humiliation felt like running in a derby where all the others were horses and I was a buffalo. Did I mention, I hated Fridays. But to top it all, I always ended the race by puking my face off, not a pleasant site for everyone to see. I really hated Fridays and thanked God for the weekend to set in so I could wash the shame off, and start Monday as the coolest girl in school again.

2

I guess, over time, I had come to take the humiliation every Friday until a new student started at Lusaka Secondary School. Bittu was also in the tenth grade, transferred from India. His father had received a year's assignment and this was his first school in Zambia. Maybe I should have been more empathetic towards him but he rubbed me the wrong way. I actually didn't want to be associated with him but instantly the entire school thought we ought to date because birds of a feather should whatever…

Bittu was a chubby kid, with enough oil in his head to lubricate a jet engine, wore pants one size too small for him and I think to save money, his father loaned him his tie which was not the exact brown color of our school. Guess he thought no one would notice – we did.

That's one thing about us brownies I never get. We spend like hell on food and education and our homes, but never on looking good. Pretty much every aunty would have an awakening moment in a foreign land where she would want to change her appearance and look more modern. But, instead of spending some money on new clothes, she would reach for her husband's pants and wear it with a Kurta*, tie her oily hair in a bun and wear lipstick that made her look like she just drank her husband's blood. You could almost always see which aunty was going through an identity crisis. They would all come from India in their Sarees* and Salwar Kameez* but after months of living in Lusaka felt like a change was needed to fit in. That's when the transformation would begin and eventually you could spot these five dollar hookers walking around in tight pants that killed their circulation from the waist down. They would be wearing Indian shiny Kurtas and that red lipstick with the ugliest slippers to complete the ensemble. I think if there were fashion police in Zambia, they would have all committed suicide.

But back to Bittu. He was a simple lad with just awkward clothes and glasses that for some reason always sat on the tip of his nose and the lens would reflect his nose pores making them look even larger. I guess it was the oiliness that shined his nose even more and eventually all you saw was a large nose with huge pores. When Bittu entered the classroom the first day, he saw me in the front row and apparently he thought, since we both are Indians, we ought to sit together. He walked in and sat right next to me. Oh my God, I could smell his entire kitchen on his clothes, his book bag even had turmeric stains and when he smiled at me I wanted to take his book bag and smack him with it. I heard others whispering and making sounds to imply that my prince charming had arrived or maybe he and I would start something together. I couldn't wait to run away. I actually wanted to run those three miles right at that moment. I wanted to make sure he stayed away from me. Don't look at me! Don't talk to me! Don't even think about it, was all I was trying to project until….

'Hi, I'm Bittu,' he smiled to show his full set of teeth. How dare he talk to me! What the hell man! Read my face and don't you dare, I looked at him.

'Hello, I'm Rushmi.' I went back to my books and hoped the earth would open up and swallow Bittu entirely. But class went on and he started to befriend me as though it was a given that being Indians, we would automatically become friends. I hated that assumption, especially now that everyone gave me the look like - look at your goofy boyfriend or look at these Indians, this is as good as it gets or something. Why? Why the hell couldn't a really stunning desi guy been here. All week Bittu walked close to me, tried to make conversation with me, but I was able to slide by without having to talk to him.

Then came Friday. All week I had tried to avoid Bittu darling, which he obviously never picked up on and lingered around me the whole time. But today was going to be even more special than I had imagined. Coach Mugabe was conspiring to increase my misery just a little bit more; he arranged to have both girls and boys run together on the track. It was a five mile run- lucky me. Bittu darling was excited to run with me. Get the hell away from me Nosy! Was all I wanted to scream out, but I contained myself. I was going to run like hell away from Bittu. Let him be the last one this time. Off went the whistle and the running started. He was so chubby and no way could he beat me. Slowly the older students reached the end, then the remaining Zambees,' (nick name in retaliation to brownies), until there it was, two hippos dragging themselves on the track side by side. Oh my God! We were like two dying Walruses. I saw his stomach bouncing up and down then I noticed my jugs bouncing up and down. His face was flushed and almost suffocating without oxygen, his hands swinging side by side and my hands swinging side by side, his heavy legs dragging on the ground and my legs dragging on the ground. As I noticed the similarities, I became more and more horrified of looking at my mirror image. Oh my God, he was exactly like me! The exact mirror image of me! Everything I disliked in him was all bundled up in me too! No, this can't be! I'm nothing like him, never! This was extremely shocking and completely horrendous. While experiencing this traumatic reflection, I tripped and fell making the other Walrus fall on top of me and then, there were two Walruses rolling on the ground. His humongous, sweaty body rolled onto my body and every inch, every part of our skin made contact. I had an out of body experience. I couldn't hear anything, couldn't say anything, everything moved in slow motion and it felt like we were rolling for ten minutes. Unable to breathe from under this mountain, I felt his shoulders, flabby stomach, and huge thighs. I was cringing, with eyes closed, until finally we stopped. I thought I ought to give birth to a baby Walrus because that's usually how it happens on National Geographic.

My world had just ended and instead of an afterglow, I had more of a Tales from the Crypt glow. I think it was better for Bittu because he seemed to have smiled all the way home. I think everyone else was clapping and cheering for us but I couldn't remember a thing. Just like in a car accident, you can't recall all the horrifying details I too couldn't remember.

I didn't sleep that weekend. The image of him on top of me was traumatic. Each time I closed my eyes, and relived those moments, I'd awaken in a cold sweat. I finished an entire bucket of ice-cream, chaat* and got a pedicure, but nothing helped. I had to face the school no matter what. Now, I really wished the earth would open and really take Bittu away.

I watched the entire series of the A-team that weekend. Just something about watching death, shootings, and murders that made my pain a little less. I had watched the A-team so many times that I could recite the dialogues and my favorite was, 'I love it when a plan comes together.'

But again, I still had the weekend to look forward to and I took four showers scrubbing myself, but still could smell him around me. Our home was a three bedroom, single story with a large garden in the front yard. We also had Cathy, my sweetest stress reliever poodle. I knew I could just play with Cathy and try to keep the trauma away.

My mother never worked, kept herself busy with parties, cooking and taking care of the home. My father worked but had flexible hours so he would come home for lunch and return by five in the afternoon. Weekends were all socializing with other brownies. I guess it was our way of staying connected in a country away from our home land. Whenever an Indian family would move into our city, we all would know about them. Where they came from, who their ancestors were, what religion, what job, what education, how many kids and pretty much everything. If anyone had a stomach ache we would all hear about it, that's how connected all brownies were. But we had our own cliques too. There were the Gujjus. These people were usually in business; most owned grocery stores, gas stations, motels, factories, clothing outlets and everything in between. Then there were the Southies. This category was given to everyone who came from any part of South India. Even though South India had multiple groups, in Zambia, they were all labeled as one. These folks were known for Idli and Dosa*, being overly smart and very, very focused on education. Then there was us, North Indians. Honestly, not sure what we were known for other than eating, being on the heavy side and kind of in between. Neither were we business savvy nor did we focus on education, just focused on life and hard work. Needless to say, we labeled people a lot; it wasn't a bias but more of a culture of belonging. When you arrived in Zambia, these labels helped you to immediately belong to a certain group and that gave you access to families that you could relate with.

3

On this weekend, our socialization was with the Northies. My mother had planned a dinner party at our home and was going insane cooking everything that required large and multiple cans of cooking oil. I really hated cooking. I think it was because my father loved to eat and my mother loved to cook. I stayed out most of the morning playing with Cathy, wallowing in my own sorrow of being a mother Walrus and experiencing the blues of after birth. I was really not looking forward to tonight's party. If anyone were to find out, the word would spread to all my friends and then the earth would have to open and I would gladly jump in.

'Rushmi, get in here and cut the salad,' my mother screamed. She was a round woman, five feet nothing and easily weighed 200lbs. She was fair, with long black hair and despite the world revolution of being health conscious, believed that it was never the food that you had to control, just the exercise. So, in an attempt to be healthy, she would walk around our yard for three laps to lose weight but enjoyed samosas, soda, heaps of rice and veg's, then to top it all, ate fried desserts dipped in butter and glazed with sugar. Amazingly enough, every party contained a conversation of how none of the aunties were losing weight despite walking three to four laps a day.

With amazing scientific research, recent revelations and facts, everyone would wonder how ironic it was that no one was losing weight and blamed motherhood for their tight blouses. But then by the next weekend, someone else would be frying the next heart attack. Life is too short and Northies believed in living, laughing and eating "so why not enjoy". Tonight the clogging of arteries was to take place at my house and some of my friends were coming.

I decided to get out of my moping mood, dress up in my finest dress, a grey knee high dress with flowers, a darker shade of grey. It had a V-neck and belt that made my waist look small. I wore my high grey heels, pulled up my long black hair in a ponytail with a grey hair band. I was fair like mom, but had light brown eyes, my most attractive feature, wore light lipstick to complete my makeup to look natural. I didn't like too much make up, but today I tried eye shadow to feel different. I think I just wanted to avoid reminding myself that Bittu and I had anything in common. When I was done, I looked at myself and reassured myself,

'I am nothing like Bittu, I am cute, attractive and a sexy woman, I am confident and smart and pretty.' With that reaffirmation, I was ready. My friend Preety was a Gujju and her family owned a clothing store. She was also in the tenth grade and went to the public school on the other end of town. Then there was Sneha, a Northie who went to private school and had a little attitude about going to a rich school. Preety and I enjoyed putting her down. Then there was Arjun. He was in the twelfth grade and attended the same public school as Preety; he was gorgeous and made me so mad that Preety had him all to herself. He had shoulder length hair, was a Prefect and had fair complexion, smooth skin and deep black eyes that just took my breath away. He was also a player; Preety told me how he dated Zambees and actually had an attractive Zambian girlfriend. Guess, being attracted to Zambees was one thing but dating was totally another, and a big deal. Our parents just would and could not accept that relationship, so if anyone was dating a Zambee it was hidden. Then there were the younger kids, so many that they gave me a headache; they just ran around harassing Cathy, breaking everything around them and messing up my room. Why people have kids I will never understand.

During our parties, the men made their own circles, women on the other end, the kids in my room and all three groups did their own thing until food was served with a final game of Antakshari. Antakshari was a singing game in which each person had to sing a song that started with the last letter of the previous song. First of all, I think this game should be banned among older parents. There is something about watching your dad sing a love song that makes you hate that song for life. Then there are the aunties who while singing are imagining themselves as the heroine of that movie, which is fine if it's a Godly song like a Bhajan*, but when it's a song of two lovers in the rain, wet clothes, or the bedroom, you could see her blushing and her husband grinning knowing that this is what will get him some. It was such a gross feeling knowing what the uncles and aunties are thinking and they thought we didn't see it, but unfortunately for ALL of us, we could see the bouncing of orgasms in the room and thinking that we are the result of these Antakshari games was appalling.

So, the guests started arriving and some little ones started running around Cathy. Poor thing, she hid in my arms and the little rugrats kept pulling her tail. She was a white poodle, just the tip of her nose was black, making her the cutest dog in the world. I held on to her, freeing her from the little buggers. Preety arrived with her parents, Kokila Bhen married to Bhupinder Bhai; the Gujjus always referred to each other as Bhen and Bhai (brother and sister), which the Northies found hilarious but this joke had been made so many times I could care less. Preety wore a white Salwar Kameez with the whole gimmick; bangles, bindi and sandals. Yes, I was not dressed like her. Being different at these parties was the goal. I think being Indians, these parties were our way of being different within our community, so I had scored one point for dressing different today. Then Sneha and Arjun arrived around the same time. Arjun's parents were older and very sophisticated; both were teachers at the high school level, were very down to earth people; perfect in-laws for me. He, on the other hand, looked like Prince William who had come to take me away from this life and together we would rule Britain. If only I could have had him in my school. That would give me so much time with him.

'Hey,' he said and walked right past me leaving a trail of his cologne. He smelled of everything masculine. I felt like I could jump into his arms and look into those deep eyes but I returned to my senses and just inhaled a little of him. I was still at the front door greeting our guests when another car pulled up to the drive way and out came my prince charming, Bittu dear.

I heard someone laughing in an almost weeping manner, oh wait, it was me. I was laughing but in a crying manner as I saw him approaching my door. Good Lord, what is he doing here? I was just about to forget all about

Friday's ordeal and here he was in my house! His parents came out of the car and were talking to my father. His dad was tall, six foot something with a long face, strong jaw and a wide nose. When his mother came closer, she looked exactly like dad with just a long braid at the back. Wow, it was like they were twins, same build, same height and same face; extremely creepy. She was not at all feminine and right behind them was my man. No, no, no! I was screaming inside, that moment the future flashed in front of my eyes, having these Siamese twins as in-laws and I was married to my twin. It reminded me of the National Geographic episode where you see a family of elephants and you can't tell any of them apart; that's what our family would look like.

'Hello.' His voice snapped me out of my coma. As I stared at his family, his manly mother patted my head.

'You are in our Bittu's class right?' Her hands touch my cheek and I think I smiled or screamed, one of the two, but dad stepped in and said how marvelous it was to have another Indian student in my class. Dad almost arranged our marriage by saying that I would help Bittu with anything he needed. Really dad! Really! Should I teach him how to do bungee jumping and hope for the best? Barely able to speak, I just stood there, not realizing that Bittu had moved closer to me and now he was standing next to me. It was like we were getting our picture taken at our wedding reception.

Walking Bittu to my room where the others were waiting was a walk of shame. He would know more about me than I had ever wanted. He would know about my room, would sit on my bed, he now knew so much more about me and being the new Indian family in Zambia, my parents would hang out even more. It was official, instead of Prince William; I was ending up with Prince Nosy. The evening went by great. The whole time, Preety had a smirk on her face implying "I get Arjun and you get Bittu", I hated her. She and I slid away for a few minutes and she kept smiling without saying a word.

'What?' I said not indulging in her gloating.

'So, haven't heard about Bittu from you. What's up with that?' She was smiling, holding back her laughter.

'Preety, shut up!' I was losing it. He was in my house and God knows if he would tell anyone about our roll in the hay, especially to Arjun. I would kill him. After seeing his Wright Brothers' parents, I actually wanted to kill myself.

'He seems fresh off the boat yaar*, come on,' Preety was trying to comfort me but still making fun of me. Even though we were all friends, I never insulted anyone in front of others. To tell Preety how I really felt was off limits, it was a very small community and eventually Bittu would find out about any comments I made. So it was better to stay quiet. But the expression on my face could tell it all. She knew it and I too knew what we both were thinking. To just top it all off, she referred to Nosy as Jeeju (brother-in-law) at which point I tried to strangle her. As we were goofing around, me holding Preety's neck while she laughed like an insane woman, I noticed Bittu standing by the door smiling.

He had a silly grin on his face; he looked like he was in love. Gag me Lord! He was in love. Oh my God! I could just sense it, he would be thinking of me tonight while he visited his beloved Pamela. That one look and I wanted to pick up a broom and smack him over the head. Preety and I just stood there until he said,

'Are you okay?' Oh no! Don't you dare start talking about the roll in the hay story, I had to think fast! What could I do to distract him for this conversation? Stop speaking. Do something!

'Let's play Antakshari,' I said relatively loud. Preety and Bittu jumped up and surprisingly responded, "Okay" simultaneously. We all headed to the living room and with everyone sitting in a circle, we started singing. The game started off and some of the Aunties had already been mentally undressed by their husbands and sometimes by other men too. One of the Wright Brothers started singing and she sang a beautiful Bhajan, it was a beautiful prayer, she actually had a lovely voice. Maybe I could call her Mom someday. Then it was Bittu's turn to sing. Singing a vibrant hero song of meeting someone special for the first time;

'Thujhe dekha tho yeah jaana sunum,'* he sang with his eyes closed mimicking expressions of being Shahrukh Khan, his head swinging side to side; I knew what he was thinking. I felt like coming into his fantasy and smacking him with the leather jacket I knew he imagined himself in. Then after another few out of tune songs it was my turn. I had to sing something with the sound ra; I knew so many love songs but was looking for a motherly, sisterly or Bhajan song but nothing came to mind. So I passed and let the game move on without me. I lost the round and was relieved to be out of the game. I could step out and let Bittu make love to himself. The rest of the evening, everyone sang while I wrote my suicide note in my journal. After people started leaving, Bittu came around and said,

'Next time you and I can be on the same team because I know a lot of Hindi songs. By the way, I am sorry about yesterday, I hope you didn't get hurt.'

I smiled but was at a loss for words. I didn't know what to say. If I accepted his friendship, most certainly he and I would be connected by the hip at school. I couldn't be mean to him either since our parents would have more of these gatherings. So I just smiled and said 'Good Night.'

That night, I watched the entire series of Star Wars; I needed the Force to be with me. I could feel the urge to go to the dark side and needed Yoda to guide me. But the more I looked at Yoda for support; his round face reminded me of Bittu.

Monday morning came so fast and I thought a lot about the long burka; I could really use it that day. I had anticipated a lot of ragging from everyone at school. I expected Bittu to sit in my lap and I expected every other guy at school to run away from me.

Entering class, Bittu had a huge smile on his face, I guess Pamela had been nice to him, but I maintained my half plastic- half serious smile and went right into focusing on my work. Mary, who sat four rows away, passed a paper my way. She was an excellent artist and had actually painted the school mural, the paper made it my way with everyone seeing the picture. When it finally made it to Bittu he looked at it and passed it to me. There it was, Mary's work of art, one elephant humping another in the jungles of Africa. There was a lot of giggling sounds coming from the back at which point Bittu looked at me almost laughing. After he saw my expression, he stopped making eye contact. That's what made him sit a few rows behind me for the remainder of the year.

4

Four hours into the flight, I shifted in my seat trying to fight for more space from the African lady sitting next to me. She seemed like she had passed out, so I decided to curl up in a fetus position and return to memory lane. Bittu had avoided me or maybe I had avoided him, but we kept our distance and soon his presence became less of an issue for me. The only time we were paired together was during the Walrus races. After the tenth grade, Bittu and his Wright brothers had to return to India since his father's contract was over. I still remember our last meeting. They had come over for dinner and with very few words exchanged, especially because I didn't want to show him the party hats, champagne bottle or my happy dance. He had done most of the talking. He gave me his address in India and said to write to him. He said he would write to me too.

'I had a good time and mostly because of you' Bittu said while standing on the front steps of my house.

'Have a safe trip,' I happily wished him, turning my back to finally let him go.

'Please do write, because I will,' he kept talking until his father honked the car and finally Bittu was a thing of the past.

He did write a lot of emails to me, sent me birthday cards, but my responses were one liner of 'all is well,' 'hope you are well,' 'we are well' and 'take care.' After a few months of these exchanges, our conversations ended.

5

It was around the time when I was half way done with eleventh grade and my studies were really getting more serious. One more year and I would have to think about college. I was really busy most of the time studying and spending less time partying. I remember when my parents had taken me to a carnival just to get me out of the house. It was the national treasures of Zambia where you could find all sorts of natural amazing things in the nation. Booths setup with Copper ornaments, animal skins, drums and other musical instruments, jewelry made from animal teeth, animal hair and all sorts of touristy stuff. It was nice to get away from work and just to breathe fresh air, so I wondered into the Fish of Zambia. Large glass tanks filled with different size fish were on display. I really enjoyed watching the tiny fish, then the larger and then the largest fish. The last tank was five feet tall and had foggy water making it hard to see anything inside. I placed my face right into the glass and saw two very large fish looking right at me. I was startled at first and then actually liked what I was looking at. They were just two very large fish with their faces right by the tank. I don't know why but it felt like they were talking to me, so I did my 'oh you're so cute, sweetie pie thing,' and then I kissed the glass with my lips on one side and the fish lips on the other side.

Instantly, the fish flapped her fins so hard that she flew out of the tank and right on top of my head! This huge thing was fluttering right on top of my head, water running down my head. It hadn't even registered to me what had just happened and this gigantic fish was now on the ground flapping, dying for water. I just stood there in immense fear and nothing was registering. Then two men came quickly lifted the bugger and dropped her in the tank.

'Second time she had done that,' said one of the guys. What the hell just happened was all I could ask, I looked around for some comfort from the bystanders and turning around I saw people laughing quietly, guess the laughter was contagious because everyone was laughing out loud as I stood their drenched in fish filth; even the fish were laughing. I just walked out completely disturbed about this whole ordeal, never had I ever seen this on National Geographic. After fixing my hair and whipping off the fish puke I returned to my parents and just demanded to leave. But they were having such a great time we had to stay.

My mother kept asking why I smelled of fish. They even took me to a booth labeled snake woman. Apparently it was a head of a woman with the body of a snake. No way in hell I was entering that booth; when my parents returned they were so excited to have witnessed the miracle they were jumping in joy like kids having seen the mother of all snakes. Anyway, the day was over and I could move on with my life. Well, the next morning, right on the front page with the heading, Fish Fun at the Fair, was a picture of me with a large fish on my head. First my dad had read the article and then they both were laughing then, I read the entire article. They wrote the whole article in the form of a fairytale copying the princess and the frog story. The ending of the article read: When her Fish would turn into a handsome prince; nope not this year. It was unbelievable.

'I always wanted you to be famous,' my mother said, holding her laughter then they both burst out laughing. They were laughing so hard, my dad rolled on the ground and my mother had tears oozing out of her eyes at their daughter's shame. Horrible parents! I pulled the newspaper out of her hands and took it to my room. Oh my God! It was so humiliating. Needless to say, the phone calls started coming and everyone called in to congratulate us on me making the headlines. Well, after that lovely step into fame, I was known as the Fish Princess. Even at school, I heard kissing sounds as I walked by and so many boys made fish faces asking for a kiss. It was a nightmare.

6

I looked at my watch and still had twelve hours of flight time to reach Chicago. I made my seventh walk in the aisle to the restroom passing by others passed out on their seats. I noticed a Gujju girl in line to the bathroom and she totally reminded me of this girl who was in the eighth grade. She was very petite and being Gujju, was skinny and shy. She was a sweet little thing and being a non-Zambie, she stood out too. One week into school and she was called flat bottomed flask. A chemistry term meaning someone with no behind - so obviously they named me round bottom flask. Meena, a.k.a flat bottom flask was so naïve and had received so much attention early on that it became addictive and she fell for it.

She became pregnant before the end of the year and dropped out of school. Being from a traditional Gujju family, the rumors spread and everyone was talking to their kids about what was acceptable and what was completely out of the question. Weekend parties revolved around Meena and everyone looked so overly concerned for her while thanking their stars for it not being their child. But regardless of what others thought, I too felt like she had wasted her life so soon. Being a mother and with some other Zambee guy with no future in mind, wow! I just couldn't do that.

After dropping out, she stayed at her parents, and to her credit she kept the baby; giving birth to a black child and married the boy. It was tragic on one part, but I admired her parents for embracing their son-in-law and trying to make it work. Social gatherings were really hard for her and I too didn't know how to handle myself around her. Did you talk about it or did you pretend like everything was all well and good? I hated myself for not knowing what to do, but the social pressures were just too hard to deal with. I could not overcome her situation, not because she fell in love with a Zambee, but because she had made the decision to give up her dreams and education and take on the motherly role so soon. I totally couldn't imagine doing the same. I guess I learned something about myself; I wanted a future for myself.

7

Waiting in line for the restroom on the flight was just one way of stretching my legs. I could use some more food but no one else was eating so I decided to just get a drink. I was finally on my own and well, it was time. So I ordered some white wine, even though dad always said that it tasted like horse pee, I still wanted to drink my wine as my way of telling myself that I was now an adult. I was now feeling very comfortable and closed my eyes again but with the wine in me, sleeping was easier.

In my last year in school, twelfth grade, Sanjay Sharma walked into my life. Having the same last name as me; it felt like destiny and I wouldn't even need to change my last name. He was good looking; wore glasses but looked sophisticated, had the sweetest smile and was decently built. He had a mustache growing already and took good care of himself. He was a transfer student from Mufulira Secondary School, a city up north and also in the twelfth grade. He also had a sister in the eighth grade; Simi. She was a sweet girl too. Getting to someone's brother is always done by pleasing the sister. So first, I made Simi madam comfortable in school. I showed her around and told her which teachers were good, introduced her to my friends, and just helped her whenever I could. I actually liked her a lot. But, as a reward, hanging out with her, meant that her brother would eventually come around looking for her and then, would find me.

So we finally spoke to each other and he appreciated my care for his little sister. Over time, Simi seemed to disappear from the picture and it was just he and I. He was older, so he talked a lot about his classes; he loved art and drew incredibly. He showed me sketches of this fruit bowl he had drawn with pineapples, apples, bananas, grapes and pears and all sorts of fruits but it seemed so real; he had drawn buildings, his teachers, his dream home and airplanes. He had such an imagination. He had imagined a bungalow in Greece where all the buildings were white and overlooking the ocean, the house was a beautiful place where we would raise our lovely family.

'You have such an imagination. Wow! Wouldn't it be great if there actually was a place like this?' I remarked in a dreamy demeanor to which he looked at me surprised.

'You know this is an actual place in Greece right, Santorini?' he seemed surprised. Well, now I felt sheepish, he wasn't drawing our dream home, he was sketching real places and that slip was a bit awkward. I held back the urge to say anything and just nodded my head. That slip was really embarrassing. Here, I was making our dream home and he was nowhere close to thinking like me. Despite spending so much time together, he was just being himself and here I was already naming our kids.

Well, as always, now the Sharma's were also getting very friendly with the other Sharma's; my mother actually found a connection in our family tree. So it was perfect, our families liked each other. I liked him and could totally be married to him. We would live happily ever after. But our love was short lived; he became the chosen one, and got accepted to a US college and after completing his 'O' Level exams, left for the US just one year into our friendship.

It was hardly enough time for our romance to blossom and fate took him away. At that point, meeting Simi was useless. She actually started to get on my nerves asking about everything. Grow up lady! Do something by yourself! I was in a crappy mood after Sanjay left because I was not the chosen one.

It had been eight months since Sanjay had left for the US and his sister and I were now the two brownies at school. She too had a long list of fans. But today was a very happy day for her; she was on her way to pick up her brother from the airport. He had spent his first semester in the US and was visiting home over the summer. She had talked all about him for the past few months telling me all the things he was getting for her.

'I asked him to get me a cd player, makeup set and perfumes, Chanel No. 5, and the new Jennifer Lopez collection,' she went on and on with her things that her brother would get her. I wanted to ask her if he would get me anything. Did he even remember me or would he even want to know me after being in the US for so long. For some reason, kids who grow up in Zambia with you would be quite normal but after their re-incarnation from the US would come back as their Royal Highness. Full of accents, attitudes, and thought they were all that; I actually wanted to be like them. I mean, so what if you have gone to great colleges and are doing amazing things in education, so what if you're going to earn six figures and so what you now dress better than some of the movie stars; God! I wanted to be like them so bad. But what about Sanjay? Would he be a big show off too? Would he totally ignore me or even recognize me?

It was all set, my mother had arranged to have the Sharma's over for dinner after they had picked their son up from the airport. Even though my mother had been forced to setup this dinner by me, I didn't want to seem overly excited about his arrival. He could have changed completely and could be just like the rest of them.

The evening had come and it was actually past eight; very late for dinner. No phone calls, no updates and we were getting quite upset about their late arrival. The whole evening went by and there were no calls from them. It was very strange and never would anyone just not show up for dinner and not call either. We had our meal and went to bed not knowing whom to call. Their cell phone was not answering so we didn't know what to do.

The next morning, having heard nothing from them, we knew something must have gone wrong. Maybe he missed his flight or maybe they had to stay at the airport longer and returned late. But still no answer on their phone. Later that day, news had arrived that on their way back, they had a really bad car accident. A truck carrying construction equipment had crashed into their car and everyone was in the hospital. Every Indian family was calling everyone sharing the news; it was terrible knowing how happy this family was and now they were in a terrible accident. I was in complete shock, disbelief and just incapable of handling the situation. I remember going to see them in the hospital the same day to find Simi doing better. She had scratches on her forehead and arms but she was doing good. Her mother had a broken arm and scratches; Mr. Sharma had hurt his back badly and was in some strange machine all stretched out and looked like he was in a lot of pain. He was scheduled for back surgery and seemed in critical condition.

But seeing them at the hospital was traumatic because they had a look on their faces I will never forget. They knew they had just lost their son. Sanjay was driving the car and had been killed. I couldn't handle the crisis, their faces, lifeless, their dreams gone and their sudden happiness followed by sudden tragic death was unbearable for me. Simi just sat on the bed speechless and cold with no emotion. Her parents were lifeless and no one cared about their own bruises, life had dealt them a terrible card and nothing seemed to matter. This was my first experience with death and it felt terrible. I was at such a loss for words. How do you empathize with a father who sent his one and only son away to build a life and everything was shattered in an instant. How do you comfort a mother whose dearest son she had waited for six months had returned just to say goodbye. And a sister, who just was a child, now grieving such a big loss; I just couldn't handle it. Overwhelmed I collapsed in the hospital.

When I returned to my senses, I was in the hospital bed with my legs elevated so blood could flow back to my brain and I could think again. I hated every moment of that day and for the first time realized how hard life can be. Nothing was the same for the entire community; it took a long time for everyone to overcome this horrible tragedy that had struck all of us. I don't think anyone ever forgot those moments and even today those thoughts live with me.

8

Remembering Sanjay had killed the buzz from the wine so I ordered another large glass, at this point the stewardess knew to fill it up to the top. Wow, I could get used to drinking; part of my conscience was feeling bad about drinking my first day away from my parents but something kept saying that no one will know. It's funny how you think no one will know but when in the face of death, you tell everyone. That's what had happened to me. It was over the summer holidays when we had our usual friends visiting and parties and get together.

But one weekend my parent's friends, the Singh's had come over for an afternoon tea. Their son, Vineet was a good looking guy almost twenty and had started his education at Purdue University. He was a sweet guy but very feminine for my taste but either way I thought he was sweet. A little too sweet, he would never say it, actually no one would dare say it, but I thought he kind of enjoyed the company of dudes rather than dudettes.

Well, the afternoon was great and he and I went in the back yard for a walk. Our backyard had large mango trees and being in America Vineet had missed Zambian fruits. Zambian fruits are the best, juicy, plump and colorful. We had a tree full of mangos, so I told him that I would climb one and get him the best mangos. So even though I had denim knee high skirt on, I took of my shoes and put my right foot in the center of the tree bark that was split in two.

The idea was to use the split to climb high enough to reach the mangos. Well, with my right foot touching the bark, I felt a soft touch on my foot and saw a cobra snake sleeping in the center of the bark! It was a black snake, who upon my touching lifted his head up and was now staring me in the eyes. I instantly looked at him and there were the two of us looking at each other. If this was a Hindi movie, our eye connection would have resulted in either me changing into a snake and doing the snake dance or him changing into a handsome man and both of us doing the human snake dance. But alas neither happened and I found myself in the face of death. Any movement and this cobra would have had his way with me and I would have gone, my life would end and never would I live to see what I could have been. Where my life would have taken me, never married nor enjoyed the life I had envisioned.

The dread of death was so overwhelming, I started crying out, Vineet saw the snake but he was totally out of his element and didn't do anything. He just stood there listening to me weeping with my foot still on the belly of the snake.

'Oh my God! I will die today, I am never getting out of this alive,' I was murmuring

'Oh God! Why me! Why me! Dying with a snake bite, so young and so beautiful, I will never make it,' now I was hysterical, sobbing and wailing myself crazy;

'God help me, I don't want to die! I don't want to die a virgin! Please don't let me die a virgin, please God I don't want to die.' I screamed hopelessly all the while my eyes were closed imagining my own funeral.

Sobbing and crying my eyes out; I looked like I was missing some chromosomes at this point. Just the thought of this snake biting me and I would be dead with just enough time to say goodbye to my parents was painful to imagine. Not getting another day to live was dreadful. I was imagining the Bollywood movie scene of the gorgeous actress in the arms of her parents, sobbing and muttering her last words. The scene was intense and emotional; at this point I was crying for the heroine. I kept calling upon God nonstop.

'Please God don't let me die,' with my eyes closed and right foot still on the bark, I felt a tap on my shoulder. Vineet was looking at me, calm and collected, he pointed to my foot. The snake had slithered away from my foot and out of the tree. So, at this point, I had been hysterical, right foot in the tree and sharing all my personal thoughts with Vineet. I didn't know what I had said but for a few minutes I continued to stand there and still kept my foot in the tree in the silence as Vineet stood patiently.

The silence at that moment was so loud that now I really wished the snake would have bitten me or swallowed me whole; it is possible, I have seen in National Geographic.

Sipping my wine and reliving those moments made me laugh; I can't believe what Vineet must have thought about me. After that day, I avoided every event I knew he would attend. Even when I saw him, I would avoid eye contact at all cost. I guess, I appreciated him staying away. The day he left for the US was a big relief.

9

Another few hours and this long trip would be over, it was getting to be a very long flight and with so much wine, I was beginning to feel a little nauseous, sleepy, and drowsy. What the hell, let's get another drink! Now I was on my fourth glass of wine. Life in Zambia had been a lot of fun. Over my summer holidays I would work at one of the Gujju's stores. I worked at a grocery store at the register for Mahesh Bhai, a man in his fifties, more than nine months pregnant stomach and his features always reminded me of a llama, same lips and long hair that covered his ears. Sometimes he would move his hair away from his face only to reveal even longer hair oozing out of his ears. He would always say to me, 'control the supply, control the money,' I had no idea what he meant but I happily agreed just so he would leave me alone.

Well, despite the ambiance of the store, I did look forward to working there for the summer. It allowed me to earn extra cash and I got to meet many people. I knew all the other teenage kids who worked at these stores in the summer. There was Meena, who worked at the bakery, Pooja who worked at the clothing store, Sonakshi at the other grocery store and Sagar at the jewelry store. Well, with so many girls working at these stores, I was most interested in getting to know Sagar. He was a gorgeous guy, tall, fair and had black eyes you could swim in. He was a really shy guy and despite my visiting his store numerous times, we were still at the meet and greet stage.

'Hello, May I help you?' he would say unable to hold eye contact and I would shamelessly stare into those pools of lust without blinking.

'Could you show me that ring?' I always made him show me the rings just so he could put it on my finger. But he was way too nice; he would pull out the ring from the stand and place it on the table each time.

'How does this one look?' I shamelessly put it on and ask for his compliments. But my saint would never get my message.

'Looks wonderful,' he would say without even looking at my hand. Standard answer he was trained to tell all his customers. So I would return his ring and try again tomorrow over my lunch break. This complete lack of attention continued for three months and .....nothing. We had not passed this stage. It was hopeless. Right at noon, I would punch out for lunch and make a speedy walk over to the jewelry store rushing to beat Meena and Pooja who also were after my man.

They would drool over my man, always talking to him in Gujarati; just to get him to open up to them. I wish I could speak that language too, but for Sagar I could do anything. He was so innocent; I really wanted to teach him everything. Just thinking of all that this saint would learn was very exciting. I had to get his attention before those Gujju Bhens got to him and took his innocence away. But I couldn't do what they were doing; I had to come up with a clever plan. I hadn't realized how obsessed I was over Sagar because I was talking to myself when the lama was standing next to me.

'What do you need Sagar to do?' he asked in a Gujju accent, chewing on something which resembled exactly what a llama would chew.

'Nothing uncle, just there is this guy who doesn't even talk to me and I just wanted him to be my friend,' I was chewing my finger nails opening my heart to this aged llama. Why, I have no idea. Well, knowing how small these communities are, the llama knew Sagar and called him over the phone.

'Hah Sagar che? Ok you come to my store now, my cashier is wanting to being your friend, why you don't accept it beta? You have to be being her friend ok so just come now now and being her friend.' He stopping talking but I couldn't stopping screaming.

'No, No Noooo No!' Gujjus call each other as Bhai and Bhen referring to each other as brother and sister because they take away all the romance from their lives. Why was he murdering my romance? How could he just call Sagar on my behalf, tell him I needed his friendship and tell him to be my friend. I felt like an ass, a real ass. The only thing I needed was to face the other ass. Well, like a good boy, Sagar walked into the store with his blue jeans and yellow button shirt, almost like a school boy, walked up to the register and stood right in front of me.

'Kaka said to be your friend, I'm ok with that no problem.' He just responded like a robot, no emotions, no surprise, like this was so ordinary while I was sweating and dying of shame. It was idiotic to experience this friendship, but here he was. So what else, I extended my hand to him, greeted him like the CEO of Google making a deal with the IRS.

'I am glad to be your friend too.' I thanked him for coming and returned to my work. At this point he returned to his llama uncle and they exchanged words in Gujarati which all sounded like names of pickles. But that day was the complete murder of my love story. He was so not the person for me. No idea about women, and no clue on signals. I had wasted three months on him and found an absolutely lack of romance from him. Wow! How could I have not seen this coming? I realized that I was such a romantic and needed a great love story to find my mate. But today, for sure it was not Sagar. I could just see his future wife saying, "Honey you now put this in here."

10

'Are you ok? Wake up, Wake up!,' I heard someone saying constantly but couldn't make out who was talking. All I could hear was a humming sound, "hmmmm hmmm", then what felt like an earthquake, I felt my body shake, then again someone was speaking.

'Are you ok? Hello! Wake up!,' then another shake and with sudden shock I opened my eyes. Around me were four stewardesses, one sitting in the front seat looking at me, two others bent down in front of me and another one behind my seat. They were all blondes and despite being a seventeen hour flight I hadn't noticed how each of them had eyes of a different shade of blue. These women were very pretty and they were all surrounded by a cloud of perfume. This stuff was the good stuff; my nostrils were having a party just by them being around me.

'You doing ok?,' the lady in front was asking, I looked at her but just couldn't speak. My head hurt like hell. I felt the African drums beating in my head and each beat sent throbbing pain right between by eyes.

'Do you need some water?' one of the ladies kneeling by my seat was asking as she touched my hand. Water, wow! I hadn't had any throughout the flight. Guess when there is free liquor, who wants water. I looked around and the entire plane was empty. Apparently everyone had left the plane but I was asleep throughout the landing. I didn't know why my head was throbbing like hell, my stomach had a strange burning sensation and I had heartburn. I had to leave too but found it just really hard to comprehend my situation. But the ladies were all so sweet and really caring for me. I had to pull myself together and get off the plane. I had one woman hold my right arm, the other my left and they began helping me stand up when it finally happened. The five meals of rice, salad, cakes, pudding, cookies, ice-cream, bottle of wine, coke and more wine consumed throughout the entire seventeen hour flight was all returned to the airline and on the four stewardesses. I vomited everything I had eaten right on the poor ladies.

The five course meal was now on seat number 15E, 14E, 15B and 13A, 13B and couple more seats, my DNA was now running along the aisle and on the lovely ladies who once were nice to me. All I heard was screaming and I think someone cursing as well as I watched the four women run like a heard of zebras after spotting a tiger, only I wasn't a tiger, I was more like a dying duck.

After giving British Airlines Flight 4873 their full meal refund, I actually did feel better but that headache was still terrible. Covered in my own bacteria, I stood up only to fall back down on my seat. Taking a few minutes to gather myself, I noticed two men dressed in nuclear gear approaching my seat. They were dressed as if I had just deposited uranium in their precious plane, but immediately, they began using large vacuums to suck everything around me. I thought I was about to lose my fingers in the vacuum. I quickly left the scientists to deal with the nuclear disaster and moved into the restroom.

Looking into the mirror I saw a pale face, blood shot red eyes, lips dry like twigs and the hair that used to sit on my shoulders was now standing erect like I had just been electrocuted. I felt like a hyena that just got beaten up. Cleaning as much of my DNA off myself, I finally walked out of the plane into the immigration area.

The immigration lines were distinctly marked, one side had the red carpet with rose petals and champagne glasses welcoming the US Citizens and the other side was the Non-Citizen aisle. This aisle had the barb wires, vicious dogs, and body scanners and every officer gave you the evil eye. So I took the path of shame and walked into the Non-Citizen lane.

At this point the excitement of being in America had vanished and all I could think about was getting a bed to crash on. It was amazing, because of the trail of puke on my clothes, it was enough for me to fly through the immigration line, and everyone allowed me to move ahead of them. I walked up to the window and a really nice looking, clean cut officer was sitting behind the glass booth. His badge said, Immigration Officer Richard Samuels. He looked like he had just stepped out of a shower. I could smell his cologne outside the glass booth and after smelling the puke on my clothes; his smell was a breath of fresh air. He went through my documents and kept looking at me, when I got a glimpse of my face on the reflection of his glass booth, I realized he was staring at a baboon. I looked scary.

It was like I could read his mind; Why do these people come to America?, was what his face said; I really looked like a monkey straight from Africa. After he had enjoyed his trip to the zoo, I collected my baggage and moved to the Custom check point. The two officers at that point looked at me and they too had that expression of "look mommy, a monkey"; I couldn't care at this point, I was just miserable.

'Do you have anything to declare miss? Livestock, Chemicals, over $10000 currency?' one of the officers asked me as he stared at my luggage. Not knowing this at that time, but if a young woman arrives in America with four large suit cases and two carry-ons from Africa, you will get inspected.

'No officer, nothing,' I said innocently, not thinking about what I was carrying in my luggage. I guess the only thing I had to declare was that I was carrying enough food to feed half of the Indian population. But other than my clothes and large amounts of food my mother had packed; I really didn't have much to declare at customs. But for some reason, the officers didn't buy that; I think it was all the ropes my parents had tied to my bags protecting their precious snacks. So I was asked to step to the side and open my bags.

One by one the officers opened each bag to find all the reasons for the obesity crisis in this world. I had several pounds of Indian sweets, snacks, dry fruit, lentils of all colors, spices and even pickles my mother had made just for this trip. As each of my clothing was opened and my underwear spread out for all to see, I watched as the real convicts and drug smugglers were casually walking out of the airport. When it was almost over, one officer pulled out a plastic bag from the inside of my sneaker, it was a zip lock bag filled with something grey. Suddenly four officers surrounded me and the main officer held the bag in front of me asking loudly,

'What is this?' My heart sank. I couldn't believe this came out of my shoe. I had no idea what this thing was, I felt the presence of the officers closer to me; I think they thought I would try to run or something and I was now being asked over and over again what this bag contained. It was like a movie scene where the pretty actress is framed by the real druggies and she gets caught in a world of sex and drugs. It was very overwhelming and I didn't know what to say; I didn't know what that thing was.

'I don't know what this is, I have no idea. My mother packed my stuff and I don't know what this is?'

I was trembling at this point and speaking very fast. I looked around me and these handsome officers didn't seem so nice looking at this point. Then another officer came, looked like their boss, he took the bag and left the scene while I stood there not knowing what was going to happen. I thought I was going straight to prison or maybe they would just shoot me. My heart was pounding even louder and I was trembling with fear; what could that be? How did it end up in my bag? I truly had no idea. I looked at the table where all my things were spread out, a huge mountain of food, shoes and clothes.

Right on top of this mountain were my Derek Jeter underwear laid out with his big smile looking at me. I never really understood baseball but always had a thing for baseball players. Derek had walked into my life two years ago when I had read in the magazine about him dating an Indian Bollywood actress. After that article, I knew he and I were meant to be. He was just adorable and gentle and I really wanted to go to college in New York just to be close to him. But I ended up getting admission in Chicago. Anyway, with Derek smiling on the top of the pile for every officer to see, I decided to hide my exposed ass and picked it up to place it away from everyone to see. That was a BIG mistake. No one informed me that sudden movements, especially in the customs department at an international airport, was not such a good idea. My sudden movement led to the officers pulling their guns out immediately.

'Put your hands where I can see them!' one of the officers was yelling while the others were in position to blow my head off. I froze to the scene of five guys all around me with their guns pointed at me while I held my underwear in my right hand.

'DON'T MOVE!' I wasn't moving at all, in fact even though Derek was now swinging on my right finger, I let go of my embarrassment and just stood there. The officers put their guns away and one of them took the underwear from my hand and took that too to the inspection room. After standing there for ten minutes barely breathing or moving a muscle, the supervisor returned and handed me the plastic bag.

'This is Vibbuuti. Why didn't you tell us?' He said in his American accent and looked at me as though I had just made a fool out of them. I had no clue why all this was happening; everything seemed so blurred and confusing. First, why the hell did my mother put Vibbuuti in my bag, Vibbuuti is a Holy powder usually used in temples. Why was I carrying it? To top it all, why was it hidden inside my shoe? Oh my God! Did she expect me to go to college or was she sending me to an Ashram?

'Officer, I had no idea my mother would pack these. I didn't know anything I promise,' I was begging at this point and speaking very fast. He actually had calmed down and two officers next to me had left the scene. Then the other officer returned Derek to me. I held Derek in my hand and felt somewhat relieved to have his comfort as the officers left me alone.

No one said anything more but to pack up and leave. I collected my dignity as much as I could in my four bags, tried to compress the food supply and exited the check point.

Finally I was out of the baggage area alive, stripped of my self-esteem but still alive. I was shaken by this incident so much that I was ready to collapse. Now, all I had to do was look for the bus that would take me away from prison to the University of Chicago campus.

Chicago O'Hare International Airport was really huge; it was completely packed with travelers and signs pointing in every direction. I went in all different directions until I found the exit towards the bus stops. Stepping out of the airport baggage area felt like I had just landed on the North Pole. It was minus something when I got out, the ice cold wind and rainy snow felt like I was getting razor cuts all over my body. All I had to cover this behemoth body was a sweater. I stood outside for ten minutes and now I couldn't feel my toes. I wasn't wearing socks, just my high heels which made me look like an idiot.

I had especially bought these high heel shoes for my trip to the US, fighting my mother until she finally gave in. Now, I looked like a giraffe walking in Alaska. Needless to say, I did get a lot of looks especially when the frost bites on my feet made them look a shade of blue. It looked like I was wearing dark blue socks, but it was just the ice cold freezer hell I was walking in. The stupid bus took an hour while I waited with a skirt, t-shirt, sweater and high heels. My hair pointing in all directions and my face turned yellow from all the puke and a splitting headache visible to everyone. I was like a homeless person freezing my ass off; still hung over. All I needed was a sign that said 'FRESH OFF THE BOAT.'

11

Finally, the University campus bus arrived, a few people got in and everyone waited as I lugged my heavy suitcases, hitting and shoving everyone on the way. The painful ride from the airport to campus was over two hours. My feet were now blue and I couldn't feel my legs at all. My nose was red and icicles had formed around my nostrils. My electrocuted hair still up. I looked like Frankenstein Rudolf. I sat closest to the heating vent in the Bus and closed my eyes to relieve the pain that was throbbing between my eyes. I was cold, tired, and ill, I didn't want to talk to anyone, didn't want to see anything, I just needed a bed. I took a cat nap on the bus. Finally, the bus stopped and parked at the University parking lot. Getting off the bus and stepping on campus was another moment closer to finding this bed I desperately needed. I got off the bus and took another half hour to get all my belongings down; I think everyone else on the bus was happy to see me leave, might have been the smell from my clothes.

The campus was lovely; large buildings with a nice curving road connecting all the buildings. This campus was alongside Lake Michigan which made it colder than the airport. The bus dropped us off at the International Students office which was in the Albert Pick Hall. It was actually the smallest building on campus and when I walked in, it reminded me of a bed and breakfast building which even made a jingling sound as you opened the door. Inside this building were more ghosts from the past, pretty much everyone looked homeless, exhausted and totally under dressed. It's like no one got the memo to bring Eskimo clothing.

Albert Pick Hall was crowded with lots of other students trying to find out where their new homes would be; all of us holding our belongings close to us and all of us carrying a lot of luggage. I could see the numerous bags roped shut were the workings of obsessed mothers who had over packed their kids bags with mostly food stuff. The smell in the office was incredible. I think the puke smell was my unique smell.

Just like the groups in Zambia, Indian students started gathering in one corner exchanging information, Europeans on the other end and Africans on another. Eventually we all got our assigned rooms, boarded the campus bus and began searching for the buildings that would be our new home for the next four years. The campus dorms were at the far end of the campus and you had to hop on the bus to get to them. This campus shuttle bus went back and forth on University Ave every ten minutes taking students back and forth from 6am to midnight.

Looking into my registration forms, I was to get off at the first building of the dormitories; the bus stopped and the driver, an older man helped me get my luggage off. He was actually very kind to put everything on the sidewalk and left. I was the only one that got off the shuttle bus. Looking around, I was still freezing in my skirt and at this point I couldn't feel any part of my legs. I had four suitcases and two carry-on bags to take from the bus stop to the building right next to the bus stop. One by one I got my bags into the main entrance, a glass double door; inside the building you could immediately feel the heat. So in and out of the warm air, I carried all my bags until every piece was in the building. Then I lugged each bag one by one to the third floor wondering whose brilliant idea it was to not have elevators; after all this was America. If everything in America is supposed to be high- tech then why the hell was there no elevator?

My apartment was in the Blackstone House apt number 3A on the third floor. Entering my very first place should have been exciting but by the time I was finally in my new home I was completely exhausted. My apartment was a two bedroom one bathroom, kitchen and small living room. It was the most perfect apartment for me. Completely empty, I could just imagine how it would look after I was done decorating it. But first things first, take a shower and go to bed, I was so ready to finally get out of the bikini I was wearing and get into some sweat pants. The shower part was great, but no bed and no bedding. No one had told us to send bedding, no sheets no blanket. That first day was a rude awakening. I took a shower and wore layers of clothes to bring back some feeling left in my legs; mom had packed lots of snacks which made an excellent dinner. For the first time I appreciated her sending so much food since my trip. But by the time I was ready to sleep, I took all my clothes and spread them on the floor, wearing multiple layers and covering myself with every shirt, pant and jacket I finally lay down on the floor. Only after had I settled down on the floor did I begin to feel my own apartment, a cold place with nothing in it, I saw myself in a fetus position trying to keep warm and I tried to feel comfortable on the hard floor but it was so cold and hard that no position felt better. I took my handbag, turned it into a pillow and then it hit me; with all the hassle of getting to this point, the climax was really sad. I looked outside the living room window and could see other dorms, the main road to the campus and lots and lots of snow everywhere.

I looked for a few minutes for anyone but in this weather I guess no one would be outdoors. The streets were empty and my apartment was empty. I began to feel tightness in my chest and was unable to breathe, I began crying. The tears were now just rolling non-stop and I was crying like a little kid saying goodbye to my parents on the first day of school. I missed my parents, my home, my room and being here felt scary. Everything up to this point had been a disaster and nothing seemed right. Coming to this point had been a dream of mine, I had always wanted to be the chosen one and today it didn't feel like a privilege to be that chosen one. I was all alone in a new country, no one to care for me, no one to depend on and no one to lean on. I had never been so alone up to this point and the revelation of being independent had been so sudden and completely not what I had expected. I was afraid. I didn't know what tomorrow would bring but today I was cold, tired and lonely. I lay on my clothes keeping myself warm and cried my first night in America.

12

The campus was open to international students, but the official school semester had not started yet. We had arrived the first week of January and school officially started the third week. It was in the 20s and without proper gear, venturing outside was painful. I had my layers on of pajamas, jeans and pants with five shirts and four socks with two sweaters and a baseball cap. After everything was on, I really looked like a freak.

My apartment was cold. The windows were all shut and the white blinds were a dirty white color matching the color outside. It was a foggy day in Chicago; wet and slushy snow fell from the heavens. I sat on the floor looking outside; never had I imagined it would be like this. It reminded me of the National Geographic episode of Alaska where animals go into hibernation. I felt like I was hiding in my own little nest, tucked away from civilization hibernating until who knows when. How was I going to do this? Make a life here, a place so depressing, so cold and very lonely. How were the next four years going to be? Would I spend the most precious years of my life in this apartment alone? What if no one likes me? What if I make a fool of myself? What if I didn't fit in? It was really hard to believe that this was the Promised Land that everyone wanted to come to, yet today, I missed my life in Zambia. I had never appreciated the beautiful weather I always had all year in Zambia, the green trees filled with fruits, our gardens full of life and healthy crops, the comfort of my parents who took care of all my needs. I guess I had never really realized how much my parents had done for me until this moment.

Staring out the window and imagining the future was very frightening. I had to depend on myself to make the right choices, had to listen to my own instincts to decide what was right and wrong, I also had to take care of myself. I couldn't afford to get sick or hurt because no one would be there for me.

Gloomy and depressed I almost cried again, but realizing that crying in an empty apartment just made it freakier; something I saw crazy people doing in prison, I pushed my sorrow deep into my stomach. I took a deep breath and decided to venture into the Promised Land. Getting into layers, I stepped into the freezing temperatures and walked down stairs of my building. I was on the third floor but this building had five floors and each floor had four apartments. The building looked new but everything was the same dirty white color of walls and doors. The bottom floor had all the mail boxes and some had numbers while others had names. I saw the names Prashant and Nikhil who were on the fifth floor, Adam and Brian also on fifth, some more numbers and then there was Shelly and Judy on fourth, Robert, Sandra, Gregg and another Judy on my floor. There were a bunch of names on the second floor but the first floor had only two apartments, one had Larry the other had Supplies on it.

I guess, I would get my name soon but thinking about my very own mailbox made me smile. Who would write to me and besides who sends letters these days? Especially the image I had of America, it always seemed like computers ruled this place and everything was done using technology, so seeing a simple thing like a mailbox was surprising. I walked outside the glass doors which opened towards the parking lot. It had only a white pickup truck parked in 1A and sure enough I too had a parking spot for 3A; maybe one day I would have my car parked in that spot. The parking lot wrapped around the building. Eight similar buildings stood behind my building. Standing in my parking spot I could see the University Ave Road that went all the way from the apartments to the main campus and in the distance I could see larger buildings, all beige and maroon that looked like the actual campus buildings. I had only been out for ten minutes but my feet were frozen, the sneakers and three socks did nothing to keep the cold out, my toes were numb and I had to return to my den. I hurriedly went through the glass doors back inside and waiting at the door was a beautiful golden retriever. She looked like a puppy and was really cute, she jumped on me and having been so alone for the first time, it felt awesome to get her love. She happily jumped and licked my hands and face, her tail swinging back and forth; I fell in love with this dog instantly. I was hugging and kissing her and within minutes my depression had disappeared.

'Mili! Mili!'; a white man walked out of apartment 1A and was calling out for his dog. He seemed to be in his sixties, grey beard and grey hair with glasses wearing thick sweat pants, white socks and sweatshirt.

'Hello.' He approached me and held on to the dog.

'Hi,'

'I'm sorry! Is she bothering you?'

'No, not at all, she is so sweet, can I play with her?' I wanted to pet the retriever.

'Sure, Mili loves to get attention,' he was smiling as Mili kept rubbing her body against my legs which was exactly what I needed, with her thick fur my toes came back to life.

'She is really a sweet dog, I have a dog at home too. I already miss her'

'You just moved in?'

'Yes, last night all the way from Africa,' I was trying to be calm and trying to show him that I was excited to be here, yet inside, I still felt like crying. Seeing his dog I had remembered my baby Cathy.

'Wow! Africa, that is wild, I meet so many kids from all over, the furthest I've been is to New York and boy that was a culture shock.' He laughed so I laughed. I wasn't sure why we were laughing.

'Mili, that sounds like an Indian name?' I was still playing with Mili who was now lying on the ground with her legs in the air asking me to pet her belly.

'It is, I just read this book by an Indian author and saw this name in it, liked it a lot so named her Mili; would you like some coffee?' his apartment door was open and at first I wasn't sure if I should enter a strangers apartment. What if he kills me. Who would know? What if he was a weirdo and tried something with me? But, what if he was normal and gave me a warm cup of coffee. I had decided a warm cup of coffee was worth the risk.

'Sure, thank you. Do you have tea?' I walked into his apartment and Mili followed us in.

'I'm Larry by the way, and you are?'

'Rushmi,' I was looking at his apartment which was very simple, couch, TV, dining table for two by the kitchen. His kitchen was full of bottles and containers and there was that wet dog smell in the entire apartment which he tried to conceal using overly strong air freshener but that combination was even worse. His apartment was nothing I had imagined people in America would live in. It was very simple and kind of an okay apartment; my view of life here was fancy sofas and large TV's and video games but Larry had none of those things.

I sat at his dining table which was a small circular table with two black chairs. He went into his kitchen, which was visible from my seat, and I saw him pour a tea bag into a cup, dropped in sugar and carried it to me.

'Thank you,' I usually take milk in my tea but felt uncomfortable asking him for so much so I sipped on this black sweet water which still felt good. Usually I would have two cups of tea at home but without any groceries I hadn't had a cup for two days and that was making me feel a bit deprived. Larry had gone into his room and came out holding a book.

'This is the book, it's called Two Possibilities, I just finished, it's really nice and the character's name is Mili, that's where I found it,' he handed me the book.

'What does Mili mean?' he kept his blue eyes on me looking for a smart answer.

'Oh…..I don't know,' I could see the disappointment in his eyes. He had thought it was a smart idea to name his dog a different name hoping it would mean courageous, or something and I had just let him down. Mili was sitting by my feet. She looked like a golden haired beauty and the name did suit her.

'I think it means beauty.' I sipped my tea calmly hoping he would buy it.

'Beauty! That she is! Wow! Perfect! See Mili, you are my beauty,' he wrestled with her while she growled and played with him. I could tell he was living alone and she was his only friend; maybe that's what would happen to me, maybe I should get a dog too.

'Larry, your apartment is really warm, mine is ice cold.'

'Did you turn up the heat?'

'Turn up?' we had never had a heater or AC in Zambia so it had never occurred to me that there might be a heating system in my apartment.

'There is a thermostat in your apartment, see here next to the kitchen just turn it up, should work, I'll check it for you.'

'No, I don't want to bother you.'

'Bother, no that's my job- I'm the maintenance guy who manages all these dorms, so if anything breaks or needs fixing, they call me.'

Great, I was having tea with the right guy, maybe he would be able to tell me more about where everything is.

'In that case, yes please, I have been freezing up stairs and without any TV, groceries or heat I had the worst night of my life.'

'I'm sorry Rushmi, you must have been freezing upstairs, do you have enough blankets?'

'No, nothing, I came here with clothes and some snack but the rest I need to get.'

'Wow! Listen, come with me.'

He walked outside his apartment but right by the door he grabbed a big set of keys and walked next door to the room labeled supplies. Unlocking it, he turned the lights on to a large room filled with all sorts of used things like chairs, tables, pans, dishes, clothes, shoes and paintings and many more things in boxes.

'This is where I keep all the crap these kids leave behind once they graduate; no one bothers to take it with them, so they just leave it. I dump it in here, you can take whatever you want.'

I couldn't believe my own happiness in seeing old, used stuff, stuff I would have thrown out in Zambia but today seemed like lost treasure. Larry left to turn up the heat in my apartment while I walked around looking at everything. I saw a couch in good condition, a dining set just like Larry's, saw nice pictures and lots of kitchen stuff that needed a good clean.

Soon, Larry came back, 'All set, your apartment will get warmed up in a few minutes. Do you like any of this?'

'Absolutely, thank you so much, everything I need is here.'

'Okay. You start putting aside what you want to take and I'll bring it up for you, but let me get you some groceries first.' He walked back out so I started picking out all the things I wanted to change my prison into my home. Larry came back again and brought a brown paper bag full of things, Mili was following him back and forth. He saw the pile of things I gathered and took two chairs and a painting with him upstairs to my apartment.

He was an old guy and I felt terrible asking him to carry so much for me, so I stopped after a few items and told him I would do this slowly over the next few days by myself so he wouldn't exhaust himself.

'Listen, you come over anytime you need anything okay.'

'Thank you so much, you're a really nice person.' Larry had changed my day, from being depressed and gloomy; he had offered me tea, furniture and most of all, he had given me company, I wasn't used to being so alone.

'Well, Mili doesn't play with everyone but she loves you so I had to help you. If you need anything just let me know. I will setup a phone line in your apartment maybe in another day,' we exchanged smiles; he went into his apartment and I walked upstairs into mine.

Upstairs in my apartment, he had placed the chairs and paintings on the side, left the brown bag in the kitchen. In the bag were a tea kettle, tea bags, sugar, and a carton of milk, cans of chicken soup and a loaf of bread. I was so touched by his generosity. His thoughtfulness and kindness made me get a lump in my throat. I was bit relieved to get his things and a bit conflicted too. Never before had I ever received donated food like this, never had I ever even worried about groceries before, my parents would just have everything I needed available to me. In fact, I usually was over fed and so many times had thrown away food, but today, someone had donated food to me. Mixed with emotions I felt very conflicted about my life in America. That day I had my dinner of soup and bread. After being so cold and hungry, warm food tasted like a gourmet meal. I thanked God and asked Him to bless Larry too.

13

It was the start of the first week and now I had to start getting myself acquainted with the campus. I got maps, class schedules and went to the book store to figure out what I was going to be doing for the next four years. I found the Harper Memorial Library, the computer science department was in the Ryerson Physical Laboratory. I went over the map and found that the campus was divided in four quadrants making it easier to navigate.

I was enrolled in the Computer Science bachelor's degree program, a program I knew nothing about. It was a four year program during which time I had to become so good that it would land me a job. I was on a student visa and the clock was ticking to get myself sponsored for a work permit or Green Card in four years. That was the time line every child received from their parents upon leaving for this great nation. It didn't matter whether I liked computer science. The mentality is that you are so young you don't know what is good for you and besides, if the money is in Computer Science then that is what you ought to do. So, here I was enrolled in my first semester with Java programming, C++, Pascal and RPG programming languages.

At the book store, getting my million dollar books, I saw warmer clothes; sweat pants and jackets with the college logos, all of which seemed extremely warm. So, I bought all of them. I bought socks, sweatpants, t-shirts, jacket, and a matching hat. I even bought myself a backpack and drinking cup. At the checkout my heart sank when I had to drop $300 to pay for my new found treasures.

Walking out, the campus was pretty and covered with snow. I had never seen snow before and always found it to be a very beautiful sight on TV. In

National Geographic, they showed amazing pictures of trees filled with snow, buildings and I saw people skiing on this white powder. I had always wanted to see snow. Now that I was walking in it, it didn't seem that magical. It seems dumb but watching snow on TV never seemed cold and today the revelation was finally made that snow is actually quite cold. I felt like these conditions were not for humans; why anyone would choose to live here was beyond my comprehension. The bottoms of my pants were wet, snow had penetrated my sneakers and I could feel the wetness in my shoes. Any part of my body that was exposed had frost bite instantly; this was not the pretty snow I had imagined.

I was famished from walking all day since the shuttle bus hadn't started running yet. I ventured into the cafeteria where I found warm fresh food. The smell was so delicious and I was starved. I felt like a vulture eyeing its prey. I grabbed a tray and took pies, fruit, lasagna, chips and soda. I think seeing all this food and not having had a proper meal to eat, I was really hungry for something warm. Now I was ready to pig out. I walked into the cafeteria and found myself in deja vu; there were three large groups of students sitting in the cafeteria. It was like the animal kingdom. Territories had been marked by the animals and you had to walk cautiously to not aggravate the males. One table had a large group of European students, another table of Africans and another of Indians. It was exactly like in Zambia. I guess we do flock together.

Since the campus was not officially open, only international students had arrived. We were now segregated into groups. I guess once we were out of our comfort zone, we did tend to stick to our own kind first. Walking into the sitting area, I didn't know where to go. Should I join the Africans? I did have a lot in common with them, but then I was Indian so guess I ought to join them. I saw many eyes looking at the new animal and dressed as a hobo, I think no one wanted me to join them. I couldn't decide whether to approach these groups or just keep to myself, so I went and sat by myself at the far corner of the room. There were other rejects sitting by themselves too. Without being rude, I started studying my animal kingdom.

The Indians here were all together. I could tell there were some Northies, Southies, two Sardars and of the twelve students, four were girls. There were more South Indians than North Indians and they seemed to know each other; probably their second year. I ate by myself but it felt like the whole table of Indians was talking about me. I saw eyes meet and one and two smiles at me. It was the mating call I saw on TV that animals do to invite the member of the opposite sex. I was being invited to meet the rest of the clan.

Over at the African table there were almost twenty boys and girls. I know from their color that many were from Ethiopia, South Africa and one guy looked like he was from Morocco. At the European table I saw seven students; I think I heard French words so guessing they were from France.

It was a lovely sight outside. The sun was shining outside, the snow covered all the trees, the temperature was very cold outside, but sitting in a warm room looking outside I saw the magic in snow I had envisioned. It was very pretty. Every branch was carrying the weight of snow and since the campus was mostly empty, the snow was untouched. It looked amazing. Lost in my thoughts I had not given the Indian table much response to their mating calls, so the stud of all males walked over to my table.

'Hello, are you new to this campus?' he asked me in his Southie accent.

I looked up to see a tall guy who looked like he was from South India, chubby with thick hair parted on the side, glasses and a very thick moustache that matched his eye lashes. He wore glasses, a navy blue sweat shirt that had FBI written in large letters and blue jeans. He looked like one of the south Indian film stars who have what I call "Birthing Hips". This was a term I copyrighted describing men who had wider hips than females. When a dance number comes on in south Indian movies, the hero shakes his large hips better than the heroine and their voluptuousness makes them ideal to give birth.

'Hi, Yes, my first time in the US.'

'Myself Anand,' he was smiling and put his hand out.

'Myself Rushmi,' I was mocking his dialect, why, I have no idea.

I felt like an ass replying in the same manner as him. Why did I do that? No idea. But it was done and I think he was taken aback hearing me respond like him. Maybe, he thought I was being a smartass or mocking him but he seemed to pull back.

'Would you like to join our table? I can introduce you to other students!' He was being very courteous and now I felt bad.

'Sure, I would love to,' I picked my tray and moved to the Desi Kingdom. Everyone was smiling and very attentive to me. I felt a bit self-conscious especially with all my layers of clothes. I wanted to tell them that this is not how I dress but it was too late. They all gave each other looks and I knew all of those looks were about my appearance. I looked pathetic. I couldn't blame them. If I was in their shoes, I too would make fun of me. In fact, I was making fun of myself. I looked like a shmuck.

Everyone went around introducing themselves, what semester they were in. Everyone was in the Computer Science program. In all, six South Indians and two Sardars. All the four girls were from the South too. So, now I was the only girl from North India in this clan.

'I am RelaxSingh,' said one of the Sardars. He wore a red turban, thick beard and moustache; perhaps in his mid-twenties. This made the whole clan laugh out loud but I actually had no idea what was so funny. Sardars usually take on the role of being comedians in most groups and this guy definitely took on that role. Every time he spoke, others just laughed. I found him quite irritating especially because I didn't get his jokes.

'And I am LipSingh,' the other Sardar spoke. He also wore a turban but had little facial hair and was also in his twenties. Now all the Southies were cracking up loud; to me it was bizarre what was so funny. This shenanigan went on for a while until I lost interest in their not so funny jokes.

'Ok, well, I should get back to my apartment; still have so many things to do. It was nice meeting you, Anand, Srikanth, Nukul, Prashant, Nikhil, Anirudh, Anya, Hershitha, Madhu, Lakshmi, Relaxsingh and Lipsingh.' Hoping to impress them with my memory of remembering everyone's name I stood up to leave. Everyone fell to pieces laughing. Maybe my Derek Jeter was showing or something but I just didn't understand their internal jokes and left the scene leaving those maniacs bursting out in laughter.

I was a little irritated about my initial meeting with this group. They were a little weird and my first impression was absolutely not cool. I had to figure out my clothing situation. Hearing the names of these students, I thought I had seen Prashant and Nikhil's name somewhere but couldn't remember where. Seeing more life on campus felt great. There were other people on campus and in another week, more should show up then maybe it wouldn't be so boring. Between the food Larry had given me and what I had brought from Zambia, I was running low on supplies. I desperately needed to get groceries but hadn't had the guts to board the bus and venture into the land of the unknown.

On my way to my apartment, I met Larry again. By week two, I felt very comfortable with him and Mili could sense me coming. She would scratch at the door and Larry would let her come into my arms. He had helped me get all the stuff I needed into my apartment and today was the last of it.

'Wow! Thank you so much Mr. Larry,' I was ecstatic to get my hands on all this old crap; old beds and sofa's which had all sorts of smells, lots of pans and a few coffee makers, rice makers, blenders, an iron and some knickknacks. I now had a fully furnished apartment. For someone who had never done any work; I was impressed to see myself already taking control of my life. I must have gone up and down hundred times but within four days I was now the owner of a fully furnished and organized apartment.

Needless to say I appreciated Larry and offered him some Indian sweets. Larry was an older white man who had worked at this University for over thirty years. He had kids and grandkids and was working just to keep himself busy. His white hair and thick glasses made him look like a professor but he never went to college in his younger years. He seemed to be happy in his life working odd jobs on campus which put his kids through college. In fact Larry told me that there were certain positions on campus that if I wanted would be a great way to make some pocket money. I appreciated having someone to talk to and Larry was a nice guy who also was very helpful to me. I think he seemed old and almost homeless. Not many people talked to him but I actually liked him. He was simple, non-judgmental and very helpful. Plus I would never forget his generosity.

Now, when I entered my apartment, I had a sofa set which I covered with my clean sheets; I had lots of utensils, a coffee maker even though I never drank coffee but it felt so American to have one, so I got it. I also had two beds, one for me and the other I put in my roommates room in case she needed one. I also had a dining table for two and some wall hangings. One picture was a multicolor flag that I thought looked pretty and the other was the symbol of our lord Ganesh which to me was ironic to have found it here in America. My room looked great. I had my bed and my clothes were all arranged in my closet, a desk to study and Larry gave me his small TV especially because I had told him how lonely and bored I was all by myself. He immediately came back with this small antenna TV that only played two channels, one was a shopping channel and the other a local TV station where I could watch the news and watch some shows something called Soap Operas.

Week one was looking up and I decided to cook something myself, in my kitchen. But before anything else, I had to get some groceries which meant I had to ride the bus. I had avoided it long enough and now it had to be done.

I desperately needed milk, bread, jam, sugar, vegetables, fruit and eggs and ketchup. I couldn't eat my mother's snacks another day.

So I geared up and dressed as a hobo in layers of colorful clothing. I stood by the bus stop which was on the other side of the parking lot and I was carrying a twenty dollar bill. I stepped into the bus only to have the driver rudely and loudly yell, 'Need Exact Change!' I just stood there looking at him. So he yelled again, 'Need Exact Change!'

'This is all I have,' I sheepishly said to which he pointed me to get off the bus. I didn't understand what to do. Where would I get exact change and how much does this bus cost anyway? While the awkward moment passed, I saw a man walk up to the driver and deposit some money. The door shut and the driver again yelled at me to step back. I was not sure of what to do and with the twenty dollar bill still in my hand I tried to hand it to the driver but this man held my hand and pulled me to the back. We sat down and the bus went off.

To my surprise, I was sitting next to one of the guys from the cafeteria.

'Prashant, from yesterday,' he said and smiled knowing that I was a little shaken up by the experience, especially because I had never taken the bus in my life.

'Don't worry, we all did the same thing, but once you do things here you get the hang of it really fast. Like, always have exact change for the bus, or get a bus pass from the campus office and keep your quarters for laundry, bring a backpack for your groceries and buy a decent jacket.' He smiled looking at my layers of clothes.

'Oh my God, everything here is so overwhelming and scary. Why do I feel like I am doing something against the law or something,' I settled in my seat and put my money away.

'I know what you mean. I felt the same way last year. You always worry about getting into trouble with the cops or something but that's just cause all this is new,' Prashant was smiling sitting back in the seat with his jeans, black leather jacket and black snow hat. He wore glasses and they seem to suit him. He seemed nice. I hadn't actually noticed him yesterday between the herds but today, he seemed alright.

'I'm on the fifth floor of your building,' he said. That's where I had seen his name, on the mailbox.

'Please don't mention this to the others.' I whispered hoping he wouldn't tell the entire desi club of my embarrassing moment. He looked at me and smiled but didn't say anything.

'Where are you going?' I asked realizing that I needed more help from Prashant especially for grocery shopping. God forbid they have a system that I don't understand. Usually in Zambia you just get what you want and pay for it, but what if you have to show your passport or something because I wasn't carrying anything more than money.

'We usually go every weekend grocery shopping and get everything we need for the whole week.'

'We? Who is we?' Prashant pointed to the other seats where the entire clan was seated. I had been so horrified that I never noticed the twelve musketeers' seated behind me. They had all witnessed my humiliation once again. This was getting a bit awkward.

'Great, just great!' I began sinking into my sweat shirt and never spoke again until our stop. We all, and unfortunately, I too had become one of them, got off the bus and marched into the Meijer shopping store. I followed the whole gang buying veggies, spices, milk and eggs and some guilty pleasures like ice-cream, soda and American potato chips. American chips are the best I had ever tasted. My mom would always allow me to eat a few while reminding me; "it's too fatty", but now I had the mother of all stores selling different varieties of chips and I was ready for them. I hadn't spoken much with the group just followed them through the checkout and observed their every move so I could nonchalantly do the same. All went fine and we took our tons of groceries and marched back onto the bus. Now I had my exact change and confidently sat in my seat.

'See I told you, easy!' Prashant whispered from behind my seat. We exchanged smiles and I felt so much better. A simple task of shopping can be so stressful in a new place. Usually, we would drive to the market in Zambia, park right outside the stores and do our shopping. The driver would carry our bags and that would be our shopping adventure. Here in America where life was supposed to be EASY, I found it to be the craziest. I had never taken the bus in my life, never carried groceries in my backpack and never lugged things on my back like a donkey. Was this the true America? I wondered.

'Rushmi, you're the new sheep, so your treat today,' RelaxSingh yelled from behind. That guy really irritated me but suddenly everyone started agreeing with him. With twelve against one, I was forced to provide dinner for everyone tonight at my apartment. I hadn't planned on any get together so soon but had no choice but to agree. I told everyone to come over in an hour. Being in my apartment all alone for a week was driving me insane. I could use the company.

Chips, soda, snacks from mom, tea and tomato sandwiches all nicely decorated on my dining table, I was set to have my very first dinner party. Usually I would have changed into a nicer outfit, but I realized that everyone was quite casual. I stayed in my sweat pants. Not long before everyone came at the same time.

'Oh my God! Look at your apartment!' Anya exhaled as she looked around in my entire apartment without even asking my permission. She just ventured into my bedroom and closet casually; very irritating. The others too made remarks about how nice my apartment looked.

'Where did you get this stuff?' Nikhil asked as he sat on my couch with his feet up.

'Oh I got them from Larry. You know? The dorm administrator?' I was staring at Nikhil hoping he would put his feet down, but he never got my message.

'Larry, who is Larry?'

'You know…. that guy who does maintenance of these apartments; he lives in 1A.'

No one seemed to know who Larry was. But more than paying attention to me, they were just amazed at how nice my place looked. I felt great, my first place was MY very own, I was really proud of it and it didn't cost me a cent.

'What is THIS?' Nikhil was pointing to my colorful flag I had displayed in the living room. Nikhil was very dark complexion and had thick hair with bangs covering his forehead. He looked very much the "overly smart one" which I think he was.

'Oh that's a flag I found, loved the colors, not sure which country it's from,' I proudly explained; but again there was that irritating laughing fit everyone started having.

'Oh my God that's no Country Flag you silly, it's the proud GAY flag,' Anya saluted the flag as she cracked up and then one by one every one walked to the flag and saluted it. Honestly, I had no idea what to do; I never knew there was a flag for being gay; but this one was so cute and colorful.

'So, who cares, it looks good,' I gloated and was adamant on not taking it down. I just wanted this constant humiliation to end and was not about to give them satisfaction by taking it down.

They sat on my couch, some on chairs, and some on the floor which was carpeted and asked a lot of questions about me. Where I was from, what kind of life is in Zambia, if I knew Hindi movies, and what program I was going for. With that interview over, I found out that they were all first generation to come out of India; they were all in Computer Science for one reason only; landing the first job. Most of the guys couldn't wait to send money back home. I could sense the burden they felt of having been sent here with the high hopes that soon these kids would make good money and send it back home.

'What do people do here once they graduate?'

'Well, usually, by your fourth year, you should have already started networking with professors and done some good projects so that they refer you to some company,' Nikhil was explaining while everyone else listened quietly.

'There is the Dean, Jay Chand, I've heard is a good connection, he looks out for Indian kids and has gotten so many kids work,' Anand was explaining as he engulfed most of the sandwiches.

'But you have time, Rushmi, just take as many technical classes as possible and get friendly with the professors. If they like you, they always help you out but stay clear of Professor Walter. He sucks!' Srikanth yelled while everyone agreed with him.

'Why what's wrong with Walter?'

'He is four feet something, very petite guy and never looks at your eyes when he talks, instead he looks at your chest while talking,' Lakshmi shrieked and Anya was nodding her head in agreement.

'And because we don't have much down there, he doesn't even acknowledge us; but for a woman he happily makes time,' Anirudh explained.

'He is so eeeeoow, can't stand him, pervert sala; it's a good thing I'm shorter than him, but…..,' Anya looked at me and giggled then everyone else started smiling. I knew what they were thinking; I was 5'6 and had a decent cleavage, so this Walter guy would have a party down there. Great point to self, don't enroll in his classes.

'What class does he teach?'

'C++, and yes it's a first year pre-requisite for other classes,' Madhu smirked in disgust about being forced to take this man's class. Okay, I was looking forward to starting the semester but not so much now.

'Then there is Penguin, she teaches algorithms class, you will have to take her in your second semester,' Madhu said.

'Penguin, that's her name?'

'No, that's how she looks,' Madhu was laughing and struggling as she tried to get the words out and everyone was giggling.

'She is very round at the bottom and wears tight black and white clothes, you can't miss her,…..it's so hilarious.' Madhu was bursting with laughter and the guys were having a good laugh at the thought of Penguin. I saw them exchange looks and saw some raised eyebrows.

'Ok, so we have a Pervert, a Penguin, anyone else?' America sounded a lot like the African zoo already.

'Oh, don't forget King Kong!' Nikhil shouted.

'King Kong, who's that?'

'She teaches Java, I think she is in the Guinness book, must be 6'3 or something and eats little kids for lunch.' Anand was smiling while others had a funny smile on their faces. It was like they had a name for every professor.

'Then there is Professor Waldo, he's the funniest, wears Waldo's hat and Rushmi, he's really goofy; but a good guy. You'll enjoy his networks class.' Nukul was standing by the food loading up everything in sight.

Hearing everyone telling me about what to expect seemed very strange. These were the best colleges on the planet and I had imagined them to be very professorial and intimidating. But now, hearing how these people were like regular people helped me feel a bit more confident in dealing with them.

'Rushmi, we have first semester books, so don't get any of them. Take ours, and also, we meet at the Tomatina café every Sunday afternoon for lunch so you must join us,' Prashant said as he enjoyed my mother's treats.

'Sure, you'll just have to show me.'

'Don't worry, we live upstairs, so just come with us, we all have classes in the same building so you can join us, and if you're taking C++, you will spend a lot of time in the lab working on projects; you'll get used to it.'

'Also, every Friday we rotate potluck so next week we are hosting the potluck,' Hershita said and I figured she was Anya's roommate. The night went by so fast, in talking about life, getting that first job, getting our Green Cards, the money we would someday make and before the end of it all, the conversation went back to missing home.

'I miss India, Yaar! The life is really something back home. Not sure I want to settle in US,' said Anand.

'I know I've been here almost three years and have not gone back once. I've missed my cousins wedding, missed so many festivals and just miss all my friends.' Nikhil was not making eye contact. He stared at the Gay flag to hide his feelings, but I could sense he was emotional.

'My sister had a baby who is two years old already and I have still not seen my niece. Sucks man!' Hershita was talking with her head down and now no one was eating, the plates were down and I sensed sadness. With her remarks, the mood changed and everyone was at a loss for words. I could see everyone in their own thoughts about how many events, birthdays, celebrations had been missed and the sacrifice we all were making for a better life. Giving up family, friends, support and our homes, we all were to spend four long years away from everything that we held dear – that was our true test in America. I tried very hard to keep my emotions in check but soon could not hold my tears back. It was time to say Good Night.

Everyone helped clean my apartment, which I thought was very nice. Saying Goodbye to everyone, I went back into my lonely apartment and felt like the wave of emotion was climbing out of my stomach, where I had tucked it away, and soon it had reached my heart. Tears rolled out as I lay in my bed watching the jewelry show that displayed ugly earrings and necklace for

$49.99 plus S+H. All the while I was tearful, I kept wondering what S+H meant.

14

After that one encounter, needless to say, just like back home, this was going to become a ritual every Friday. We would rotate whose place to have the potluck and each would bring a dish to share and believe it or not, we agreed to play Antakshari like good old times. I was just amazed at how similar life was in America for me to life back home.

The following week, Anya and Hershita were hosts to our potluck. They lived in the third building down on the fourth floor. Even before entering their apartment, I could smell spices, curry and BO from the second floor. Upon entering their apartment, the smell was so strong that I almost threw up. Their apartment had no furniture and everyone sat on the floor. They had sheets spread out on the floor and pillows lying around. In the kitchen, they had a few cooking utensils and they used paper products for daily use. I did see a few framed pictures of family and they also had a picture of a south Indian God hanging in the kitchen. I think cooking in an apartment with all the windows closed killed the circulation and they had the heat in their apartment so high that the smell was sticking to everything in their apartment including the people in it.

Ever since I had met these guys, I could smell the same odor from their clothes. At first, I thought it was because of bad hygiene, but now I could understand why they smelled. Indian cooking has a lot of spices and if you don't have proper ventilation, it sticks to your clothes. If you don't wash your clothes regularly, this smell gets in deeper and deeper; on top of that, add sweat to it and the smell can kill small animals. Anya's clothes smelled of everything she was cooking, they had made rice and samber and something sweet was what I could gather from smelling her. The others had brought chicken, potato subji* and I took a pie to their potluck.

Baking was the one thing I felt was my specialty. Everyone loved my pecan pie and before dinner, the desert was gone. That day they all made me promise - I was to always bring pie to every potluck. Being my second potluck, I was looking forward to hearing more about college and what to expect in my four years at this college. But soon I became flabbergasted by the conversation that took place in their apartment. The guys were lying on the sheets, I sat with my back on the wall and everyone was now talking about marriage.

'My mother told me that I'm up to four lakh in India,' Srikanth smiled while the others raised eyebrows in approval.

'I already got a marriage proposal and they are already willing to pay up to two lakhs, but once my degree is completed and I get a job, that number will double for sure,' Anand was gloating.

'What are you talking about?' I was completely out of my element, had no clue on what they were talking about.

'That's right, you're not from India, you have no idea,' Nukul replied

'Idea about what?'

'See in India there are certain standards, if you are a high school graduate you get so much money from the girl's side at the wedding, but once you're a graduate from an American college, we're talking about lakhs.' Prashant explained excitedly.

'Wait, you're talking about dowry for you to marry someone?' I was appalled at what they were talking about.

'I don't like that word, it's called investment, see our parents are putting so much into us, so obviously they want their return on it,' Prashant was still talking but I think I was looking at all the guys in complete shock.

'So wait, your parents invested in you but didn't the girl's parents invest in her?' I hadn't realized but I was raising my voice.

'But the girl will live with the guy so she will add to the living expenses plus, it's nothing new, I mean this has been going on for centuries,' Prashant was becoming defensive. I looked over at Anya and Lakshmi but none of them seemed to find this strange.

'So if I married one of you, how much would I have to pay?' I shot a dirty look at the guys, at this point I was getting a bit pissed off because they had so quickly diminished the value of a woman and were already adding up numbers of their future bank balance. Totally disgusting!

'Look, it's the cycle of life, girls want to marry guys who have good jobs, make good money, and have a car, a house and all that good stuff. So what's wrong in the guy looking for a girl who is already loaded? At the end, this money is there for both of them to start their new life together. So some money the guy brings some the girl brings,' Prashant sat next to me as though explaining to a child.

'But what about love, I mean don't you marry someone because you are in love?'

'Off course, the love part is great, and we will all love our wives but that has nothing to do with the system of exchanging money.' At this point I was not sure if I was wrong or if they were wrong.

'So, if I married you, how much would I have to pay to buy you?' I made sure I said buy just to sound derogatory.

'Well, you're different, I mean your educated in the US too, so I would marry you for only one lakh,' Nikhil laughed and the others again joined him. At that point, I was the only one not laughing. I realized that it was a centuries old dilemma and despite being in America, the land of equality, these guys were still locked in the same world as their great grandparents. It was no use arguing or destroying their vision of what they were worth.

'But Rushmi don't listen to them, I will give you one Lakh to marry me!' LipSingh intervened and the hysterical laughter started again. I really don't like this Sardar.

That day I realized that I was such a romantic. I believed in falling in love, finding that one person who would want me more than my money, not that I had any. But hearing them all talk about their future plans, I felt so naïve. I had never even fathomed something like this was happening in the world, people were calculating the worth of others based on their income potential.

Yet, for women, we were still lower in the food chain than men. It was an awakening moment.

15

Once the Semester started the campus was full of activities. Life became so busy with finding out where my classes were, who my professors were, what books to get, running from one class after another, lots of books to read, and projects to plan for and people to meet. Each class started with ground rules, deadlines, expectations and endless chapters to read. I hadn't realized what had hit me the first few weeks of the semester. I hadn't had time to clean, cook or even call my parents. My focus was on knowing what classes I had, making that A in each class and getting from one class to another. After the initial two weeks of running around, I finally got the hang of my schedule and calmed down. In these two weeks, the stress level had been so high that I had drained my chips supply and with my baggy clothes hadn't realized the extra pounds I was carrying.

I was invited by the International Student Organization to attend an orientation during the first two weeks and meet with the Dean. The name on the card said Jay Chand, same name Prashant was talking about. Jay Chand was the one who helped the Indian students find jobs after graduation. I wanted to take this chance to introduce myself to him so I made sure in between my classes, I walked over to the Dean's office.

Walking into the administration building, I was impressed with the navy blue carpet with golden flowers, the velvety curtains, the fancy lighting and impressive stairs leading upstairs to where the offices were located. At the reception an older lady was seated talking on the phone.

'May I help you?' she stopped talking on her phone and smiled at me.

'Yes please,' I showed her the invite from the Dean.

'Go straight up, first door on the right,' and she returned to her phone call. I walked upstairs and knocked on the door that had a name plate outside "Dr. Jay Chand, Dean."

'Come in,' said a loud deep voice.

'Hello Sir,' I walked into his office where stood a large wooden desk almost like the oval office, a sofa set, same carpeting as the lobby and a large American flag on the side wall stood off a wooden handle.

'Can I help you?' said this older Indian man, maybe in his sixty's, grey hair, glasses and very clean cut. He seemed very polished in his demeanor and extremely professional.

'Sir, the orientation, your invitation had said,' I held the invitation in front to show him.

'Oh, welcome, please come in,' he shook my hand and I sat on the single chair of his maroon sofa set. I was nervous meeting this man; he was the one man on campus that could help me get my first job. I really had to impress him.

'I am Dr. Chand and I wanted to make sure I meet with international students especially those from India and offer my support whenever you need it. What are you majoring in?'

'Computer Science.'

'Good, where are you from?'

I gave him the whole story about my past and he seemed very interested and seemed to care about my future goals. He gave me his card and told me that I should count on him whenever I needed any help. We shook hands again and I left the building. He seemed like a really nice person, very gracious and extremely involved in the lives of us Indian students. It was like he wanted to take care of everyone at his University. I was so happy to have met him. The Indian gang had described him as being overly motherly to the point he could breast feed. I didn't see that in him. What I did see was a fatherly figure watching over us.

Finally, I got my first semester schedule together. I had classes' everyday mostly in the mornings. I had to stay in the lab during the evenings to learn the new computer languages, figuring out the code for our projects and just getting comfortable programming, something I had never done before. I had also met my professors, all men, older and all white. I also met Professor Walter; I had recognized him immediately as I saw him talking to a girl before class and saw his eyes fixed on her chest. Even during class, he walked around the room and stopped close to women who were at least a B cup.

I spotted Penguin who almost made me laugh because she actually did look like a penguin. Dressed in black tight pants with a white and black striped top she wobbled back and forth as she walked. It was quite funny to see her walking in the corridors and I could see the other kids exchanging looks as she passed.

Since my four classes were mostly in the mornings, I had more time in the afternoon, so I picked up a job at the library. This job helped with getting extra cash. Larry had told me to stop by the Library the first week before all the jobs were taken and luckily I was hired right away. Nikhil, Madhu and Srikanth were in some of my classes but I hardly saw the others except on Fridays at the potlucks. Every experience was a big change, the classroom settings, the way the professors interacted with the students and I also noticed how casually students talked to their teachers.

I was taught to never argue with a teacher but here students were always in discussion with professors. I found it very hard to speak up in class let alone ask questions, but in college you got more points for asking questions and participating in discussions. The kids felt comfortable discussing topics with the professors. I really enjoyed this part of the American culture.

Our assignments were all given to us the first two weeks and were due at the end of the semester. But this C+++ project was a nightmare. We had to design some code that would take in a list of supplies used in a building construction project and based on requirements and construction dates, would determine when supplies were to be reordered. My first reaction was, What? For someone who has never done this before, how was I supposed to even start doing this? This was the start of reading huge books, learning about arrays and complex algorithms that helped suck the life out of me.

Every evening after work, I marched into the lab, where all twelve nerds sat together coding the night away. Nikhil helped me a lot; in fact, it was like he did everything. Even understanding what he was doing took a lot of time on my part. Professor Walter offered to give me one on one tutoring but I respectfully declined and always carried my books close to my chest any time I had to converse with him.

I met King Kong who scared me a lot! She was a big woman and wore mostly black clothes. I think people have a misconception that black is slimming but they forget that if you see a 6' woman in black, it's quite scary. She was not only tall; she was heavy too which made her even more intimidating. I was glad I wasn't in her class this semester.

With classes in the mornings, working at the Library in the afternoons, then coding the night away in the lab, my life was no longer lonely. It was just exhausting. I walked fast, ate fast and had started talking fast too. Getting into the Desi club had helped so much. I had friends who were there to help any time I needed anything. They explained things to me that seemed very confusing at first and they provided me with a home like feeling whenever I missed my parents. But the down side was that their smell was getting into my clothes too. When all twelve were in the lab you could see other students leave immediately. It was like a cloud of BO walking around. I had tried to get used to it but sometimes it was just unbearable. That's when I would take a break and walk outside the building just to get fresh air. These guys were my friends but not close enough for me to tell them about their little problem. I knew this was not because they were dirty; they just cooked way too much desi food. My only hope was that maybe their professors would tell them.

Working at the Library, I was fortunate to meet other non-desi students. Everyone on campus needed the Library for projects and research, so working there meant I met everyone on campus.

I met so many interesting kids from all over the world. So many kids had come from Japan, China, Chili, Brazil, Sri Lanka, France, Australia, and I even met one girl from Nepal. I got to know everyone from Africa and knowing I was from there too made others very friendly with me. The kids from Africa included kids from Ethiopia, Kenya and I was the only one from Zambia. But belonging to the same continent connected all of us and suddenly I had my African family too.

My African friends were all very cool kids, very down to earth, and had heavy accents that I loved to hear. Being around these guys felt like I was not the only one struggling with being homesick and their friendship felt very familiar. Everyday these guys would meet in the Library lounge and spend hours talking about home, classes, and play African music. I had really missed the music the most. I immediately connected with Rayani, Eskima and Musasha; these guys were from Ethiopia, had a coffee color complexion and came from the same town in Ethiopia. They shared an apartment outside campus and also had a car, a Honda Civic.

Rayani worked in the evenings at the local hospital at the flower shop, Eskima worked at the Gym and Musasha worked at the Deans Office doing some research work. All three majored in Nursing and were in their second year. Rayani was a slender girl, tall and extremely beautiful and she knew it. She had dated everyone on campus. Once I even caught her making out on the second floor of the Library and had to ask her to leave. Eskima was also slender but shorter and very sweet. She had a pretty smile and was very friendly towards everyone. Musasha was my height, slender and eyes that looked like he was wearing makeup but it was all natural. He was very good looking and he knew that too. He reminded me of Ian and immediately I had a liking for him.

At the Library, I worked with Julie who was white and majored in Psychology. Julie belonged to a simple family and came from some farmland area. She had never lived in a big city and found it fascinating to know that I was from a different planet.

'Africa, what's it like there? I mean do you live in homes or huts?' She had asked me at our first meeting. I looked at her pale white face, pink lips, blue eyes and blond straight hair in complete amazement. She knew so little about Africa and most of her knowledge came from National Geographic.

'We do have houses, roads and buildings you know.'

'Oh, I always see this show where they show Africans eating snakes and drinking blood.'

'Yes, I see those shows too- they are called the Masai tribe and the show is about strange things around the world but that's not a common thing,' I said sarcastically.

'Well, I've never been out of Kansas so guess you can say, "we're not in Kansas anymore Dorothy".' She laughed in a squeaky voice.

'I'm not Dorothy,' I was confused what she meant and why did she call me Dorothy?

'Never mind,' Julie smiled and went back to her work, shelving books. She and I would shelve books, photocopy, check out books, place items on reserve and answer phone calls. The Library was huge with five floors and the lounge was the first thing you saw when entering the first set of doors. Passing the second set of door were you actually in the Library. Upon entering and leaving the Library you had to pass through a detector that would beep if you carried a book outside the library without checking it out. The work was not at all stressful, in fact, there were days when it was slow and I could catch up with my class reading.

I also met Samuel; he worked in the Library's computer lab providing technical support. He was from Morocco and was here as an exchange student. He looked Asian but slightly African so he was kind of a mix. He was a very sweet guy majoring in anthropology. There were other students who also worked at the library but some of them didn't look friendly. Some looked overly stressed and some didn't interest me. But the most fun part about working at the library was helping the athletes.

My favorite was the volleyball team, the men's team. Wow! There were fifteen hunks that were stunning and very HOT. They were tall with broad shoulders and I LOVED them in their uniforms. They had white and blue slacks with blue shirts and they all hung out at the library trying to study but none of them looked like they could read. I made it a point to shelve books on which ever floor these guys were "studying". I had read about all of them in the school magazine, there was Ryan – 6'1, blue eyes, blond curly hair, loves cooking and majors in Literature. Chad – 6'4, darker blue eyes, black straight hair, loves to play guitar and majors in Political Science. Well, lets just say I had studied the volleyball team very closely and because games were free to students, Julie and I had promised to watch every game that semester.

But with every pot of honey, bees will come too. With the athletes come the cheerleaders too. These girls would come in with their blond hair, tight clothes and skinny bodies and flirt with our men right in front of us. Shamelessly they would giggle and find excuses to touch and hug these guys. Pissed me off! They were all over these boys and unfortunately, these guys didn't seem to mind. So basically, I spent all my energy shelving books, parading around them and didn't get noticed because of these blonde beauties. At times, I felt like Cinderella while the cheerleaders were my step sisters then there were moments when I felt like the Beast and these girls were Beauties. These girls were shameless and I never saw them pick up a book and when they did, they held it upside down.

'The steroids they take probably makes them gay,' Julie would always say after having stood in front of them and still never getting noticed.

'Well, I never give up so easy' I said as she and I leaned over the checkout counter eyeing our prey get massages from their cheerleader sisters as we called them.

'Even if we go top less - they might still not notice us Rushmi,' I glanced over at Julie who was barely an A cup.

'We can't say never until we try,' we looked at each other and just burst out laughing. She and I were comfortable in sharing our insecurities and consoled each other in never getting any response from our Ryan and Chad. But she was so sweet to me, she always complimented me and I returned the favor too. It was the only thing that kept us from sinking into deep depression. Some days she would experiment with dark makeup and bright red lipstick to get Chad's attention. She reminded me of the Zambian $5 hookers whenever she wore her red lipstick and green eye shadow.

One time Julie wore a "shorter than short" dress and climbed up the ladder to shelve books close to where the volleyball team was studying on the third floor. Watching her climbing up, the guys thought they were in her way and got up and moved to another spot. Lucky for Julie, Professor Pervert was on the same floor and seeing her up there, he found himself a good spot and enjoyed the show. She immediately came down and threw the books on the table where I was sitting watching her shameless act.

'I hate them!' She said, and then walked towards the bathroom to hold on to what little pride she had. I went after her and did what every friend has to do.

'The guys are talking about you and laughing,' I said.

After making her feel worse, I would then build her up. I would build her self-esteem, put down the guys, really degrade the cheerleaders until she felt good about herself to open the stall door and come out. This cycle would end for the day and start the next day again.

Six months had past so fast of classes, shelving books, parading in front of the volleyball team, coding nights away, potlucks every Friday and Tomatina every Sunday. It was ironic that life just passed us by so fast and I had gotten into the routine of things. I hardly had time to miss my parents, had almost no homesickness, and made so many friends that it began to feel like I belonged. Life was systematic; it required time management and also a lot of discipline of getting things done on time. In Zambia getting up in the morning was an ordeal, keeping up with my homework was tedious and my parents constantly pushed me to be organized. But here, I was all alone, completely dependent on myself and somehow I was doing it all. I was on top of my tasks and doing so much more without anyone helping me. I was really proud of myself.

16

Sitting in the library cafeteria, Julie and I would often discuss our techniques to just get acknowledged by Ryan and Chad but the cheerleaders would never leave them alone. During one of our scheme sessions, Julie and I were having coffee at the cafeteria when a really handsome blue eyed blond guy sat at our table and opened his books. Guess there wasn't another table so he sat with us. Julie and I looked at each other and took out our books in an attempt to look smart and busy. She opened her Psychology book and I took out my large Computer Science book. The larger the book, the smarter we looked. But unable to even read a word in front of that blue eyed hottie, I pretended as though in great thought and turned to Julie and said;

'Paapu!' our code word for hunk. I had taught Julie some Hindi words so we could easily describe the people that took our breath away. Julie still glancing at her book and doing an excellent job of studying turned to me and said,

'Paapu, bhohot sona hai,'* nodding her head and holding back her urge to smile, Julie could barely get her words out. Her blushed pink face on the other hand was saying a lot.

'Thank you,' the guy looks at us grinning ear to ear.

Julie and I had our mouths open in complete shock! This blonde had understood us! Crap! His dorky smile made it completely embarrassing. We thought we were being sneaky but this guy figured it out. We both were still in shock and with our mouths open, I didn't know what to say.

'Mera naam Rich hai,'* said this white blonde guy in almost perfect Hindi accent. I noticed my mouth was open and so was Julie's and we looked at each other and started giggling. Oh my goodness! Never had I imagined this situation, we both were red in the face, but we both picked up our stuff and walked away quickly back to work.

'Ahhhhh, shit!' it was just unbelievable, what the hell, I'm so embarrassed!' I was hiding my face in a brown paper bag. Julie was hitting her head against the checkout table and we both were frazzled by this whole experience. During our insaneness, Prashant walks up to the check-out counter and confused to see one hitting her head, the other covered with a brown bag he said,

'You both on something?'

'Heehee very funny,' I pulled the bag and saw Prashant, standing with our hottie. He was still smiling and was breaking into a laugh which he tried very hard to control.

'This is Rich, he just started school and has come from India,' the hottie was still beaming at us. Julie had stopped banging her head and she and I shook hands with Rich.

'Bhohut acha laga apse milke,'* he showed off his Hindi. Not knowing what to do to get over this awkward moment I realized I had to break the ice,

'Apse milke acha laga paapu' Rich burst out laughing and now Julie and I too were giggling away. Prashant was standing watching us three laugh at an inside joke.

Rich walked out of the library with Prashant and we watched him leaving until finally looking at each other we burst out laughing. We laughed out so hard that I had tears in my eyes. Julie was on the floor lying flat on the ground in a laughing fit.

That evening Rich came back to the library and came looking for us. Julie had already gone for the day so I was there at the counter. Seeing him at first felt a bit odd but this encounter was just so strange there was no way I could ignore him. I smiled at him standing on one side of the counter while he stood at the other end.

'Hi,' I said sheepishly.

'Hi,' he was smiling showing off his perfect set of teeth. He didn't look dorky at all, he looked good.

'So that was some introduction.'

'Yeah, oh ….a bit embarrassing,' I was struggling to keep eye contact because he knew we thought he was good looking.

'Well, I think you're cute too if that helps.'

At that moment he stole my heart. The very first time an amazing looking guy that I liked thought I was cute too. He made my day and the embarrassment skyrocketed and I was tongue tied to say anything.

'I just moved in with Prashant until I find my own place. Do you want to walk together?,' he was asking to walk with Me? He lived in my building and he thought I was cute, at that point I felt there was nothing else to do but to say yes.

I clocked off from work, carried my backpack and he and I started walking towards the shuttle bus. But if we took the bus this moment would pass really fast. I wanted this moment to last just a little bit longer.

'Mind if we walk?' I said sounding as though I usually walk which I never did.

'Sure,' he would have agreed to anything that moment. We both started walking on this long sidewalk from the library towards University Ave towards our apartments. It was a lovely 45 min walk and gave us plenty of time to talk.

Rich was a really nice guy; was very flirty with me and knowing that I already thought he was cute, he flirted even more. He had spent two years in India as a missionary teaching English in Calcutta, Pune and in Rajasthan. He had been to more places in India than me and spoke Hindi very fluently. He knew about all the festivals, Gods, Ceremonies and foods. He was in his third year of Computer Science and had taken time off for his church to spend time teaching English in different parts of the world. He had also traveled to China, Cambodia and Nepal. He asked a lot of questions about my background. Once at our building, he walked up to my floor and was about to bid me goodbye,

'You know if this was a Sharukh Khan movie there would be a song right now,' he smiled pressing his bottom lip and I couldn't hold my laughter. Feeling very shy for some reason I thought about inviting him in, but hesitated and said goodnight.

Hearing him climb the stairs up to the fifth floor, I played the hit song from Sharukh Khan's DDLJ* movie while I lay in my bed staring at the ceiling. This was the first time when everything had gone right, unlike all my previous encounters with cute guys, this was the first time when it had felt just right. I fell asleep to romantic Hindi songs with even more romantic dreams.

The next day leaving my apartment, I saw Rich coming downstairs and seeing each other, we smiled. I thought we would walk together today too but right after Prashant and Nikhil came down too and with them with us, we took the bus together to campus.

Rich was in the Desi* group before leaving for India and returning he fitted right in our group especially because of his Hindi. He started joining in our Friday night potlucks and made the best Channa* dish. These potlucks were about cooking as close as possible to home cooked food like mommy and sitting around talking about classes, projects, graduation and getting the mighty Green card. In a way, it was like our support group in a foreign land.

Rich became one of the desi crowd boys hanging out with us all the time. But he also became close to me. He was in the computer science program as well and spent every moment with me. I found him very attractive, his ability to speak Hindi was awesome and he was aware of the Indian norms so he behaved himself. I liked him a lot.

17

Being with Rich, whose full name was Richard Peasland, I felt like he was more like me. He understood India, but he thought like an American, he respected other cultures but he held on to his beliefs. He was smart, handsome and really social. He knew Rayani, Musasha and Eskima; he knew the kids from China and he also knew the volleyball team.

He knew how much Julie and I drooled over them, so one day he brought some of the guys including Chad and Ryan to meet us in the Library.

'Guys these are my friends Rushmi and Julie,' there they stood four of the most handsome men on campus, fresh out of the showers, in uniform smiling at us, and shaking hands with us.

'Rushmi, that's an odd name; are you in a Rush all the time?' one of the hunks said I think his name was Gabriel or something. I was so anxious and overly excited to get so much attention from the volleyball team that I couldn't think straight. I wanted to impress them, I wanted to say something cool and I wanted to show them that I had watched most of their games.

'I watched your last game, you guys lost didn't you?' What the hell was that! Why in the world did I just say that? That was neither cool nor sporty. It was actually very bitchy of me. Probably the stupidest thing anyone could have said but I had said it. Julie's eyes stopped blinking and Rich was startled and everyone else just stood there staring at me. I really needed my Derek Jeter underwear that very moment.

'Well, we should be going,' Ryan headed out of the double doors and just like that they left. I had no idea why I just did that but my first impression had sucked. Even if Rich told them that I was a good person, I too wouldn't want to be my own friend that moment. I hid my face in my hands and waited for Julie to do her thing.

'Are you insane? What is wrong with you? You are an idiot!' Julie was yelling at me, she seemed really mad.

'I'm sorry, really sorry I don't know what happened but I mean it's true they did lose,' she was rolling her eyes and walking away from me. I had never seen anyone shelve books with such rage. She shelved nursing books in the political science section and accounting books in the biology section. She was pissed.

'I hate you! I hate you!' that's pretty much all she had to say. I gave her space and stayed in the lounge sulking the rest of the day. I had fumbled and messed up, made a complete fool of myself once again and I sucked. Those were my only thoughts. But it was so hard to keep my cool. It was really intimidating to talk to American boys and sounding cool in front of them. It was so much pressure to say something smart or funny. I was really confused. Plus, all this in front of Rich, the one guy I liked the most, witnessed me being a total ass. I felt like crap.

Confused and rejected, I went home and took out a birthday present I had gotten from my father, a hard covered book. It was covered in a golden border, had small red flowers and in the center was the word in gold - "DIARY". I opened the white lined pages and started writing;

"Dear Diary, today I made a total ass of myself…….".

After that incident, Julie forgave me and I promised to keep a low profile whenever or if ever Chad or Ryan came over to talk. I would give her the lead in talking to them. But every time the guys would come over to the library, they would say hello and go to the second floor to study.

'At least they know who we are!' I excitedly said to Julie who always returned with a frown. At this point, I shelved books on every floor except the one where Chad and Ryan sat.

18

A year had passed and my studies were coming along great. Two semesters down, I had understood the system of classes, figured out bus schedules and made great friends. Yet, still no roommate. Someone had booked the apartment with me but never showed up. The word was that my roommate would come in a few months so I was still living alone.

During the Christmas holidays it was very hard for me. There were no classes and pretty much everyone on campus had either gone home to family or just had gone out with friends. Julie had also gone to see her parents. The desi guys had all decided to drive to New York and spend their holidays there. But I didn't feel that comfortable sharing a motel room with so many guys. I had become close to these guys and they were all very nice, but sharing rooms, sharing their smell and sharing bathrooms was out of my comfort zone so I decided to stay back. I would have gone too if Anya and the other girls had agreed to share another room but they didn't agree and they felt comfortable staying with everyone in one room.

The campus was empty with hardly any cars, the weather was dull but one light was still on. Larry was at home, for Christmas? Throughout the year, I had taken Mili out for walks, he had dropped in to say hello but I had never really had a lot of time to chat with him. Knocking at his door, I found Larry looking frail and alone at home. He opened the door but before saying anything he had a coughing fit.

'Hey, you ok?' looking at him, I could tell he was sick. He coughed and looked so thin. I helped him get back into bed and searching in his kitchen, I found cans of soup and bread. Quickly I made him some chicken soup and brought some warm bread with a hot cup of tea. He must have been starving because he engulfed everything quickly and his color returned.

'I hadn't eaten all day, had been sick since yesterday but today, couldn't even get up to make some coffee,' he had a very country accent. Looking at Mili it looked like she hadn't eaten either. So I cleaned her bowl and fed her dog food and bread.

'You live alone?

'Yes, since my wife died thirteen years ago, I have been alone,'

'What about your children and grandkids?'

'They live far away,' he was getting up to put the dishes away.

'No, you sit, I got it.' I picked up his dishes and the additional ones around his bed and went over to the kitchen and started cleaning his place. Larry had the same kind of two bedroom apartment as mine so I knew it well. But he had furnished it very badly, with lots of old appliances stored in one room, the other room he used as his own bedroom.

The kitchen had simple dishes and everything looked really old. Even his curtains were yellowish and kept light from coming into the room. I opened the curtains, dusted his sofa and covered it with clean sheets, washed his dishes, threw out old stuff from his fridge and cooked him some rice and dal.

I even got some vanilla candles to freshen his apartment, finally the smell of fresh food filled his apartment and the smell of medicines and wet dog was gone. I had cleaned his floors and bathroom so he wouldn't have to worry about any of it.

'You don't have to do this'; Larry was now standing up by the door of his bedroom looking a lot better.

'No worries Larry, I hope you're okay? Do you need anything else?' I had never forgotten how Larry had taken care of me and doing this for him felt good.

'Thank you so much, I've been so used to being alone had forgotten how nice it was to have company, thank you,' He was very appreciative. It felt good to help him plus it was Christmas and I didn't want to be alone either.

I made some tea for myself and we sat at his kitchen table talking about his life. His two sons lived in Texas and California but never visited him because he had married another woman. After the death of their mother, Larry had married one of the son's housekeeper. The second wife was ten years younger and not very educated and Larry's sons' disapproved of him marrying Elma.

'Elma was the nicest woman I had met after a long time and she just won my heart the first time I saw her. After the death of Marla, my first wife, I had moved in with my son. Elma was my son's housekeeper. She took such good care of me that we fell in love but the boys wouldn't hear of it so they sent us away the day I married Elma. Since, I have been living here but she too passed away with Breast Cancer.'

Larry was looking at a picture of Elma. She was a simple lady dressed in a white dress with straps and a white flower in her bun. She was an African woman with a big nose and pretty eyes and on the heavy side. But even today as Larry looked at her he smiled as though she was still here.

'My sons said that they would never accept her as their mother so since then, they have never spoken to me again. I do get pictures of grandkids but that's about all I have with them,' he showed me pictures of a very white family with lots of kids. He had just received this picture in a Christmas card that read – "Merry Christmas from the Stevens."

We had talked for four hours and it was evening, but with no school and no one around I invited Larry over for dinner at my apartment. This was going to be a special Christmas dinner. I asked him to bring the wine and I would make us a great Christmas/Indian dinner. He was so thrilled about our dinner, he even took out an old fake Christmas tree he had hiding in his room. With all the decorations out, he setup the tree in my apartment and decorated it with so much happiness, he even sang the Rudolf song for me.

By the end of our dinner, I knew names of all the Deer and learned so many Christmas songs. The tree was beautiful, the dinner was amazing with chicken curry, rice, fruit cake, and salad and wine, we were enjoying the evening. Larry brought his Frank Sinatra CDs and asked me to dance with him. It was so sweet, I felt like he was my grandpa and in our loneliness we found a friend in each other. While dancing he whispered in my ear,

'This sign is Hitler's sign,' pointing to my Ganesh sign he smiled at me. I was puzzled at first and didn't believe him but he chuckled and said the picture I had taken from his storage was the sign of Hitler. I gave it a look again and giggled, wow! I wonder if any of the other guys had known all this time that the Ganesh symbol is clockwise but Hitler's is an anticlockwise swastika. I picked up the Hitler sign and took off the Gay flag and returned it to Larry.

'Thank you so much but I will not be needing these,' we both were smiling.

'I'll see what I can find in storage to replace these, but first a little something for you,' he was holding a little box wrapped in a bow.

'It's Christmas. We all get gifts,' he handed me the box. I wasn't sure where this was going. Suddenly I felt worried. I had thought of him as my grandpa, I hope he isn't thinking anything else. Why is he giving me a small golden box? What if it is something very expensive? What if he is so lonely and looking for a third wife? What should I do? Still perplexed with my own thoughts, Larry placed the box in my hand and waited for me to open it. Unsure of what to do I hesitated, but seeing in his eyes the thrill of offering it to me; I had no choice but to accept it. I opened the box and found a key.

'This is the key to the laundry machine, you don't have to use quarters anymore just insert it into the slot and it will run for free, but as long as you don't tell or share it with anyone.'

'Yeah!!, this is the best gift ever!,' I was so thrilled as though I had won a million bucks. For a student on a tight budget it was the best gift ever. I felt so guilty thinking Larry was about to propose to me. Seeing his key, I hugged Larry and felt comfortable knowing that he was a cool guy.

We drank more wine and listened to his CD.

'Larry, who is Frank Sinatra?' Larry turned to me in complete shock.

'WHAT? Only the most famous actor, singer,' Larry looked like he was almost mad at me for not knowing.

'Okay, I mean remember I grew up in Zambia, I bet you don't even know the A-team or Star Wars'; I was hoping to calm his disbelief.

'Oh….yeah, I do, dialogues like *Let the force be with you*, and *I like it When a Plan Comes Together*,' Larry knew every dialogue. He had made his point, I knew very little about American culture, American classics and everything American.

'Okay,' I said sheepishly in seeing that he knew a lot more than I gave him credit for.

'But do you know the Zambian national anthem in Swahili?' I was being a smart ass. Larry rolled his eyes and I knew he thought I was a FOB with very little knowledge about this great country.

'Ok you're right I have very little knowledge about America, the kids in class say things like "*And may your first child be a masculine child*" and everyone laughs but I don't get it.'

'Don't tell me you haven't seen The Godfather?' Larry stood up out of his chair and looked like he was going to pass out.

'Nope,' I said almost afraid to tell him. Now Larry had lost it. It was unimaginable to him that I had such little knowledge about American culture.

'Now, I don't care what you have to do, these fifteen days of Christmas break, you and I are watching a lot of movies. Wait, let me get the first one,' he put his wine glass down and went downstairs only to return after a few minutes with his VCR and video tapes. He struggled with the old TV but got it setup. My first lesson on American culture was to watch The Godfather.

Watching the movie for three hours, he explained every dialogue, every scene, how many academy awards it had won, and every actors name and history. I now knew that for best actor Marlon Brando received an Oscar, the breakthrough movie of Al Pacino, and also learned some of the famous dialogues like, *"I'm gonna make him an offer he can't refuse", "A man who doesn't spend time with his family can never be a real man", "Fredo, you're my older brother, and I love you. But don't ever take sides with anyone against the family again. Ever!"*

By the end of the movie, I tried reciting some of the dialogues, tightening my jaw and squinting my eyes I tried to imitate Marlon Brando and said,

'First you come into my home on my daughter's wedding.'

'STOP! please stop,' Larry put his hand blocking my face a clear sign I sucked at being the Godfather.

'Don't ever try that again especially in public. One thing American is to know who should imitate and who shouldn't, you definitely shouldn't.,' Larry rolled his eyes away from my face in complete disgust. He pissed me off so bad. He didn't know who he was messing with. I could imitate a lot of people, every good Hindi movie dialogues was my thing and that day I promised myself that I would work on my Godfather skills-at least in private.

After the Godfather, there was no stopping Larry. The next morning, early, he came back to my apartment but this time he brought A Wonderful Life, a must see he had said especially during Christmas.

Watching the amazing character of George Bailey, I enjoyed his famous dialogue, "*What is it you want, Mary? What do you want? You want the moon? Just say the word and I'll throw a lasso around it and pull it down. Hey. That's a pretty good idea. I'll give you the moon, Mary.*" This movie could very easily have been a Bollywood hit; it had all the makings of a great Hindi movie, romance, pain and success at the end. I really enjoyed this one.

We had spent three hours early in the morning already watching the movie. With the weather outside still below zero degrees, there was nothing else to do but continue watching movies. So, we ordered Pizza and stayed glued to the TV. That day we heard Frank Sinatra's songs, we watched movies of Elvis Presley, and watched Miracle on 34th Street, Goodfellas, Bonnie and Clyde, Big, Groundhog day, and The Wizard of Oz.

After watching the Oz I finally understood what Julie had said the first time I had met her in the library, "we're not in Kansas anymore Dorothy". It took me a year but finally I got her joke…funny.

Early the next morning, Larry brought in a big pile of pancakes and a bigger box of video tapes for day three of Americanization. He started by playing the movie, Field of Dreams, a Kevin Costner movie. We were in the middle of watching Field of Dreams when I revealed to Larry another big secret.

'I don't understand baseball or football,' Larry almost had a heart attack. Just the thought of someone not following football was unimaginable to him. He was a big fan of the Chicago Bears and couldn't even imagine life without Football.

'You poor, deprived, withdrawn child- I had no idea about your condition, I have to teach you sports. You will never survive in America without learning all the sports people are crazy about; there is baseball, football, and basketball which are the three main ones. Follow these three and you'll make a lot of friends. By April baseball will start, you ARE going to a game with me but first let's learn football. For now, let me get my tapes of games.'

Larry had been mumbling to himself, quickly he marched downstairs to gather something. But I was a bit tired of watching so many movies; yet had no way of saying no to him especially now that my lesson on sports was about to start.

After a few minutes, Larry came up with a bag full of tapes and pushed one in the VCR.

'This is the Super Bowl' 86, Bears against Patriots, one of their best games,' he sat close to the TV like he had never seen this game before.

'What's the Super Bowl?' I looked at him confused why he was biting his lips and seemed in pain. He was shaking his head in disbelief, took a deep breath and went to work with me. Taking a paper and pencil he started drawing on a piece of paper.

He drew the field and labeled positions, he talked first about offensive positions, quarterback, fullback/running back, halfback/running back, wide receiver, left and right offensive line men, guard, and center.

'You want your wide receivers to be good runners, you want your left and right offensive line men to be the heavy guys and you want your quarter back to throw accurately,' Larry was very serious about his football and I knew I couldn't joke about any of this stuff. I had to pay attention or else he would get offended. This thing was like a religion to him. He was so passionate about football and I could see how determined he was in making sure I got the game. So I paid full attention to his Football 101.

'Then, you have the defense that blocks the offense from scoring. You have the defensive linemen; these are the heavy guys doing most of the blocking. The cornerbacks are the fast runners who go after the wide receivers and the linebackers attack the runners and quarterback'

'A play usually begins when the quarterback takes a snap from the center and then either hands off to a running back or a tail back, passes to a receiver or a running back, runs the ball himself, spikes the ball or takes a knee'

'What's a knee?'

'That's for later, stay focused on the basics,' Larry spoke as though he was talking to a four year old. But I appreciated him taking the time to teach me. No matter what classes I take in college, no one would have taught me about American culture the way Larry did.

After a few hours of talking and multiple sheets of paper and three cups of tea, I had a basic understanding of American Football.

'I think I get it! So there is one League called National Football League (NFL) within it there are two conferences - National Football Conference (NFC) and the American Football Conference (AFC). These consist of teams that play against each other, the surviving teams play against each other in the Super Bowl which usually takes place around January. The next Super Bowl is on January 28th. The field is 100 yards and at 50 yards called mid field the teams start playing. There is offense and defense, quarterback, whose ultimate goal is to get the ball in the end zone. If the ball goes into the goal post or end zone it's called a touchdown.'

'Good now here is a list of some of the teams,' Larry handed me a list, my job was to remember names of some of the Football teams, on the very top was the Chicago Bears.

By the end of the night I had managed to remember the Redskins, Giants, Dallas Cowboys, Miami Dolphins, NY Jets, Arizona Cardinals and Denver Broncos. Hoping to impress Larry, I recited them but he wasn't the least bit pleased. He made me watch four Super Bowl games explaining every detail of the game.

During my enlightenment of American Football, I had just remembered an incident in the cafeteria where Chad and his buddies were eating and watching a football game. When the team had scored everyone was cheering including the cheer leaders seated next to them. Just to fit in, I had really tried to sound cool and sporty so I joined in the cheer and said, 'What an amazing home run, wow! Yeah!' I was cheering and giving everyone high fives. They had all exchanged looks which I took as-oh she is so cool-but today realized they were thinking that I was a complete idiot. I was probably the first person to score a home run in a Football game. This would require five pages of journal writing to wash away.

Fourth day of Christmas holidays and I had watched four super bowl games, and seven American classics. I was wondering what Larry had planned for me today. In anticipation, I made a few things to eat because once Larry started talking about football; he wouldn't even give me a break to go to the bathroom. I made rice, chicken, dal, salad and chips with dip. Right on time, Larry knocked at 9am with more video tapes.

'Today we cover baseball,' he put his stuff down and started again with the paper and pencil concept.

'I know Derek Jeter plays baseball for the Yankees!' I was thrilled to know at least one thing about baseball.

'What position does he play?'

We looked at each other and I hid my face in shame. I really didn't know anything more about Derek. I had been in love with him yet knew nothing about his game. So today, I was going to learn everything about the game.

Baseball was a bit easier for me to learn. The positions were easier to understand, pitcher, first, second, and third base. Derek played short stop. There was right, center and left field, a home run was when the ball went out of the field and the batter was allowed to walk on base, if the pitcher threw four balls. A player was out with three strikes. After his hours lecture, I felt very comfortable with my ability to understand the game.

We watched two of the World Series games and I found out the names of some of the good teams – Atlanta Braves, Chicago White Sox, and NY Yankees and NY Mets, and San Francisco Giants.

In fifteen days, I had watched forty movies and absorbed as much of the American sports as I could. We had watched three of the World Series, five Super Bowl games, and two basketball games. Baseball was much easier for me to understand and now I could tell whether it was a strike or a ball even before the umpire. I could actually follow the pitches and knew most of the players' names on the Yankees team. Actually, I not only found out that Derek was a good player but his team members included other hot players like Alex Rodriguez and Andy Pettite. Larry pushed me to learn the names of the players on the Chicago Cubs or White Sox, but I kept messing up their names and went back to the Yankees.

'Move to New York then!' Larry growled at me but I found that extremely funny, he was so passionate about his sports.

I was so thrilled that now I could tell a touch down from a home run, could follow an actual game and this year I would follow the Super Bowl. There had been so many incidents when the kids in class would talk about a game and everyone would immediately bond. But I just nodded my head without any clue on what they were talking about. Finally, I would have something to add. It was actually quite interesting too.

It was New Year's Day and the whole place was quiet. Everyone was away from campus. The desi gang was at Times Square. I was in my apartment remembering all the New Year parties I had been to in Zambia. Every year, in Zambia, we would have halls rented, decorated with balloons and party favors and lots of food for everyone. The entire town would be at the party and we all would dance the night away.

My last New Year's Day was in Zambia and that's the day we had received an email confirming my acceptance into this University. My parents were happy and sad at the same time. They had spent so much money filling out college applications, spending hundreds of Kwacha on visa fees, air tickets and spent close to thousand dollars for putting my name into a Green card Lottery. Having spent close to six months on the entire process, I had finally been accepted into this college. That day, our New Year eve party was a bitter sweet moment. We three held smiles during the party but inside, I knew there was a lot of sadness, fear, excitement and anxiety.

Today, a year later, I was in my apartment alone. It was ok I told myself. Larry had planned on getting a cake and some extra goodies and we were going to start 1999 with another movie. This was part of growing up too. Not every moment has to be of your liking, even though this was not the best New Year's party, it was still an experience.

Larry brought the movie The Graduate, with Dustin Hoffman. He said it was one of his favorites and I even saw Larry move his lips repeating the dialogue – *'For God's sake, Mrs. Robinson. Here we are. You got me into your house. You give me a drink. You... put on music. Now you start opening up your personal life to me and tell me your husband won't be home for hours. Mrs. Robinson, you're trying to seduce me.?'*

He was so funny, a man in his sixties so fond of movies and crazy about sports. He was truly what I called an American. He really was a nice person, so down to earth, so accepting and very charming. Never had I imagined myself spending New Year's Day with an old white man in my apartment. In one year my life had changed so much. But despite my struggles, I enjoyed every moment. Being on my own, learning to handle everything that was coming my way was helping me grow into a confident adult-at least I felt more confident. The attitude I used to see in kids returning from America felt as though they were being snooty. But today, I realized it was just the opposite. This experience in America didn't make one snobbish; on the contrary, it made people humble. Despite having the comforts in Zambia, I enjoyed myself in America. That's the day I understood all the kids returning to Zambia and why they behaved the way they did. They were not being arrogant as I had seen them but rather they were just confident, independent and hard-working kids.

Christmas Holidays and New Year was over and now it was back to life again. Soon everyone started returning from their vacations and Larry's lectures had come to an end. He had successfully taught me about movies, sports and most importantly given me company in my loneliness. Now I was ready to start year two of my life. The campus was filled with life again, freezing cold temperatures still covered all of Chicago and everyone was starting their busy lives with the new semester. After Larry's first incident of being ill and no one watching over him, I took it upon myself to make Larry breakfast every day. I delivered it every day before heading to class. I couldn't promise him more than this because of my schedule but at least I would see him each morning and ensure he was well. Whatever I made for myself, I would make for him too. I also fed Mili before leaving for my class. Some days, Larry kept the door to his apartment open so I wouldn't wake him so early. I felt like he was part of my family.

19

Life in college was going by really fast; I was already in my third semester. I was taking five classes, working ten hours a week and the projects in class were keeping me in the lab every night. On one of my usual busy days, exhausted from coding all day I went to work at the library which seemed relaxing. It was 3pm and Rayani was reading in the library lounge for a nursing quiz but her eyes wondered every time a guy walked in.

'You are such a flirt Rayani,' I commented as I sat next to her sipping on my cappuccino.

'So? These are the best years of my life, when else will I enjoy myself?' She winked at me. She looked pretty in her black high neck sweater and the guy walking in had definitely noticed her.

Musasha walked in soon after and we all drank our warm coffee. We talked a lot about Africa and exchanged some of the music we used to listen back home. I had missed Zambian music. The sounds of the beating drums, the accents and not appreciating it then had not even brought one CD from back home.

'Come over today, we have a party at our apartment and all night it's my kind of music,' Musasha smiled.

'That sounds great. I would love to go,' thrilled to finally get a break and dancing was one of my favorite things to do.

'Ok, pick you up after your shift,' it was set. After work around 8pm they would pick me up. I was wearing jeans with a blue sweater, not really party clothes, but with no time to go back I didn't have a choice.

Later that evening at their apartment, which was a two bedroom apartment on the ground floor, they had a few chairs and a large dining table filled with chips and dip. They had lots of beer and pasta and pizza too. No one seemed to care about the food, but everyone was holding a beer bottle. I got a bottle for myself and started jamming to the loud African music; it wasn't Zambian music but very similar.

I saw Rayani, wearing a black small dress, Eskima was wearing brown pants with a white shirt, Musasha was wearing a white traditional outfit and the others were also dressed semi casual. I saw Chad, Rich, Samuel, Ryan and Gabriel, and I also met people I had seen on campus, there was Chang, a really good programmer in his third year from China. There was Brian, the quarterback for the college football team.

Amongst the crowd, I enjoyed watching everyone dancing on the floor and just having a great time. I hadn't been to a party this whole time and was so excited to finally be here. The party went on for four hours, and then I saw people talking and laughing out loud. I then heard the guys giving each other high fives and then I heard them saying,

'We are in!' Chad, Samual, Gabrial, Musasha and Rich left the apartment. Rich hadn't spoken to me at all, he was so occupied with his friends, I thought maybe he hadn't even seen me. Then Rayani come over and said,

'Let's go.'

She took my hand and took me towards her car where three more girls including Eskima joined us and off we went. I really had no idea what to expect but soon we arrived at what looked like a club. The Chippendale, exclusively for ladies was displayed in a neon sign. It looked like a fancy bar and lots of women were entering the door where two large body guards stood.

Entering the club, I was first blinded by the darkness then walking around the corner we entered the stage area, all carpeted in pink, there were tables setup and women were drinking around the stage area which was lighted with bright lights.

'What is this place? Is there a show?' I looked at Rayani who looked like she was really looking forward to the night.

'Just relax and enjoy the show.'

The lights went dim and then came out two men, wearing a tuxedo collar and bow tie, bear chest and black underwear. These men were very muscular, tan and greased up. When the music started they started dancing in a manner that actually shamed me for even watching but the other girls started screaming and whistling and cheering. Oh my God! I was in a strip club watching grown men strip! I stood in complete shock watching grown men move their bodies in ways I didn't know they could, I found it to be extremely weird and embarrassing.

Watching these women drooling over these guys and these men who were really nice looking dancing like that was strange to me. I had heard about these clubs in Zambia but had never been to one. Today, I just felt ashamed to watch these men. Then more men started coming on stage with even less clothing and these women screamed even louder.

Then these men jumped off the stage and started dancing around the tables, one on each table rubbing against women who screamed and placed dollar bills inside their already small undies which looked more like strings. Then this Arnold Schwarzenegger lookalike sneaks up behind me and starts shaking his hips around me. He grabs hold of my hips and starts grinding next to me. I didn't know what to do. I started laughing hysterically while this man is dancing around me. I mean, there is something about a really good looking man dancing erotically next to you, I couldn't handle the excitement and started laughing obnoxiously. I think he was waiting for a tip but I didn't have anything on me. I looked inside my pockets and only found three quarters. I pulled out the quarters and inserted them into this man's underwear; he stopped dancing immediately – gave me an angry look and walked away. As he walked away, two of the quarters fell on the ground and I burst out laughing even louder.

Rayani kept dancing with these men and putting dollars in their underwear. She worked hard for her money every day at the hospital but today she must have spent almost $100 on one guy. Even if I wanted to tip the guy, I would still put pennies down his underwear. Thinking to myself, I giggled and stayed back and sipped my ice water observing this part of American culture.

I didn't enjoy the strip club as much as I enjoyed watching these women going nuts. They seemed so thrilled about this whole experience, and Rayani seemed even more insane. I was amazed at this whole experience. I guess I was mostly concerned about dancing with one of these guys and with my luck he would turn out to be my next professor, so I stayed back. This was not my kind of fun. It was way too strange for my taste. Leaving the club that night, the girls were thrilled and had enjoyed themselves. We left the club close to

2am and I was glad to be back in my apartment. That night I did giggle as I wrote in my Diary thinking about such clubs in India, I bet my birthing hips guys would be ideal for this job.

Next morning, I was typing away in the lab when Nikhil came over with the school paper,

'Guys check this out! Look, Rich is in the paper!' He placed the paper on the table and everyone circled around him. On the second page was the headline, "Students Behaving Badly", there was a picture of Chad, Gabrial, Samuel and Rich and Musasha standing around police cars! After everyone had read the article I finally got my turn.

After leaving the party last night, the boys had gone downtown looking for a hooker according to the article. During their search for the right woman, they tried to pick up this blonde woman who turned out to be a cop! Everyone in the lab was laughing. Holy crap! They had been arrested and were in jail the whole night. I was speechless, and to think that I was at that party. I was good friends with these guys; what if I had gotten in trouble? What if the desi crowd knew that I was with those guys? What if I had gone to jail? Imagining myself calling my parents in Zambia to say that I had been arrested in a prostitution case gave me chills just thinking about it. Everyone had been laughing and cracking jokes about these guys but I was truly frightened. Samuel was also involved in this mess and he was from Morocco. How would he explain this to his parents? I couldn't even imagine him being a part of this; this was totally out of character for him. He probably was at the wrong place at the wrong time. I too was so naïve and could easily get into a situation like this without even knowing. Just going to the club last night with the girls was one thing but what if there had been drugs? I too could be in the papers. I should be more aware of where I'm going and with whom. That day I promised myself to be more careful.

I worried about what would happen to Samuel. What was it going to be like to see Rich again plus poor Chad and Gabriel, their team would really be upset about all this. These guys now had a criminal record. How would they finish college? What about their families? How would they explain this to their parents? Anything like this amongst the desi crowd and parents lose it. The embarrassment and shame that something like this would bring was just unimaginable to me. I prayed that never should I get into anything like this again.

Knowing that these guys were going out to buy a prostitute changed my entire view of these boys. I was conflicted on what I was feeling. I was disgusted to think that they would hire a woman to use and actually pay her for pleasing themselves. They would all share one woman was a thought that I couldn't brush away. But then again, I saw my girlfriends go crazy over men doing the same thing. They too put money in men's' underwear and enjoyed watching them undress. It was a very different culture. Living in Zambia, I had never been introduced to this concept, but it seemed like kids in college were very familiar with these issues. This chapter in American entertainment was very unsettling for me. I felt that the boundaries Indian parents put on their kids sometimes prevent them from doing something outrageous like hiring a prostitute. With the fear of letting our families down, we usually stay away from all this so maybe there was something to Indian expectations. While American culture was open and independence focused, Indian culture provided the boundaries within which to find that independence.

A few weeks later, we had heard that these guys had been in jail. They now had a criminal record and Samuel had lost his visa and was going back home. The whole campus was laughing at their case but underneath their laughter I could see so many students thanking their stars for not being caught. I was one of the students thanking God over and over again.

20

It was January 28th and the Super Bowl XXXV was being played at the Raymond James Stadium in Florida between the AFC champions, Baltimore Ravens against the NFC champions, NY Giants. Larry wanted to watch the game on the big screen, so we went to the student lounge area in the cafeteria where other kids had also had the same idea and watched the game.

I sat amongst other students and without much effort was fully engrossed in the game.

'Jermaine returned the ball to the New York yard line,' I was explaining to Larry who had missed some of the game during his bathroom break.

'Baltimore score touchdown pass to the wide receiver some Brandon guy,' I think that's his name,' during Larry's second bathroom break.

'Penalty against Giants…..,' during Larry's third bathroom break.

'Ravens advanced to the 24-yard line but missed a field goal,' that was during Larry's fourth break. He was drinking a lot of beer during the game and went to the bathroom way too often.

It had been an amazing game and more so for me. My first Super Bowl and I had fully understood it. Larry was very proud of me. I felt like America is so connected with its sports and anyone really wanting to understand this culture has to learn this part as well. I was so grateful to Larry who had given me this chance. Now there wouldn't be any home runs in football.

'Larry, thanks to you, I got it, and loved it!' I hugged Larry for all he had done for me.

'Now it's your turn,' looking puzzled Larry didn't know what I was talking about.

'Just wait and see,' we reached home and I played the only Hindi movie I had brought from Zambia to help during my homesickness- Sholay.

'Indian Classic movie, you're going to love it,' I made Larry watch the entire movie without forwarding any songs and in between the movie he dozed off. I woke him up, making sure he understood every dialogue. Throughout the movie, he kept asking me if the two heroes' in the movie were gay because they kept holding hands and hugging each other. He thought the women were a bit chubby and found the villain to be average looking. But he loved the violence in the story and was very intrigued by the scenery of India. He almost ruined it for me, my very favorite movie and he had dissed some of the good parts. Once we were done, he got up to leave.

'And?' I asked him.

'Too many songs and very little nudity,' he commented and left my apartment. That was the beginning and end of Bollywood 101. Maybe next time I should get a Madhuri movie that would definitely peak his attention.

The third semester was going on its high pace as usual but with no volleyball players and no Rich, we desi kids were very fixated on our studies. Every potluck had a discussion about Nikhil and Anand getting closer to graduating and finding their first job.

'I met Jay Chand today, he seems to think that I should have no problem getting into this company,' Anand was very giddy and excited about imagining life after college.

'Imagine man, a nice house, car and better furniture, I will not take any crap from my apartment, all new stuff,' Anya was day dreaming.

'I need to send money to my parents soon; my sister is getting closer to marriage but dad wants to know how much I can send him and when. So he can plan for her wedding.' Nikhil was already feeling the pressures of family and their expectations. He was still three semesters away from graduating and already his parents had started asking him for his future income. If only they could see this wonderful young man working his butt off and living on $250 a month budget and getting perfect grades. Instead of giving him room to breathe, the expectations and responsibilities on his shoulders was getting heavier and heavier.

I still felt blessed because my parents had never placed so much pressure on me. They actually had never asked about my future job nor put pressure on me. For my parents, grades were their only concern. Nothing less than an A in each class was their only rule. I was amazed at myself because living with my parents in Zambia; I had gotten terrible grades. I had never taken any responsibility or interest in my studies. Yet being on my own, this feeling of making my grades, keeping my GPA at 4.0 and being cautious in spending and budgeting all came with being independent. This had been the best thing for me to grow up. I actually understood why in America kids move out at 18. It finally made sense to me.

21

With the fourth semester in full swing, the rush of buying books and figuring out schedules and finding classes, meeting with advisors all came pouring down on me. I had Penguin and King Kong but was really glad to move away from the Pervert. I had met with my advisor, attended classes, bought my books and did five hours at the library. Having spent all day on campus, I was ready to lie down. Taking the bus home I could only think about making a sandwich for myself and then taking a nap.

I had been out all day returning to my apartment at 8pm to find the lights on and Indian food and dirty dishes in the sink. There was a big mess in the bathroom of dirty towels and a big pool of water on the floor.

'What the hell?' I murmured to myself. It's not a break in unless the thief was an Indian hungry dirty person who took a shower before robbing me. It can't be Larry because he never uses my things. Looking around I heard something in the other bedroom. I knocked on it and opened the door. Standing stark naked was a man bending down to put lotion on his legs.

With his rear end in full view, I froze. Someone was screaming. Soon I figured it was me who was screaming. I was screaming while still watching this man. Now he too was screaming while running to grab his towel which was lying on the floor in the bathroom across the bedroom.

Watching this man run from the room then outside into the living room then into the bathroom picking up his towel while screaming like a girl was a very weird sight. But to my disappointment, I was just screaming, not running out or afraid just screaming. Seeing him naked reminded me of those hilarious monkeys who have extremely large red butts and constantly groom themselves. I wanted to leave but at the same time I wanted to see because this was my first time of seeing a man – the whole of him. It was not as endearing as I had imagined. Once the towel was on, I came back to my senses and attempted to get out of my apartment.

'Who the hell are you?' I turned around facing this person who was now half naked and half covered with MY towel.

'Who the hell are you?' this strong voice spoke back almost accusing me of wrong doing.

'This is my apartment. How did you even get in?'

'Don't you even know how to knock.'

'Did you break in?'

'How dare you see me naked!' we were both talking at the same time. We must have been really loud because Larry heard us from the first floor and came running upstairs.

'Hey, hey calm down you two,' Larry tried to come in between us but we both were still pointing our fingers at each other.

'Rushmi, this is your roommate!' Larry spoke on top of his voice.

'Roommate! My Roommate!' I was screaming now.

'This is ridiculous, how can I have a male roommate? I can't live with him!'

'Rushmi, calm down please let's sit,' Larry was pulling my arm to sit at the table and the other man was also quiet.

'Bobby, you might want to wear something,' Larry gave the other man a nod and the other man got up quickly to get dressed.

'Rushmi, listen I opened the door for him, I'm really sorry, but we waited for you all day and the poor guy hadn't eaten anything since 5am, so I just let him in,' Larry was trying to comfort me.

'Roommate! Larry, are you kidding me? There is no way I'm living with a man. You know that, how could you allow this? You know me better than that!' I was so upset at Larry and more so grossed because a man had been in my apartment without my knowledge.

Just then the man came out of the empty bedroom wearing blue jeans, white shirt and he had a silver bracelet on his left wrist, gelled hair and I think Polo after shave. He didn't wear an under shirt and his hairy chest was sticking out of the shirt collar. Dressed up he actually looked very nice. His face was very soft, softer for a man and his lips were pinkish in color, for a guy he was my height, and weighed maybe 110lbs possibly in his early thirties. Knowing I had seen ALL of him, it was a bit hard for me to make eye contact and I think he felt the same way. Plus, this was the first time I had actually SEEN a guy and from what I saw it was freakish.

'Rushmi meet Bobby, Bobby this is Rushmi the girl I told you about,' Larry was sitting between me and the other man. We didn't say much initially but I couldn't understand how they could assign me a guy for a roommate. This would not work at all.

'Hi,' this little voice said.

'Hi,' awkward was the only sound coming out of me especially because I was imagining him sitting in front of me naked grooming a monkey. I guess those sights are hard to get out of your system.

'Rushmi, this is Bobby, he is the son of a professor here on Campus. Because of some issues with his dad, I had to find him accommodations elsewhere just for a few days. I know you didn't want a male roommate, but I felt it would be safe to have Bobby. He is a very good boy and I swear he will never be in your way. It's just until he sorts out things with his father.' Larry touched my hand and I knew he wanted my help.

'What's going on Larry? You guys up to something illegal?' I had a bad feeling about this.

'You guys getting me involved in something illegal? I'm not getting involved and Larry you know my situation. I can't let my parents down by getting into trouble. How could you do this to me?' I was in shock that Larry would use me like this.

'I am so sorry but it's not Larry's fault, it mine. I asked him for a favor and he could only think of you who could help,' this man was talking to me. Suddenly he seemed humble and honest.

'My father is the Dean of the Business school, Mr. Jay Chand, I think you must have heard of him in various events around campus?' Bobby was staring at me and I could tell in his eyes something was very wrong.

'Go on.' I listened carefully.

'I just need to stay away from my father just for a few days that's all,' Bobby sat up and looked at Larry.

'If you want my help then you need to tell me everything or else just leave,' I was way too scared of getting in trouble especially after the case with Samuel. Exchanging looks, Bobby took a deep breath in and with Larry's nod of approval, Bobby began telling me his story.

'Well, I happen to have stumbled on something my father was doing that well, basically, is taking advantage of students and making a lot of money off of them,' Bobby seemed ashamed of talking about his father.

'Wait, What? I don't understand.'

'There are a bunch of people on campus that work with my dad to exploit students and make money off of them.'

'But he seems so nice,' I remembered him from the orientation night and this man seemed like a really nice person. What is he doing that's so wrong? He has a PhD in something but I remember his speech, it was very inspiring.

'You see international students who come to this country have little idea about the rights and wrongs of America so, basically my dad looks for such people and then sets them up in a scam to get money out of them for years.'

'How?'

'During your third year, you get invited to my dad's place, he dines and entertains and takes care of the students, becoming their father figure. Then he talks about your future and getting that almighty Green Card. He knows these hard working students have huge responsibilities and no one they can trust. So, he gains that trust, shows them that he cares. Specifically those students who do well in their studies and are looking to get settled in the US. He targets those students. He promises you an H-1 after graduation and a job right after college with the promise to getting that Green Card.'

'That actually sounds really good up to now,' I was not getting the point.

'Yes but if it's too good to be true it probably is. You see he claims that from your third year, you have to deposit $1000 every month into a BOND as he calls it, which will be the deposit towards attaining that Green Card. Then, once you graduate he gets you hired by his own Consulting Company which is run by his buddies. This company gets you an H-1 for six years during which 80% of your salary is taken out as commission and after abusing you for six years with working over 100hrs a week, he then applies for your card. Plus, he puts up these kids in terrible living conditions to the point where they become so scared of life outside this company. If anyone tries to leave, well they just can't.'

'But it seems so risky. Anyone could complain against him.'

'Well, you think about it. If he holds your H-1 and you pull the plug, you get deported too. Plus, he's getting you that Green Card, so these naïve students think that another six years of suffering is justified for the benefit of their families. By the time you figure out their scam, you're a few years into this process. You've invested thousands of dollars; why would anyone go up against him? This company isn't openly run by him; it's all covered up so nicely that no one knows who is actually running the show. I mean, I don't even know who all is involved and who actually is in charge. All I know is he's making a lot of money and a lot of people are involved.'

'But why aren't you with him enjoying this money?'

'Because I hate him,' Bobby held a stern look on his face that showed his hate for his father.

'Okay,' I said sarcastically and totally not buying that as a reason to get involved.

'I have a personal vengeance against him, plus this is wrong and someone has to do something, so better I do this, this way no one else has to take the fall.'

'This is all really interesting but what has this got to do with me?'

'Well, nothing specific but I have a plan to deal with dad but needed help and Larry thought you would be the one to help me out.'

'What is this great plan?' I was curious what they had in mind.

'Well, it's a bit strange but I think it'll work. All I need from you is a place to hide for a while.'

'Excuse me? Hide! That right there sounds illegal, no way,' the only thought in my head was spending time in jail.

'Listen ok, so going through my dad's computer, I know that he has a million or so in his account and in order to make this right, I need that money to help these students whose H-1 visa's they control.'

'Keep talking.'

'Well, the idea is to find a way to help these students maintain their status but putting dad out of business.'

'How?'

'By creating a new company that will take over the existing students' visas.' But to do that I need funding to open this company and that's where you come in.'

'How?' This was sounding more and more like a Brad Pitt movie.

'I faked my own kidnapping and asked my dad for $1 million dollars. This will be a good start to opening this company, but until I get funded, I need a place to hide.'

'Are you insane?!' I was almost about to laugh! This is silly. I think he's been watching a lot of Hindi movies.

'No, really, I just need money to start another firm that will take over the current H-1s then find these kids legit jobs. If I cut off his supply of new students, he will be out of business really fast. Really, it's the only way. We can't let these kids get deported. What's the point of doing that? They might as well stay with him rather than be sent home.' Bobby was talking as though it was no big deal but I was in complete disbelief. This guy was smoking something. He had the right intentions, but kidnapping and million dollars, come on, who's he kidding? This was totally insane.

'So, you take money from daddy through ransom, open your new company, but how will you get him to transfer his current employees and where will you get them work?' I had to start poking holes in his theory because he was thinking theoretically, not practical at all.

'I am not sure. Maybe pay them for every H-1? I haven't figured out this part yet.' I knew it! He had terrible plans and with his silly kidnapping, I could easily get in trouble. No way was I going to be a part of this. No way.

'Well, why even go through this process at all? Just get into this business with him then take over the company and ruin it from the inside out. I mean, he is your dad, if you want in, he will take you right away. So why go through all this?'

'Because I can't do this alone. I can get in and break his company from the inside, but I need a person on the outside to take care of these kids. While I break the company from the inside, I do need someone on the outside to deal with these kids. Just taking over from my dad's operation might allow me to break up his little scam, but I still need someone to get these kids new jobs. I need a person on the outside to help me. Besides, it's not that easy. There are multiple levels to this scam. One is the direct money students pay my dad each month that he receives in cash, so no traceability. Then he sets them up with Blossom Consulting for their H-1s. Blossom collects money each month from these employees' salaries and puts it into a fund called Vantage Funds. Vantage is a private fund managed by my dad's friend and this fund gives returns which are distributed amongst him and his buddies. I don't have all the details, but this is all I was able to gather from his office.'

My head was spinning with all this information. Even if it were all true, what is it that I have to do? My thoughts were all over and with so much to swallow, I wasn't sure how the pieces fit together.

'So again, whatever you're planning on doing, why me again?'

'Look, I already staged my kidnapping and sent dad an email requesting ransom for my safe return. Until then, I needed a place to stay. Larry thought since you don't have a roommate, I could hide here until I got my money. Once I get it, I will be out of here. But he thought you would be the right person on the outside helping me.'

Bobby seemed very serious and looking into his eyes, I could tell he was going ahead with this operation whether I helped him or not.

'Well, thank you Larry for your trust, but why not hide in a hotel or something? Why my place?'

'Because, we can't trust anyone seeing him. No one will even consider looking here, especially because I have been asked to keep an eye on the dorms. We know that no one will look here except me,' Larry jumped in to defend Bobby.

'But, Larry, I mean keep him with you, keeping a guy, especially with all this kidnapping stuff, I mean, I could get caught and even go to jail for all this.' Remembering Rich and his incident gave me chills.

Larry held my hand, 'I would never have brought him here unless I was sure it was safe for you. Look, I promise, this won't be more than a week. Jay Chand would never let Bobby's kidnapping leak out to the press to avoid unnecessary attention to himself. So we expect to get paid, then Bobby returns home and no one will know. Plus, Bobby, well, he is gay so don't think of him as a man, just think of him as a woman.'

I chuckled but looking at Bobby's face, I knew he wasn't too happy with Larry for revealing his secret. Well that explains him moisturizing his legs earlier.

Thinking back at this conversation I was baffled about how quickly things had changed in my life. Wow! What just happened here? I was happily minding my own business and now suddenly here I am in the middle of some swindling scheme that didn't concern me. I didn't want to get involved in something like this. Besides, maybe he ought to get help from these students instead of me. I don't want to get in trouble. I have to turn them down, no, I can't get involved with this. So, I had decided. I wouldn't get involved, it was way too risky.

'I will pay you $100,000 for keeping me here for a week!' Bobby was standing in front of me looking deep into my eyes and I could tell he was serious.

'What! $100,000! For a week!' I don't think I had seen that much money before. This would easily get me through college and my Masters.

'Okay, you've got a deal,' I quickly shook hands with Bobby. Well at least I had thought about it for a second and maybe it was worth taking some risk. Besides, a 100K is a lot! In Zambian currency I could buy a hundred cows, get a huge piece of land and run an entire village for years.

'Now what?' I felt a bit greedy about agreeing so fast.

'Well, dad received the ransom note yesterday, he hasn't called the cops, haven't seen anything on the news so he has until Wednesday to make the money transfer. All I have to do is hide here for four days.'

'Okay four days, four days…I can do that, you ARE gay right?' I smiled at Bobby but looking at his expressions, I could tell he hadn't come out of the closet yet.

'Fine, so you stay here, use the kitchen and all, but stay away from my room please and yes, get your own towels please.' I gave him that look that says - stay away from my stuff.

'Larry, you keep an eye on everyone around the dorms and Rushmi if you can linger around dad to see if you can find out anything. I will stay here waiting to see the money in the bank account. Oh! One more thing, don't change your behavior please. I mean don't act at all suspicious, no one should know ok?' Saying this, Bobby walked into his room and closed the door.

'Get some rest Rushmi and thanks again. Trust me you're doing a good thing.' Larry walked over to the door.

'Larry,' I said in a very serious voice, 'should we put up the flag again?' Larry chuckled and walked to the door closing it behind him. It was almost 2AM and I was wide awake thinking about this unbelievable situation. I was more excited about having $100,000 in my account in a week. It was pumping adrenaline in my system. Wow! How would I spend it? Besides, having a man sleeping in the room next to mine was also strange for me. Even though he was gay – nonetheless, a man and sharing an apartment with him for four days seemed like I was doing something wrong. What if my mother found out? What if the other desi kids found out? What if he wasn't gay? What if I changed him and he becomes straight?

All night I kept having strange dreams of monkeys…not sure why.

22

With Bobby in the house, it was weird the next day to find him making eggs in my kitchen wearing a yellow robe. Really? Robe? What is he? The Heff or something? But seeing him in his yellow robe took out all doubts I had last night about him being gay. He was gay, without any doubt.

'You want some?' he pulled out a plate and offered me some eggs and toast.

'Okay, thanks, I haven't had anyone make me breakfast since I got here.'

'Well, hope you like it,' he actually had made really good eggs.

'So, what's the plan today?' I asked him while chewing down my breakfast.

'I have to make some calls and keep a low profile. I need you to keep an eye on dad and, oh yeah, I need to send him a video of my kidnappers abusing me. You be my kidnapper and help me make a torture video.' He walked into his room and picked up the camera and duct tape.

'I thought you tape me up and with some makeup place me in the bath tub and pretend to drown me. I think that should make my dad pay up fast.' I just watched him speaking like a child watching a magic trick. Is this guy for real? I mean isn't this like Al-Quedaish?

'Is it really necessary?' I couldn't imagine faking this, it was that bizarre.

'Rushmi, you don't understand these people. They are like parasites, they suck the blood from innocent people and until you hurt them where it really hurts, they don't react. My dad would crumble watching a torture video of me. It has to be done.'

'What's this thing between you and your dad?'

'Another time ok?' he walked into the bathroom and started the water.

'Yeah okay, but if your dad loves you so much then why not fix it with him, I mean he can't be all that bad. You're probably making this into something that isn't even there. I mean maybe he is really helping these kids out, he seems nice to me.'

'Oh nice? You think he's nice? Okay, let me show nice,' he grabbed his phone and dialed a number.

'Hey, Shrini, it's me, listen I need you to show a friend floor J-71. Yeah, I know, but she is Indian and no one would even know she doesn't work there. Okay, I'll send her now.'

Turning the phone off, Bobby wrote on a piece of paper and handed it to me.

'Rushmi, go and see how nice my father is; here is the address. It's on the outskirts of town. Go to this address and a good friend, Shrini will meet you at the parking lot. Show her this paper and she'll let you in to Blossom Consulting.'

'Blossom Consulting? What's that?'

'The company that works with dad and hires these students giving them H-1 visas; go watch how he treats our students, go talk to some of the employees.'

'Bobby, long hours and less pay are expected abuse from employers who give us H-1s. If he doesn't do it, I am sure someone else will. Once companies have your H-1 they have you by the neck. So..,' he didn't let me finish and walked closer to me.

'Just go and see okay?' Bobby was standing in front of me and waiting for an answer.

'I'm going, alright, watch here I go.' Well, guess I had no choice but to check it out. Bobby seemed like such a drama queen; anyway my classes didn't start until the afternoon. So, I agreed to first go and check out this company, Blossom Consulting.

It took an hour getting there. Bus 7, 13 then 415 to finally Senter Rd. Standing at the bus stop I could see this was the business end of the city. Tall high rises, lots more traffic and people all dressed in suits. As I walked up Senter Rd, my building was the third one from the stop and it was huge. It had glass windows and as tall as my apartment building. Walking into the parking area, I saw it had a large parking lot, stairs going up to the large fountain and behind the fountain were two revolving doors. This place was actually very pretty and I hoped that maybe someday I would work here.

Waiting at the parking lot was a petite woman; she was wearing a khaki pant and white shirt. She was Indian, big pretty grey eyes, long beautiful hair and she looked like she had just showered. She had a darker complexion and judging from her long thick hair, I guessed that she was from South India.

'Excuse me, I'm looking for Shrini?' I smiled at her, but she never returned the smile. She kept looking around then she nodded and just said to follow her. She had a soft voice, slight Indian accent and very serious demeanor.

'Has Bobby told you anything about this place?' walking around the cars, she took me away from the main entrance and somewhere behind the building.

'I do know that this is a company run by his dad, it hires lots of graduates but nothing else,' I almost bumped into Shrini as she had stopped walking.

'Wait, that's all he told you?' She seemed irritated like I had just wasted her time.

'Yes,' I said almost scared to tell her, I thought she would yell at me or something.

'I can't take you in like this! We need to talk.,' looking around she moved away from the building towards the cars. Finding a spot behind a white car she sat on the edge of the car that was not facing the building.

'Rushmi, I've worked here for four years right after graduation. In this building, there are several floors, the top floor is where you find the executives and these guys are the ones who get contracts for the company. They go out and talk to clients and deal with sales and all. You will see a secretary, few offices of Vinod Thaka CEO, Shahil Kapoor COO, Meena Kapoor who is Shahil's wife and HR specialist, Rupa Sinha - head of Sales.

These guys run the entire show. But you go down a floor and you find the programming lab, all servers, PCs, and hundreds of programmers working on various client projects. These are our students. We don't go to client sites; rather we do everything in house. Any on site jobs or client dealings are done by the executives who then bring everything back in house. Go another level below and you find the living quarters for the employees. We actually live in this building. We are given accommodations at a cheap rate, mainly because from what we make, we can't afford a place of our own. We get large rooms to share amongst many others, men on one side and women on another. Another reason to keep us close to work is because we program for over 18 hours a day. With the pay we actually earn no one can afford a place of their own. We have bunk beds, shared bathrooms and a shared kitchen where we all get our meals. Rushmi, life in college was far better than this lifestyle. Whether you're sick or tired doesn't matter you need to be at work. It's like a prison down there.'

'Well, why work there then?' I could sense the frustration Shrini was feeling and I felt angry at what was happening in there especially knowing that Indian's were doing this to other innocent Indians.

'Many of us came to the US with only one hope, getting jobs that would help our families back home. My dad sold his land to get me here. What am I going to do? Go home empty handed? This is one of their criterion, they target the desperate ones. I have been waiting for the end of my six years knowing that at the end they do apply for my Green card. After that I can work anywhere and start making some real money. But it's just getting too much. None of us have gone back to see our parents. My sister keeps sending lists of things she wants me to get for her, but with this rate we get paid $400 a month, which I have to save because at the end of these six years they ask for another $7000 to apply for the Green Card, so that means I end up with nothing!.' Shrini took in a deep breath and closed her eyes. This silence was louder than her words.

This was incredible! What a great gimmick of looting these poor kids. I was a bit baffled and saddened. I could see in Shrini's eyes how terrible things had been for her. I sensed she was the eldest in her home and this pressure must have been killing her to send money back home but just not able to. I felt really disturbed to even think that this was awaiting me after my graduation.

'I couldn't help my father with anything, not during my sister's wedding, not when they lost their house not even for my younger brother's admission. He thinks I'm not sending anything because I have changed. But what can I do?'

Shrini was now looking away with her eyes damp- I could feel her pain. I felt awful at her state, she seemed very sad and disheartened.

'So, why are you guys going after them now? I mean, don't you need this job?'

'I would have continued this lifestyle, but when Bobby got involved I decided to help him. He told me about his plan where we could save the students and their status in the US, and get us all out of this Green Card trap. Besides, he is the son of Jay Chand so if anyone can do something it's him.'

'How does Jay Chand fit into this?'

'Oh, he's a sneaky man. I hate that guy! During the third year when you're almost done and looking for direction, he invites you to his mansion and dazzles you with fancy dinners and gives you a taste of his luxurious home. He plays a Hindi movie in his home theatre and treats you like one day you too can have what he has. Then, he gets close to the students, finding out about their backgrounds. He never gets the students who come from rich backgrounds because he knows they have options. But he targets the ones who are desperate or swamped with responsibility. He gets you in his house a few times until he has fully convinced you that he can get you this interview. So you get setup to be interviewed by this Vinod guy and you suddenly feel relieved that you have a job waiting for you the day you graduate. Until then, Mr. Jay Chand is your father figure, always checking up on you to make sure you never even consider interviewing any place else. Even today, he acts like the father figure to these innocent kids who still don't know his role in this scheme.' Shrini spoke of Jay in a disgusting manner.

I had again been so naïve, meeting Jay Chand; I had been so impressed and almost fallen for the same trap. I couldn't believe how nice he behaved. How caring he had seemed and how it had felt so good to have his support. I totally would have followed his advice; he was so convincing and really behaved like a father every time I had met him. Hearing this about him was very disturbing.

'The only reason I know that Jay Chand is involved is because there was this student, Abbas. He had graduated top of his class, he had trusted Jay and confided in Jay Chand about the working conditions at Blossom. Abbas had hinted that he would get the police involved. Jay had promised Abbas to not call the cops because he would deal with Blossom Consulting, saying he would do something about it. Well he did! He told his buddies at Blossom and they got Abbas arrested on possession of child pornography. Abbas was a Muslim man and knowing what this would do to his family, he killed himself. Burned to death. No one has dared to speak against these guys since. We call it the six year *bunvas.*'* Shrini was nodding her head in disagreement and hopelessness.

My head was spinning. This seemed very strange and just too thought out. I was outraged and horrified to hear this torture that was being done to well-educated kids who just wanted to get a life in this country. This was not what anyone of us would even begin to imagine. Trusting teachers is what we all have learned to do in life. I couldn't believe this was even doable. Besides, one Indian doing this to another Indian, it was despicable and unbelievable. I just could not imagine. These poor kids trapped in such a mess-how can these people do this to them?

'Why is Bobby helping you guys? I mean isn't he on their side?'

Shrini finally smiled. 'Life is strange Rushmi, Bobby would join his dad and make loads of money, but he got involved with this guy, Roshan. Roshan was from India and working at this company. Roshan told Bobby everything about this place and actually Bobby did his own investigation and found out how much money his father was making from this scheme. When dad found out that Bobby was involved with Roshan, he was pissed off. He called Roshan's parents in India, knowing that his father was not well; he told them that Roshan was a gay prostitute. Receiving this call from a respectable and convincing man like Jay Chand, his family believed him and well, his father couldn't take it. His heart gave out. Then, they cancelled his H-1 and sent him back to India where I'm sure life must be hell for him. Bobby didn't take this well. Bobby had previous issues with his father for leaving his mother years ago, but I think this incident with Roshan just went over the top. Since then, Bobby's been trying to bring down this empire. I would never have joined in but Bobby convinced me and he sent my parents money on my behalf and that meant I owe him at least some help.'

'Show me what's happening inside, I have to see it for myself.' We both started walking towards the back of the building.

'So, listen, there are 300 agents down there, and,'

'What! 300! Unbelievable! That many?'

'Yeah, I mean, that's how they make so much money. Imagine the amount of work they're getting for zero cost every day. But getting you in has to be from the back door. Now remember with so many of us inside, people may not know that you don't work here. But in case you get stopped and asked, say you work in QA team 41 ID 7334 name Vesali Patel,' saying this important piece of information in half a second, Shrini started walking towards the building back door.

'Wait, ID 7734 QE what?' She wasn't listening to me and ducking from the windows, we made it to the back of the building. There was a beige, large metal door without a handle but something has been keeping it from closing completely. A small bottle cap had kept the door from closing shut. Shrini squeezed her finger between the spaces and pulled the door open. She went in first and I followed behind her. The entry inside was a long corridor with tube lights, what seemed like an endless path finally reached the end which had stairs leading down and up. Shrini took the down stairs that lead to double doors that were also kept open with a pen this time. But before opening it, Shrini signaled me to get down. Bending down on our knees, she looked at her watch and waited for a few seconds. Then opening the door, she pulled me inside as fast as possible. Almost chocking my neck, again waited 10 seconds then she grabbed my hand and pulled me as she sprinted to the left and suddenly turning left again.

It all happened so fast, all I saw were more beige doors and more tube lighting. We must have ran and stopped a few more times until the last turn led us inside a big hall.

'The cameras rotate every 10 seconds in the corridors and inside this hall there are two cameras in each corner. From here on, don't act suspicious just act like you work here.' She walked towards the serving tables where lunch was being served. She picked up a plastic tray and walked up to the tables that had dal, rice and yogurt being served. I was too busy looking around at hundreds of Indian kids in the cafeteria chit chatting on these long benches. The walls had pictures of Indian Gods and Goddesses and to the front of the hall were two serving areas and behind the serving tables, I could see the kitchen where other Indian men and women were cooking. I felt a firm hand pull my arm and Shrini was giving me the look which said, don't look like you've never been here before.

She pulled me closer and pushed me in line to get food. I got a lump of rice and a runny dal poured in my plate and followed Shrini to the benches. Sitting down on an empty table, Shrini began eating and told me to do the same. But looking at my plate, I didn't have much of an appetite.

'Every day, one room is assigned cooking responsibilities, so some days we get North Indian food, other days we get south Indian Samber and Dosa. Today it's Marathi food.'

But I wasn't so keen on knowing their menus. I wanted to look at these kids, who looked tired and worn out. I could actually tell the new employees to the ones who had been here the longest. The older employees looked like they had aged. It reminded me of the concentration camps I had read about. I saw a man who actually looked like Gandhi, same glasses, no hair and thin who was quietly eating his meal and not talking to anyone.

'That guy is Asoke, he's leaving in four months. I know he should look happier but he's horrified. Once he gets the Green Card where does he go? Where will he live? He even got a request for an interview but it's in California, doesn't even have the money to get there. He's actually thinking about staying here, which if he does, he gets moved upstairs closer to the execs offices and can get a bigger pay check and can go to client sites.'

Looking around I saw a woman, in her twenties, thin with a long braid. She looked like she was from South India. She was sitting next to a man, also in his twenties, and both of them were eating lunch together, but neither was talking.

'That is Shoba and Mihir, they came from India and got married in college here. But after getting hired by Blossom they have been stuck here for three years. When Shoba got pregnant six months ago, she had no choice but to drop the baby because Blossom could not allow any time off. With no health insurance and no place to raise a child, they had no choice. In fact, Vinod's wife took her to a doctor and had the procedure done.'

Shrini took in a deep breath and went back to finishing her lunch. But for me, watching the depression in that couples' face hit me very hard. My mother had lost her second child in her second month of pregnancy and she mourned the death of her child ever since. She had told me that the biggest punishment for a woman was to lose her child. I think that's why she was overly protective of me. Watching Shoba sitting there with her head down, with nothing to say, reflected pain and extreme sorrow. It was too much for me to handle. I was fighting my tears back.

Putting our plates away, I followed Shrini out of the cafeteria and took the stairs down to floor J-71.

'Living quarters,' Shrini opened the doors and knowing the cameras were on, she causally walked in because her shift didn't start for another 45 minutes. She was allowed to use the cafeteria and living quarter's area any time until her shift. Once her shift started, she would be restricted to the lab area. I walked in and found doors all labeled with numbers, they had ID numbers 2224 – 2234; 2235-2245 and so on. She lead me to my ID number, 7334.

'Look around and meet me outside in five minutes,' Shrini walked away. I entered the room and found what can only be described as a prison cell. It had fourteen bunk beds with hospital like sheets; the walls had pictures of family members; with no windows, the tube lights were making the room look like a Hospital.

I saw a small TV, table and closets filled with suitcases, maybe seven or so that were piled on top of one another and clothes sticking out of them. The floor was bare and at one corner I saw pictures of Gods and Goddesses decorated with flowers. You could hear the radio from the alarm clock but because we were in the basement, it had a bad signal. I felt suffocated inside and just turned around and opened the door to get out. Shrini was waiting for me outside. I think my eyes told her how I felt. This place was depressing. It was congested, had no privacy and felt like a mental hospital. There were common bathrooms around the corner which were not maintained too well because I could smell them from outside. Just being in the basement I felt claustrophobic and I couldn't imagine being in here for six years! I felt suffocated and realized that I was sweating. All I wanted to do was to get out of here.

We walked out of this floor, upstairs to the cafeteria floor, where kids were still eating and then we walked up another floor to the programming floor. Opening these doors, I saw a huge floor filled with tables and computers and hundreds of kids typing away. It was a sea of kids on large tables, seven on each desk. At least this room had windows and just getting natural light into the room felt good.

'You get seven kids on each table that have to work with a Project Lead. On the walls you can see all the projects that are currently being worked on. On the white boards you can see projects in the pipeline, and on the Project Lead's desk are monitors where he can see who is on shift and who is not.

They make this room the most comfortable so you want to be at work instead of downstairs where it's suffocating. Okay, we have to go now. My shift starts in five minutes. I have to get you out, if I'm late they deduct from my paycheck.' Shrini closed the door of the lab room and turning back she bumped into Asoke.

'Where are you going?' Asoke had a soft voice and he was looking at me.

'Oh, I don't start until another five minutes, going to drink some tea.' Shrini motioned to me to follow her.

'Wait! Don't think we've met. What is your ID?' Asoke pulled out his hand to shake mine. Crap! What was my id again? 7774, 7734, or 7334, shit, my mind went blank. I shook his hand and said,

'If I keep talking to you my five minutes will be done,' I walked away smiling but inside my heart was racing and my underarms were wet. I had never been this afraid in my life as I was at that moment.

Shrini and I rushed out onto the stairs and walked down, making it out again into the corridors. Ducking the cameras again we got out of the building. I took a deep breath of fresh air and was relieved to get out. My lungs had been depleted of fresh air and my head felt dizzy inside this concentration camp. Being in the open, in the fresh air, I took in deep breaths until my heartbeat went back to normal. What I had just seen was unbelievable. Kids being kept like prisoners. Working like dogs, in suffocating conditions, these kids were being robbed of a great future just for the mighty Green Card. Was it really worth it? All this suffering for what? To make it in America? This life that everyone wanted, was it really worth it? At what expense?

'I have to run, bye.' Shrini shut the door and she was gone. I stood there for a minute taking in all that I had seen. I think at that moment, I was so grateful for my own life. My apartment, my freedom, my friends and even my library job seemed a blessing at this time. I thanked God for what I had. The days I had cried for being lonely or being away from my parents was nothing compared to what these kids were dealing with. Added to this was their desperation in providing for their families back home. It was too much. Holding back my own tears, on the ride back home, I replayed what I had just heard and seen. Jay Chand, Bobby, Asoke, Abbas, Roshan, Shoba, Mihir, the cafeteria, the dorms, the lab.

It was a living example of a concentration camp. These poor kids trapped in a system they had no idea about and Blossom targeting the most desperate. Oh my God! How low can a person go? This Dean was supposed to teach and guide us, these people were Indians and well aware of how much parents sacrificed to send their children to America. How could they do this to their own kind? How does one crush so many just for their own happiness? It was pathetic and disgraceful. I felt disgusted, angry, sad and very emotional. I got off the bus and walking into my apartment, I finally remembered my ID, 7334.

23

I got home close to 2pm and totally forgot about my classes that day. I didn't feel like going today. This was the first time I had missed a session in the 19 months I had been here. Opening my apartment, I saw a black dome affixed to the top of my door and even before I put the key in to open, Bobby opened the door. Our eyes met and looking up at the dome, he said,

'Installed a security camera, just in case.' Not another camera I thought. Getting in, I just sat by the kitchen table while Bobby made some tea. We hadn't talked yet.

'Listen, I don't want the $100K. Just make them stop.' I was embarrassed about even thinking of money; all I wanted to do was to help. He held my hand from across the table and gently squeezed it.

'Thank you.' We sat together sipping tea and no one said much for a while. The thoughts of Asoke and Shrini filled my mind. After sitting together in silence, I asked Bobby about his own story.

He was the only child of Jay Chand. Jay had divorced his wife when Bobby was seven years old. Since that age, Bobby had spent half his life at his mother's the other at his father's place. Jay Chand was a lonely man and his only pride and joy was Bobby. Jay could do anything for Bobby. But three years ago Bobby's mother was about to take Bobby back to India and have him settle there. However, she met with a tragic car accident and passed away. After her death, Bobby moved in with his father. Bobby had already graduated with his Masters in Computer Science and being the only child, Jay begged him to move in and today, father and son living together.

'My father has a very bad habit of gambling. He gambled away almost everything we had and that's when my mother left him. Even today he continues to gamble everything he makes. I think that's one of the reasons he got into this business because his salary wasn't enough to satisfy his gambling addiction.' Bobby spoke softly and I could tell he was embarrassed to even tell me all this about his own father. I could sense that he still loved his father but still wanted to do the right thing. I admired this monkey for standing up to his father.

Bobby worked at Emerging Technologies as their chief architect specializing in back end integration and design. During one of his father's "dinners" some of the international students had been invited. It was during these dinner parties where he met someone who was a foreign student and who respected Jay Chand as the fatherly figure. I assumed this someone was Roshan, but Bobby wouldn't mention his name. This someone became good friends with Bobby and through him, Bobby found out what his father was doing. That someone helped Bobby see his father's true nature. Bobby had seen the incident with Abbas, he had seen his father conversing with Vinod and witnessed the child pornography setup that they had used to trap Abas. But things got out of control when Jay Chand found out about Roshan and Bobby after which Bobby never saw Roshan again. Roshan had vanished and asked never to contact Bobby again.

Bobby had tried to confront his father, but the more Bobby dug deeper, the more he realized that it was not only about Roshan. Hundreds of kids were being used to make Jay and his buddies rich. Bobby didn't just want to stop his father but rather wanted to free every Roshan in that company. He wanted to end this business of software slaves, as he called it. Knowing the pressures these kids had from their own families, Bobby wanted to make sure that these kids were not deported. Success to him meant getting these kids legit jobs with proper benefits and helping them achieve the American dream. He was adamant about not getting even one kid deported.

Bobby kept talking about all his plans until someone knocked at the door. We both panicked and Bobby looked on his computer, the camera was beaming images to his laptop. It was Anand at the door. Why was he here? I didn't know what the plan was but Bobby signaled as he walked into his room. Once he was in, he closed his door. I took a deep breath and opened the main door.

'Hey, where were you?' Anand walked in with his backpack. I had totally forgotten about meeting him in the lab to work on an Html project he was helping me with.

'Shoot, so sorry, I wasn't feeling well at all. I'm so, so, sorry Anand, I should have called you.' Anand had been so good to me and he was in his last year but took the time to help me on my projects. I knew he had a thing for me but I could never get past his birthing hips.

'You're having two cups of tea?' He pointed to the two half full cups on the table. I was baffled about what to say. This lying, sneaky thing was so new to me. Not knowing what to say, I panicked and just froze. Anand stared at me and I could tell he was very suspicious.

Just then, Bobby opened his bedroom door and walked out with his laptop. He walked in and smiled at Anand.

'Hi,' Bobby said to Anand as he stood in front of me. Anand and I stood there in shock. I had no clue on how I was going to explain Bobby to Anand.

'Rushmi, who is this?' Bobby stood in the living room where Anand and I were, the three of us looked at each other and Anand's mouth dropped open seeing a man in my apartment. He had been trying so hard to make something happen between us and today, seeing Bobby coming out of the bedroom, shook his poor psyche. I knew what he was thinking.

'Hi, I'm Bobby, Rushmi's cousin brother.' Whew! Hearing him say brother brought so much relief in Anand. Anand gave a big smile and shook Bobby's hand tightly as if he was here on my arranged marriage meeting.

'Nice to meet you sir,' Anand went on his "I'm going to impress Rushmi's family mode". They sat down and Bobby went on talking to Anand about his major.

'Yes sir, in my last year and already have an offer! Will be working for a few years at a consulting firm and they also promised the Green Card. So in six years I hope to be well settled here.' Hearing Anand talk so excitedly about his future plans, hearing him repeat the story I had just seen 300 kids go through was very heart breaking.

Anand was an amazing student. He had a very promising future, was very hard working, and was so excited about graduating. I wasn't going to let them do the same to him. I was not going to have him become another number. I was going to tell him everything. Just then the phone rang and I went in my room to take the call.

'Hello? Hi mom! I'm good, yes, school is great, yeah okay,... WHAT!.' Are you insane? No! I'm not being rude. But are you serious? No, not at all, no, I'm not going to! I do love you, but, no, yes, you did sacrifice so much, yes I am the only child, I know. I will fast every Monday, but I am not ready right now. No! Mom I have to go to class. We will talk soon, give dad my love. Oh, when do the results come out for the Green Card Lottery? Okay, give me the website and what email did you give them, okay, bye.'

I had only been here two years and my mother was already planning my wedding! Is she insane? How can she even expect me to be fixed in some arranged marriage? She had become so restless about my well being, extremely worried about living alone in America that she already started looking for a guy for me. She had completely lost it. I would not even consider marriage until after my Masters. Besides, I would like to find someone on my own. She was an insane woman. But knowing my mother, there was no stopping her. She would pester me until she got her way. She always used the guilt charm of "you're my only child" and "I was in labor with you for fifteen hours", and "you don't love me anymore", or "you must already have a boyfriend gimmick." But, I had to be strong. I had to stop my mother from running my life. She insisted I start fasting on Monday's to find a good husband. This was going to be another big battle for me. But worst of all, she was hooking me up with Bittu!!! Where the hell did he come back from? I thought I was done with that Walrus. How did he manage to enter my life again? This was way too much. I was writing furiously in my journal.

Now I was really getting a migraine. Outside my room was Anand trying to impress my gay brother. Bobby was faking his kidnapping and now my mother was arranging my marriage to Bittu! How did my life change so suddenly? This last part was the hardest to handle. I couldn't brush it aside. Is she insane? How the hell did Bittu get back into the picture occupied my head so much that for a while I had forgotten everything about Blossom Consulting. Bittu had moved to India and joined the National Defense Academy program and his parents had kept in touch with my parents. His great grandfather's sister's son's wife was somehow related to my mother's side. Because of this connection, I was being promised to Bittu darling. But Bittu? Really, is she insane? I need more tea. I went out and found the two still chatting. I made more tea and sat down to join their conversation.

'Rushmi, this is interesting, Anand has already developed an operating system, won competitions in programming and Mr. Chand is helping him with his career path. Let me guess Anand you're the eldest at home?' Anand was thrilled to hear Bobby inquiring about his family. He totally thought Bobby was doing what my father would do in choosing a groom for me. Poor guy had no clue.

'Actually I'm the only son sir.' Anand was happily telling Bobby his life history. I hated him calling Bobby sir, typical of an arranged marriage interview. All that was needed were garlands and some Indian sweets and this marriage would be all set.

'I have two sisters and my father, he is a school teacher. One sister has had her marriage date set up for next fall just to give enough time for me to get settled in a job. I am really hoping to be able to attend her wedding. I haven't gone back in these four years! After she is married, I am looking to do my Masters too.' Anand was beaming with pride. I knew he was a great guy, simple person who was really sweet. I liked him as a good friend, but just not to be my boyfriend. Knowing he was getting into this trap made me feel even more angry towards this Chand guy. Worst of all, these Indian boys are the pride of their parents. With mountain high expectations from parents back home, these kids work their butts off to support their families. Just knowing where Anand could end up made me more upset about this whole Blossom Consulting crap. I had to do something. I would do whatever to help Anand. I was totally with Bobby in bringing down this firm.

After Anand left, Bobby and I sat in the living room.

'How are you going to do this? I want to help.' I was energized and willing to do whatever to help my friends.

'Well, you know the risk, I mean it's a risky thing and we could get caught too.'

'It's worth taking the risk than letting more kids into that hell hole. Look, what if we just tell all these kids the truth?'

'No, it's not that simple. These kids won't believe it. Even you didn't believe this until you saw the building. We can't take kids to that building, it's way too risky and Shrini has already taken a risk. Besides, what good will that do? We need a better plan.'

'Okay so what?' I was biting my nails and felt energized to do some real damage to this Blossom Consulting.

'We have to target the back bone of this operation. So many people are involved in this, and we can't trust anyone. I mean no one. Especially professors. You'll never know who all is connected. We have to be extremely careful.'

'Look we are smart kids. You're telling me we can't outsmart them?' I was adamant about him taking a drastic step.

'Rushmi, come with me.' Entering Bobby's room, I saw a large white board with pictures and a chart.

'What's all this?'

'This is the information I have so far. Look, here is my father and I know the head of the Computer Science department and two other professors are in it too. I have seen these professors coming to our home a few times. So, I think they are in it too. Here is Blossom Consulting run by Vinod and his group. I also know that all the money from the students and the firm are not directly paid back to these guys because I checked dad's bank account. He gets paid from the University and an investment fund call Vantage that sends him monthly payments of large amounts.

Vantage is a privately held investment fund. If you search them on the net, you can see that you can join them only through private invitation. They keep their investments very secret. This makes everyone in it clean and undetectable. Every semester they get around 10-15 kids that they hire and today our count is close to 300 employees.'

'So you said you intend to start your own company. What would that do? Will you get their existing employees to transfer over? Why would they let you?' I felt frustrated for not being able to come up with good ideas.

'I'm not sure how I would do that. I thought, first let's stop their supply of kids. So, first thing to do would be to stop the current students who are graduating from joining Blossom. Ideally, I would want them hired at my firm. At least to get us started.'

We were both sitting on his bed looking at this maze of pictures and charts. He was right. First rule of business, you control the supply you control the money. Where did I hear that before? But how could we just open a firm and hire students? We need a legit business, enough revenues to allow us to sponsor for H-1s. That means we would need to have clients and projects for them to work on and make money. It was like opening our own business. We had to start our own consulting company.

'Bobby, we can't do this alone? We need more people to help.'

'We can't trust anyone Rushmi. One person blows this and we're done. The more people getting involved, the more people might go to jail with me.' When Bobby said jail, I realized that I had to keep everything hidden from my friends. I didn't want to get any of them in trouble. In fact, I didn't want to get in trouble either. But for Anand and everyone else, I was willing to do anything.

'Okay, you get the money first. Let me stop by the Dean's office and see if I can find out anything. Besides, if your picture is plastered on TV today, Anand will be the first to tell everyone anyway.'

I didn't want to sound too scared but I was freaking out inside. I could end up in jail and maybe meet Rich and his buddies. Talk about seeing the bright side of things. But the alternative was also unacceptable. Maybe, if I notified the media that would certainly shut them down. But again, everyone at Blossom would get deported too. So, that was not an option.

Exhausted from thinking all day about this, I finally went to bed that night. Tossing and turning, I thought of all the ideas I could come up with to make some change to this Jay Chand gimmick. If we wanted to end the supply chain, maybe we could just expose him of wrong doing then no student would trust him. Maybe if we made a video of Blossom Consulting and show the world how these kids were living, then maybe we could stop them. Maybe, if we….. my head was hurting until I finally fell asleep.

Early next morning, I picked up my backpack and left to see the Dean. This was serious, I had to be really careful. Entering into the Business Administration Building; I saw a beautiful chandelier, large paintings of past presidents and the same secretary sitting at the center of the big hall way.

'Hello, I'm here to meet Mr. Jay Chand.'

'Sure, do you have an appointment?'

'No, I don't, but it won't take long.'

'I am sorry, but he is not to be disturbed today, he is very busy today.'

'Okay, is it okay if I wait here in case he gets done sooner?' I know he's busy lady, in fact I know he must be freaking out because his son is hiding in my apartment. I hope he is suffering was all I felt.

'Sure help yourself.' The lady went back to her work.

Sitting on the cushiony red velvet chairs, I could see upstairs, the office door to his room was open. He was on the phone and seemed panicky. He was moving his hands and shaking his head. Pacing back and forth, he seemed upset. Watching him in his expensive suit and clean cut hair and glasses, he made me mad to think what an animal he was inside. He had seemed so polished and so nice the first time I had met him. But this guy was such an abusive, insensitive and selfish man, he disgusted me.

Just then, I saw a man, also in his late 50s, rushing into Jay Chand's office. I recognized him from his picture on Bobby's wall, he was that Vinod guy. He rushed upstairs and entered Jay's office shutting the door behind him. Then, few minutes later, Professor Sunil Sharma, who was my teacher this semester, entered the building and went upstairs too. Then Mr. Jain, the html guru, joined the rest of the scumbags upstairs. I waited another half hour to see who else was in on this but no one else joined them. These guys were all talking and Jay was sitting with his head in his hands and looking clearly unhappy. I actually felt a bit glad to see the agony in Jay Chand's face.

Leaving the building, I walked to my apartment instead of taking the bus. As I walked home, I kept thinking about a television show I used to watch a lot in Zambia, The A-Team. It was my favorite show and every week this team would come up with plans to rescue someone. That's what we needed. We needed our own "A-Team". But how? How could we form a team when we couldn't even tell anyone about Blossom and Jay Chand? Besides, who would believe us?

Jay Chand was obviously upset about his son being kidnapped. The others were consoling and judging from their reactions, it was clear that they had not contacted the police. Scanning through all the information that we had so far, I kept trying to figure out how we could beat these guys are their own game. We knew their supply of graduates, we knew they had Jay creating the pipeline of graduates…..Vinod was getting contract jobs …..His wife was managing the operations of Blossom. Bobby had said something about supply chain……control the supply chain…..I remembered my time in Zambia working at the store where Sagar's uncle would make his suppliers happy because he knew that his business was dependent on his suppliers. So if we wanted to start, we had to get newer kids rescued first…but how?…..

these kids graduating needed proper jobs that paid well, that could sponsor them…..maybe if we found another company to hire them….but, that was close to impossible to find work for 300+ kids……sucks…could it be that I am not as smart as I thought I was?….Why can't I think outside the box?

By the time I got home, I had completely convinced myself that I was a retard. I couldn't think big at all. I was a bigger monkey than Bobby. The only image that kept popping in my head was of Bobby checking for head lice in my head. Bobby opened the door and after debriefing him on what I had seen, we added more pictures to the white board. We now had a tree showing all the branches of people feeding into their scheme. On the one side there was Jay Chand and other college professors who were supposed to be looking out for us. On the other side there was Vinod and his buddies who ran the concentration camps. Then, there was Vantage, the gold pot that fed everyone in the system.

'Rushmi, if we have to do this then we need to start by stopping their supply of new kids first. But, that all has to start by having a company of our own. We need money to move forward. We need capital to even start doing something and lots of it.' Bobby was saying exactly the things I had been thinking, I felt a bit hopeful about my mental capabilities. Bobby was right; the only way was for us to have our own company. This mission felt like we were about to venture on a climb and not just a small hill, rather, a huge mountain climb. Bobby was smart and I, with my limited intelligence, were diving into something so big, God help us all. I was scared.

'Rushmi, I still need the kidnapping video.' Two days had past and Jay Chand had another day to pay up the ransom for his son. Larry had joined us and now we were duct taping Bobby, his hands, legs and mouth. Then, Larry used makeup to make a really good black eye and for the bloody lip, well, Larry punched Bobby. Now, we had a swollen bleeding lip, black eye and duct taped Bobby. It was very convincing. Filling the tub, Bobby tried to lie inside, just then Bobby started mumbling behind the duct tape. After opening his mouth he said,

'Add a little hot water! They won't see the cold water in the video, idiot.' I hunched and added warm water to make it more comfortable- guess I got carried away in our torture plan. Placing Bobby in the tub, his body completely submerged inside, Larry laid electrical wires on the side while Bobby imitated being electrocuted. All this recorded on his camera. Bobby took another video, this time he removed the bathroom curtain and my shampoo from the video. He was very careful the video had no clues about where this was taking place. For being a rich, spoiled gay person, Bobby actually was smarter than I gave him credit.

Then, Larry stood Bobby in front of the Nazi sign and took a video of Bobby holding the newspaper to reveal the date. It was a bit scary to see both of these guys so comfortable making this torture video. I wondered if this was their first time.

Bobby had setup a secure network from my apartment, using encrypted messaging, he sent over the video to his father's account. He also added the time line and bank information where money was to be deposited.

'Where will you get this money sent? I mean, do we do a mission impossible deal where suit cases are left at the road side? Do we make an exchange like in the movie Don in a fancy restaurant? Maybe we should get paid in diamonds that I collect at a casino?' I was staring at the two of them but neither spoke. They exchanged looks and completely ignored me.

'I have an account here; the money gets deposited in my own account. Dad thinks once it's in there, my kidnappers will use me to empty the account into another place. Well, I will move it to a new account and no one would expect me to know where it went.' Bobby sounded like he was so mature coming up with his online gig but my ideas would have worked just as well. I was ok with his concept too.

'Your plan will work too. Mine was just as good.' I walked away realizing that neither Larry nor Bobby saw too many Hindi movies so it wasn't their fault about not being as creative as I was. I would teach them over time.

It was evening and I had missed all my classes. I spent the day brainstorming with Bobby and I completely forgot until the doorbell rang. It was potluck time at my place. In comes my twelve hungry desi crowd for the evening dinner. It was supposed to have Indian food for my twelve hungry desis' who were standing outside my apartment.

'Oh shit! I totally forgot. All my friends are here.' I was panicked and didn't know where to hide Bobby. But even bigger than that I had no food to feed this hungry herd. A group of hungry students is even scarier than the time I had encountered that snake. At least the snake would sting me and then leave, but these kids had to be fed well, or else…

'Can't you send them away?' Bobby was putting away his computer and covering up the family tree in his room.

'Are you kidding? These guys are hungry. If I send them away they might eat me.' I was searching in the fridge for options. I had uncooked cauliflower, some peas, potatoes and some kind of meat.

'I don't want to be seen by so many, get rid of them!' Bobby rushed towards his bedroom door and shut it behind him.

Opening the door, the herd rushed in asking for dinner. They all came right in and some sitting on the sofa, some at the kitchen table and some snooping in the fridge looking for food.

'I'm ordering Pizza today!' Pizza is not food. Especially the ones that are sold close to colleges. They know students have a tight budget so they offer a large pizza for $5, but I know that it would take me four days to digest it. It has artificial cheese with artificial coloring and I know those mushrooms are not safe to eat. But as a student, you learn to eat anything warm and cheap.

'NOOOO!' LipSingh, Anya and Nikhil synchronously yelled. As a student, pizza is something you eat every day. But potluck night was desi night with desi food only. I had to cook for these guys. I couldn't get rid of them otherwise. However, if I start cooking now, these guys would stay longer. With Bobby hiding in the room, I didn't know what to do to get rid of them.

'Rushmi, where is your cousin?' Anand was walking to Bobby's bedroom and with the manners we all have, he opened the door to find Bobby lying on his bed.

'Please join us sir.' Bobby was startled to encounter so many students at once and now he had no choice. He came in and met everyone. But from the look in his eyes, I knew he was annoyed with me. I took every chance to avoid eye contact but the negative energy coming from Bobby was making me uncomfortable. He was mad. I didn't want to jeopardize his mission, but I really sucked at getting rid of these guys. Besides, he should know that Indian men don't listen to women.

The evening went the best it could and Bobby got to meet the entire gang. Everyone talked to Bobby about their career goals, their majors, and their dreams. Anya helped me make rice, canned channa and cauliflower subji with roti. The questionable meat in the fridge was left to rest in peace. We all enjoyed a really good feast that day and by the end, Bobby felt at ease with the group. He had found out that RelaxSingh's real name was Kawal Singh and Lipsingh was really Lukvir Singh.

'Don't you get it? I am Relax Singh, get it Relax?' Kawal was trying to explain to me his idiotic joke but it still wasn't funny. I gasped at having been made a fool for more than two years and not getting their jokes.

'What is so funny of putting stupid words next to Singh? How is that even funny?' I asked everyone hoping they would support me. Everyone looked at me and burst out laughing. I really found these Sardars annoying. LipSingh is not funny, but for some reason everyone seemed to get a laughing fit.

'She called you LipSingh for over a year!' Bobby was laughing his butt off.

'What is so funny? I don't get it.' I hadn't finished saying this and everyone laughed even louder. I just don't get what was so funny.

'She is such an ABCD, "American Born Confused Desi".' Lip Singh said still laughing out loud.

'I'm not an ABCD, maybe ZBCD.' I tried to gain some votes but no one bought it and they laughed at me the whole time.

'You know what would be to die for? If we watched Dada Khondke* movies with her.' Prashant and Hersita gasped and eventually everyone was cracking up.

'Who is Dada Khondke?' I was all for Hindi movies but never seen Khondke movies.

'Anand, you have to show Rushmi - Andheri Raat Mein Diya Tere Haath Mein.'*

'That's the name of the movie? Sounds like a religious movie.' I heard Diya* and that's what came to mind. Now, the whole group was falling apart, laughing hysterically. Bobby and Anand had tears rolling down with laughter. I just was so out of my element. I had no clue why.

'Anand please teach Rushmi this religion.' Kawal Singh didn't finish saying this and Nukul had a coughing fit until everyone stopped eating and laughed the whole time. I was so irritated.

'Why was this so funny would anyone please explain?' I was beginning to feel like an outsider when in fact Bobby should have been the outsider. Yet, he seemed to fit better with my friends than me.

'Rushmi, I promise you, we all will watch that movie together the day you graduate. But until then, no distractions. Okay?' Madhu held back her laughter and no one would explain any further. But the exchange of looks continued throughout the night and every now and then the word Diya kept coming up.

Of us twelve students, I was the only one in my second year. Everyone else was in their third and fourth year. Every one of them had been contacted by Jay Chand and in fact, been at his home for dinners already. Anand had paid Jay Chand $1000 each month for two months already. The others too had started planning on doing the same. All these students followed each other into this mess and made it even easier for Jay Chand and his buddies.

I couldn't believe it! These friends of mine, the kids I really felt so close to were already part of their scheme. Maybe by the time I was to graduate, I too would have gotten into this mess. I guess I had never asked my friends before, but Bobby found out that all these kids came from poor families. Their parents had big expectations from these kids to send money once they had their first job. Just like me, my friends worked at coffee shops, at the gym and in the lab, but every penny they saved was now ending up in Jay Chand's bank account.

Some of these kids came from homes where parents had sold their houses back in India just to be able to send them to America. Some had taken all the money out of their parents' retirement fund. Some had taken on hefty loans just so that these kids could get an American education and make decent money.

These kids had been given a chance to come to America and attain a great education, but at the end, had to work their butts off to eventually provide for everyone back home. The amount of pressure and the level of expectations were immense. This pressure was enough to make these kids sacrifice themselves for the sake of family and that is what each kid in Blossom was doing, sacrificing themselves. And that is what Blossom was targeting, the desperate, the needy and the unaware.

My heart ached to see this room full of brilliant kids who had no clue on what awaited them right after graduation. That evening, after our Antakshari ended close to 2am, everyone left my apartment. Bobby and I began cleaning the kitchen.

'Your friends are really nice.' Bobby was filling up the trash bag.

'I know and you have to do something to protect them. You can't let them go through the same shit. We have to stop this! No matter what! We just have to.'

'I know, believe me, I know.' We cleaned the kitchen and went to our rooms.

I know neither one of us slept. I was up all night imagining myself in Asoke's shoes then in Anand's shoes. Thinking about Shoba and Mihir coming to this country, their minds filled with dreams of making it big. You imagine making enough money to support your family. You come to this place, live on a small budget and work extra hard to make good grades. Sacrificing your own happiness, you live away from your parents, your friends and everything about you is left behind only so that you can become a better person.

People like Jay Chand slash your dreams and take away the little hope you have, they abuse their powers. Just like machines they make these kids work day and night. It was so disturbing to think that a person like Anand would end up in a place like Blossom; it brought tears in my eyes. He was really good in his field, he was simple and kind and I could see as he approached graduation, his eyes lit up with the thought of starting a new life and a new job. I was not going to let him end up at Blossom.

24

Wednesday morning, one more day to see if Bobby's plan had worked. My phone rang just when I was making toast.

'Hello? Hi Mom. Okay, yeah, oh I didn't check, the Green Card Lottery is today? Let me check, no, I didn't call Bittu. No mom, not now, I am really busy. My goodness please stop pressuring me. I do love you. I do, mom let me think about it.' I hung up the phone, holding back the urge to throw the phone out of the window.

'Who was that?' Bobby stood by my bedroom door in his red hearts pajamas and no shirt. I had seen Bobby, I mean seen all of him, but without a shirt and cute pajamas, he looked very handsome.

'There she is again! My mother, she will never give up. I almost wish I could sue my own mother for mental anguish - would make a lot of lawyers into millionaires. She insisted I call Bittu and talk to him. NEVER.!'

'Bittu? That's his name? Wow! Sounds charming.' Bobby smiled, almost happy to hear my anguish.

'Forget it Bobby, no way I'm ending up with Mr. Bittu.' I logged on to my laptop and started my search on the immigration website.

'What are you doing?' Bobby sat next to me and now his cologne was getting to me. I was beginning to get interested in a man who was not available, but again, maybe I could convert him.

'Before coming to the US, people coming from third world countries get a chance to enter in a Green Card Lottery. Today the fifty winners are posted on their website. So mom wanted me to check.' Bobby brushed against me as he sat closer to look at my laptop. Even though I was focusing on the computer, something about him shirtless and those really cute pajamas made me a bit distracted.

'Here, let me do it. You don't even know what you're doing. Are you sure you are in the Computer Science program?' Bobby took over the laptop and started searching. At that moment I felt so protected by him. He was so comfortable to be with, down to earth guy who totally would have been awesome for me except for that one thing. Julie was totally right, all the good ones are either married, in love with their mothers or gay.

'Talking to my mother is like being kicked in the balls if I had any.' I was telling Bobby about my mother, he stared at me totally surprised at my analogy. I guess knowing that he was gay made me feel like he was my girlfriend and I could tell him anything. But talking ill of my mother in front of Bobby who had lost his mother was inappropriate.

'What does she want?'

'She is hoping for me to marry Bittu who was in school with me. You have to meet his parents, they are like Siamese twins.' I giggled imaging Bobby meeting the Bittu clan.

'Sure, I would love to meet them on your wedding.' He chuckled, but I didn't find that funny. I picked up my pillow and started smashing his head with it. Now, we both were hitting each other with pillows. If this were a Bollywood movie, he and I would wrestle to the ground, then our eyes would meet, and then we would break into a lovely song. But, alas none of that happened. Bobby hit me harder until I moved away and he won the fight. I escaped his torture and went to the kitchen.

'RUSHMI! RUSHMI!' Bobby was yelling for me. I thought it was a trick to get me to come back and he would hit me again, but he walked into the kitchen with the laptop and showed me the screen.

'Oh my GOD!!, OH MY GOD! OH MY GOD!!!' I couldn't believe my own eyes. Looking at the screen of the Immigration website, I had actually won the Green Card Lottery. Fifty people out of seven thousand that had entered the lottery had won and one of the winners was me. Unbelievable! This was unreal! Nothing like this ever happens to me. I never win anything. In fact, in elementary school we had secret Santa bring gifts for kids and I was the only child who never got her gift because my secret Santa had measles. Being the last day of school, I never got a gift. That's how bad lucked I am and today to actually win the biggest lottery was incredible.

'Yeah!!! Holy molly, are you serious? Oh, my God!' I was jumping and did a dance. Thrilled, I took Bobby by the hands and we danced around the living room. He was a great dancer and together we danced around the kitchen.

'I have to call my mom! Oh my God!, I can't believe it. Just like that? In the next 10 days I get my fingerprints and boom! I will have my card. This is unreal!' People had spent five years getting this damn card. This card meant I could work anywhere I wanted, this card meant my tuition just dropped like half, this card meant achieving the American dream. My whole life had just changed and now everything I had imagined was possible.

I felt crappy complaining about mom when she had actually done a life changing thing for me. I had never won anything and this just like that, wow unreal. Maybe I won't sue her. But this also meant…., crap! She would never let this Bittu thing go. I could just hear her gloating, "You never listen to me, see, I'm always helping you, trust my opinion and marry Bittu." I would have to fight her even harder –not an easy task.

In my sprint of excitement I had forgotten everything else that was happening in my life. Bobby, Blossom and Shrini and everything else we were doing. It was so tempting to drop everything and to walk away from all of it. I could easily make my own dreams come true. My face must have shown some of these feelings to Bobby because he said;

'Congrats Rushmi! You know you can still walk away from all of this mess and start your life. You don't have to be a part of this. I wish everyone else was as lucky as you.' Bobby gave me a smile, but behind that smile were doubts about me reconsidering helping him anymore. It did cross my mind. I didn't need to deal with any of this and I could easily graduate and easily find a great job. If I wanted I could just ask him to leave and never worry about Blossom any more.

'Bobby, don't be silly. I'm happy, but still with you, my gay friend. This doesn't change anything okay?' He smiled. But there was some doubt. I had my own doubts but giving up on so many friends was never going to be one of those doubts. I just couldn't see my own friends end up at Blossom.

I was really, really, happy and called mom. She was thrilled and played the "I Told You So" card over and over again. She brought up Bittu thirty two times and used the "I was in labor with you for twenty five hours." This number keeps going up every time I talk to her. She used this card to force me to call Bittu. She repeated his phone number three times, but agreeing to it, I never wrote it down, oops!

The day went by contacting INS, getting all the forms together to submit and setting up dates for fingerprinting. I had a lot of forms to fill out, had to make appointments for back ground checks, get my birth certificate and a bunch of other applications to complete before the end of the week for INS.

While I spent the day calling my parents and getting my forms together, Bobby was glued to the TV making sure his picture wasn't on the evening news. While watching TV, he changed the channel and joining him, we both watched a movie. We watched *The Firm*; a Tom Cruise movie of how he overcomes a very intrusive Firm.

'Rushmi….,' Bobby was calling me to pay attention to the movie. I sat up on his bed watching the movie in great detail. We both listened attentively and then, we looked at each other. Not sure what Bobby was thinking, but I was thinking that Bobby looked a lot like Tom Cruise. Looking at Bobby's face, I could tell his mind was working but I just didn't know what. So, I started pretending as though I too was thinking of a good plan. I sat their moving my lips up and down doing math in my head just so that I could look like I was thinking. Sitting in silence for a few minutes, Bobby looked at me.

'We need to setup our own company, now the time has come.' Bobby logged on to the web, pulled out docs to incorporate a new firm. He was sure about one thing; we needed a new company that would allow all the H-1 kids to transfer over so that they could still be able to stay in the US.

'The new company has to be under your name.' Bobby casually said as though no big deal.

'Are you kidding? ME?' Just like that he wanted me to be the owner of a software company, was he kidding?

'Bobby, I don't know how to run a company?' I was still questioning his thinking but Bobby was already filing our incorporation papers and putting my name in the President/Owner line. I have seen this type of scene in the movies usually a Halle Berry movie with John Travolta, but in reality I was no Halle – well maybe a little bit.

'Rushmi, I'm going to be right there with you. I will tell you all that you need, but you have to be the face of this company.' Bobby was typing away on his laptop and totally ignoring my anxiety attack. I could barely mange myself and he wanted me to be the face of an entire company. He wanted me to handle 300 employees? He wanted me to be responsible for 300 lives? I wonder if Sonia Gandhi felt like this when she was put in a similar situation. She made a sacrifice for India so maybe I should do that same for Indians everywhere.

'I think this is a mistake, I can't do it Bobby.'

'Rushmi, listen, it's the only way right now. You have very little to lose. If this doesn't work, at least you tried, right?' Bobby finally looked at me and I could see that he was desperate.

'I wouldn't even have thought of this earlier, but with you getting your Green Card, it makes it all this easier. Don't you see this was a sign, you, yourself said you never win anything so this has to be a sign. I will provide you with everything, but just cannot be the head of this company. My father would find out easily and all this would end.'

My heart was pounding fast; I was conflicted with fear and anxiety and confusion. But, he had a point; it was ironic how I had just won the lottery. Maybe it was meant to be.

'Okay. But you have to be there whenever I need you.'

'Promise, will be there every step of the way.' He went back to typing and printing papers.

Bobby worked on the plan all day. After seven cups of tea down, he had a working plan. He sat down to teach me the basics of Business 101. How to incorporate a company? I spent the whole day on my laptop reading websites, figuring out what types of incorporation to have; how to designate board members, which in my case, I was the only member. We needed a bank account with money in it to setup the S-corporation.

After signing a few papers, reading a dozen websites and calling a tax accountant, we had ended the day by being incorporated. Living in Zambia, even paying monthly bills takes four people to run to the bank, get notarized checks then run to the water company, run to the gas company and make the payments. Here in America, you can do everything online including starting a company. Amazing!

'Our company name will be Sahara Solutions.' Bobby took in a deep breath of relief, 'it is the right name.'

'Sahara? Like the desert?' I was looking at Bobby impressed with his knowledge of African Geography

'No, you Confused Desi, Sahara means support in Hindi.' Bobby rolled his protruding eyes. He really seemed so gay to me. His expressions and use of eyes was so not manly and to think I found him attractive was ridiculous. But, I still hoped to change him some day.

With Sahara Solutions being born, our new corporation needed funding. We had to show assets to start our business. By tomorrow Jay Chand would come through with the ransom money. This money would be the seed money for Sahara. Even though Bobby was sure his father would send in the money, I had my doubts about daddy really paying up for his son. With his gambling addiction and personality, I wasn't so sure he would part with his money so easily.

'I think it's time Rushmi.' It was time to put pressure on Mr. Chand. Bobby sent out an email telling him time was up. The money had to be deposited tonight or else his son's body parts would start coming in the mail.

'That's pretty weird Bobby, sending your father your body parts. Which part are you planning on sending him first?' I giggled as I watched Bobby think about the "what if" his father never sends him the money. Was Bobby ready to find out how much his father loved him? Was he ready to face the fact that his father could let Bobby remain in the kidnappers hands and never part with the money? This was the biggest test in any child's life; seeing whom their parent loves more: money or them. For some, it's an easy answer, in my parents' case, well they would choose me, I think.

Bobby seemed a bit torn in what he was doing. Here he was trying to ruin his father but if his father sent the money it would prove to him that his father loved him so much. Was he willing to still hurt the man who loved him so much? Could he continue to hurt his father knowing that his father had spent a million on saving his life?

'You still want to go through with this?' I had to ask. Here I was sticking my neck out and going along with his idea, taking the risk of running Sahara Solutions, but if Bobby was second guessing himself, I needed to know, Now.

'Rushmi, you know when a child goes out of line? Parents stick by the child until he gets back on track. Today, dad is off track and it's my job to bring him back. He will send the money. I just know it. The challenge he does have is to get everyone to collaborate in putting together this million because dad alone doesn't have the whole amount with him. Everyone is probably collecting the cash and they have to, because if dad notifies the cops, they all run the risk of getting unnecessary attention. So they will send it.'

Bobby got up from his laptop and went to the kitchen. Whenever he was stressed he would cook something. That night, while Bobby made sandwiches, he and I kept the laptop screen up, waiting for the money transfer to take place. The pressure was so high at this point. We desperately needed this money to even begin our plan. If the money never comes, there would be very little we could do. With no money, Sahara would die even before being born. I was feeling the pressure. With anxiety flooding my system, I needed something to ease my tension. I ate and ate and ate. But Bobby, on the other hand, was so stressed that he couldn't eat. So he cooked to ease his tension and I ate to sooth mine.

I must have eaten seven cheese, tomato, and mushroom sandwiches, had three milk shakes and four samosas. Now I felt sick. My stomach hurt and the pressure was pushing everything down really fast. I had to use the bathroom. I took Bobby's laptop to the bathroom just so I could keep an eye.

'Where the hell is my laptop?' Bobby yelled from the kitchen.'

'I have it in here.' I yelled back from the bathroom.

'Gross! Who told you to take it in there?' Bobby was furious.

'Relax! Girls are not as bad as guys.' I chuckled.

'Yeah right, you're worse than me.' At that point, I had very little to say. It was true. Bobby hardly ate any food. He was a fit person, loved to cook but didn't eat as much. Plus, every morning he took a shower and put on a ton of cologne and smelled amazing all day. Me, on the other hand, enjoyed my meals, took showers at the end of the day and wore perfume when it was an emergency.

'I need a new laptop.' I heard Bobby talking to himself. He made me laugh.

'We got it! We got it!' I screamed from the bathroom. Within seconds I was outside with the laptop yelling and dancing. I held the laptop in my hands and was jumping up and down all thrilled about successfully achieving step 1 of our plan. We had received money in our account. I hugged Bobby tightly.

'You didn't wash your hands did you?' Bobby had stopped smiling and he pulled away immediately. I looked into his eyes that reflected disgust and I knew he was never wearing those clothes again.

'What's your problem dude?' I placed his laptop on the table.

'Problem, my problem is that you stink.'

'WHAT?' He can't be serious? I don't stink, maybe I don't smell good, but definitely don't stink.

'You and your desi friends all stink of food.' Bobby walked over and opened the windows.

'What do you mean I stink like my friends?' Was he referring to the food smell the other desi kids have? Was he serious that I smelled too? I know the other kids smelled of desi food but he included me too. Could it be possible? Have I merged into the smells from the other kids? Did I really smell?

'I think it's all the desi food you all cook that sits inside your clothes, hair and everything else. Yes, you all stink. Why do you think I keep the windows open in my room? I mean it's freezing outside but that's the only way to keep my room free of your odor. Why do you think I wear so much cologne? Come on, don't you guys smell yourself?' Hearing Bobby was the biggest shock of my life. I was one of them. I was one of the smellers. I was now carrying and delivering BO. No wonder handsome guys had not asked me out on a date in these two years. I guess over these two years maybe I had become used to smells. Knowing that I too had a cloud of stink around me made me really conscious. I opened all the windows and using Larry's magical key started washing everything in my apartment. I even used the Poison perfume I had been saving for my first date.

Bobby had been so relieved to know that his father had sent in the money. In fact, his father had sent the money within three hours. $400K had been deposited into the bank account with an email message back asking for few more hours to deposit the remaining $600K. Bobby had been absolutely correct. No police had been involved. Guess they really didn't want cops investigating their lives. They had kept everything so hush to avoid any unnecessary attention. But more importantly, I saw Bobby happy to see that his father still had emotions and feelings for his son.

Watching the money in Bobby's account was confirmation that our plan was working. At least step 1 had worked! We had the money, all $400K in Bobby's account. I had never seen such a large amount of money – it almost felt like just a number. I was so tempted to cash all of it and actually see it for myself. How does $400K look like? Money was powerful but never had I imagined it to be of such great strength. I felt a rush of power especially thinking that I would actually own that money.

Getting that money into Bobby's account was one part of the plan. Now we had to actually move that money into Sahara Solutions. We had to get a cashier's check from Bobby's account. But if Bobby went to the bank in town, it's possible someone from their group would be waiting there for him. He and I sat staring at the laptop which displayed the Bank of Chicago website showing $400,000 deposited.

I wondered if we could use another branch away from campus, where he could walk into the bank and ask for a cashier's check. What is the worst that could happen? Jay Chand could inform the bank to inform the police but there is no way the cops would be involved. If he wanted, Jay Chand would have done this earlier, so police was not going to be an issue. Even if Jay Chand wanted, he couldn't have people at every branch waiting for us. Maybe it wasn't going to be such a big deal. I wanted to tell Bobby what I thought but my stomach gave in again and I rushed to the bathroom again.

'What did you put in those sandwiches?' I yelled from the bathroom.

'Maybe you should eat less.' Bobby yelled back.

'Maybe you should.' I didn't have a comeback. After a few minutes in the bathroom, I walked out pressing my stomach. I had lost all the sandwiches and now felt drained. I also sprayed my perfume again and with the windows still open, I was saved from Bobby declaring my apartment as a nuclear site.

'Larry and I will go the Bank outside Chicago so no one sees us, we will do this first thing tomorrow morning, We will have to drive out tonight.'

'Do you want me to come?' I sat at the dining table pressing my stomach that was still hurting.

'No, you stay here. I don't want people to see me with you. If I get caught at least you are still away from all of this.' Bobby picked up the phone and called Larry. It was very exciting to plan this whole gimmick just like in the movies when the good guys make a plan and try to beat the bad ones. Watching Bobby getting ready and Larry, who was in my apartment talking to Bobby, thinking about driving out to the bank and me being the lookout sexy girl felt like we were in a movie. Must have been the whole excitement but I had the urge to say it, uncontrollable urge to say it and finally I did say it,

'I LOVE IT WHEN A PLAN COMES TOGETHER.' I was grinning at Bobby. He returned a look that changed my grin to a sheepish smile. Guess he didn't watch too much of the A-team. Larry had looked at me and walked away as though he didn't even know me.

'Haven't you watched this program called the A-team?' I tried to educate Bobby.

'I used to love it, not anymore.' Bobby rolled his eyes at me as though he was soooo mature. I think Bobby was not as sophisticated as he acted and I know inside was a little child dying to come out. It was just a matter of time.

'Come on man! Come to the dark side. Say it, just say it, you love it when a…?' I enticed him to say it but he walked away. Oh well, someday he has to come to the dark side and that day I shall win.

Bobby had taken a smart suit to look like someone who had a lot of money. He took his black pants and jacket with a blue shirt and darker blue tie. The plan was to drive all night and in the morning change into his suit before making it to the bank.

By 9pm Larry and Bobby left my apartment driving out of town to get that cashier's check for $400K. I sat in my apartment alone still staring at the bank account figure. Within an hour, that amount jumped from $400K to $1million! I stared at this large number and to think this actually reflected money was exhilarating. I had $35 in my account and that had made me so happy. Seeing so many zeros was unbelievable. Just like that, I was staring at $1 million. This money could make my life very comfortable. This money could change my life forever. I had never seen that amount in my life and maybe never again would I see it. I called Bobby and told him that he would need a bigger cashier's check. His father had paid the ransom.

'Awesome!' He said that one word and hung up. But I was too excited to stop thinking about this money. I needed to eat something. I found some chocolate icing in the fridge and used that to celebrate our first victory. Sitting in my cold apartment all alone, I was way too anxious and excited to sleep. Everything about the day was circulating in my head. The numbers with all the zeros, the title of being president of a company and the fear of being caught was in one moment exciting then extremely overwhelming. I was having a panic attack sitting in my bed constantly thinking about everything. I had opened all my windows and it was freezing in my room but I couldn't close the windows. It would take at least one week to completely get the smell out. So, until then, I had to keep my winter jacket on. Watching the jewelry channel was driving me nuts. Who would pay so much money for junk like that kept me irritated and when they displayed a statue of an emerald Walrus, I almost fell off my bed.

I remembered my Walrus. Bittu was back in my life and my mother was trying desperately to ruin my life. But, standing up against her was no easy task- maybe larger than Jay Chand. I had to find an alternative to Bittu. Maybe Bobby would be my replacement especially because converting him was still on my To Do list.

I got off from the bed, in my SpongeBob PJs and walked into the kitchen. I made myself a strawberry shake and sat in front of my laptop. I needed a backup plan to deal with my mother's obsession with Bittu. I decided to setup my account in Matrimonial.com.

WELL EDUCATED, ATTRACTIVE, CAREER FOCUSED DESI GIRL LOOKING FOR MR. RIGHT. MUST BE AT LEAST 5'9, EDUCATED. NORTH INDIAN PREFERRED – SOMEONE WHO ENJOYS EVERYTHING DESI IN AMERICA.
"It's not about finding the right person; it's about being the right person."

I was allowed to post a thirty word description about myself and what I was looking for in a man. Most of the time people just look at basic information like height and weight and then after exchanging basic information you setup a phone call. So, I decided to be as discrete as possible. I didn't give out my email ID, rather created a new email address. I didn't even post a picture, my thought was to get pictures from guys and then correspond with only the ones I thought were good looking. I wanted to come up with a really neat user name. Most of the time you see user names like, Dreamboy or MrRight, but I wanted something smart. So, I listed all my attributes in a list:

Beautiful, Intelligent, Girl, North-Indian, Professional, Looking for Educated, Smart, Match. There, I had a list of all the things that described me and my needs. I thought it was an educated, smart idea to create my username by putting together the first letter of all my traits, B,I,G,N,I,P,L,E,S,M. With the ID only being nine characters, I had to drop the M but at last it was done.

I had posted my matrimonial advertisement. By posting this ad on this website and giving my email address, the flood gates were open to meeting eligible bachelors. I would search for Mr. Right myself and this would be the answer to my Bittu problem. If I found the right person for myself, I could easily push Bittu out of my life for good.

Finishing the shake, I went back to bed and put some Frank Sinatra music to help me sleep. It must have been 3am when I finally dozed off to sleep.

During the night, Bobby had decided to drive in Larry's truck to the bank in Michigan. This bank was seven hours drive, but it was the only way to be far enough so no one would recognize him. Getting into a closer bank, someone would definitely take notice or recognize Bobby and that would have ruined the entire plan.

At the bank, getting the cashier's check was no hassle. It was very easy for him to get in, show some id and get his check. He called me the minute they both were driving back. We now had the funds to bring Sahara to life. They both drove back right after getting the cashier's check. It was 1130am and I had barely woken up from my late night sleep. I was just getting a cup of tea when Bobby knocked the door. Both Larry and Bobby walked in looking tired. They had driven back and forth nonstop. Bobby was still in his suit and despite being overly tired, he still looked like he had come out of the shower. He showed me the two checks, each for $500K.

Holding these checks for a million dollars in my hand, I had thoughts of running away to some place European, meeting a desi James Bond guy and living a life of luxury and romance. Then I snapped back into reality and realized that the next step was mine.

'Here, have some tea.' I gave Larry and Bobby something to eat as they stretched on my couch. Larry looked frail and weak. He had not been doing so well lately and I was really worried about his health. I had made Larry breakfast every day for the past year and now Mili waited for me to feed her instead of Larry.

Bobby handed me the two checks saying that not all the money should be deposited at once. I was to keep one check in the safe to deposit later while depositing only one check into Sahara Solutions account. This was to avoid unnecessary attention.

'Rushmi, now it's your turn. Get over to the bank and deposit it into Sahara. But, I know you, don't act like a movie star or something; just be yourself.' Bobby warned me like I was a child. I wasn't like that at all. I mean, it wasn't like I compared EVERYTHING to the movies.

I knew what I had to do. I had to take this money and deposit it into my company's account, show them the incorporation papers, get a check book and finally get Sahara Solutions standing on its feet. I wanted to go with the theme of acting all cool and smart like Bobby who had dressed in a smart suit for his part. So, keeping Rebecca De Mornay in mind, I dressed in my black skirt, white shirt and put on a black jacket to look as cool as Bobby.

Standing in front of the mirror, I looked at my black heals, knee high skirt, white collar shirt, black coat, my pearl necklace and earrings. I looked at my hair pulled back in a bun and standing up straight like any confident CEO I looked at myself in the mirror. I looked like Penguin's daughter. Immediately I changed into black pants and dark blue high neck sweater, opened my hair and wore my favorite gold earring set. Now I looked like the new CEO of Sahara Solutions. I looked like Madhuri* in the movie Beta. In fact, if this were a Hindi movie there would be a song in the back ground right now.

Leaving Bobby and Larry at my apartment to rest, I went to the nearest bank on campus. I opened a new account under the name Sahara Solutions. The bank manager was a nice old lady. She was whiter than snow white and very nice to me especially when she saw my deposit. She offered me coffee and then two more people came over to help me. The whole process took an hour. At the end, I had my account setup. My deposit stamp, checks and incorporation documents were all ordered and within ten working days I would get my debit card.

'You are very young to be the President of a Software company.' The white lady behind the desk smiled and said to me; reading her badge she was Ms. Kayla. I was not sure what to say. I was distracted by her name, Kayla meant banana in Hindi. Just thinking about a desi with that name made me smile.

'Are you ok?' The lady asked again and that's when I realized that I had been staring at her badge which was stuck on her breast area. So, basically I had been staring at her chest. After that moment of weirdness, I stopped looking at her chest and moved my eyes to her mouth where she had spinach stuck in her teeth. But my staring at her mouth made her even more uncomfortable and she stopped smiling.

'Yes, I'm fine, just a lot of work.' I had to pull myself together. I was overly anxious and overly excited. I reminded myself again that I wasn't stealing money, I was depositing money. Why was I so anxious? I took in a deep breath and tried to calm myself down. But for someone who has less than $50 in the bank to suddenly having $500K, the nerves definitely start getting the best of you. I was trembling, moving my legs, turning on my sides as I sat in the chair, rolling my hair, fiddling with a thread that was coming out of my sweater the whole time.

'Nice seeing you hear Rushmi.' I heard a voice coming from behind the glass office where I was waiting. Turning around I saw Jay Chand standing outside the office. He seemed tired. At that moment I thought that it was all over. Somehow he knew. He had found out that Bobby was living with me and he probably had police officers waiting to cuff me. He probably would have me hung in this bank at this very moment.

'Are you ok?' He came into the office and was now standing in front of me.

'Fine, sir.' I think that is what I had said but with the flood of horror, I couldn't even hear myself. He opened his mouth to say something but the bank manager walked in.

'Sir, the money from your son's account has been moved.' The bank manager had just finished saying that and Jay immediately turned around and left with the manager. My heart was in my throat and I thought I was going to throw up. Somehow I kept everything in and as soon as my account was setup and the money was deposited, I got the hell out of the bank.

After jogging back to my apartment, I gave a cool, two thumbs up to Larry and Bobby who were still sleeping in my apartment. Without saying a word, I went into my bedroom, shut the door and passed out on my bed. My head hurt, my lungs were on fire, and my stomach was hurting because my pants were killing my circulation. I had never been this scared before; that very moment of seeing Jay Chand had been horrifying. For sure I thought I would be in jail. After a few hours of holding myself in bed, I decided to clear my head by checking on my matrimonial ad. Logging in, to my surprise I had over 2100 email invites! What? I knew these sites were useful in meeting people but why so many? Was I the only woman left or something? I read my first email and it read:

"Dear Bigniples, I would be very interested in corresponding with you especially because I am all about nipples……", Oh My God! My brilliant idea had turned out to be not so brilliant. I had been so careful in creating a smart and educated ID, but once the letters were all together, I hadn't realized it spelled: Bigniples! I had over 2000 perverted messages in my account. This was not the correspondence I had in mind. Men are so disgusting, they only think in one direction; none of these guys even stopped to think that my ID might mean something else. I tried to change my user ID but the damn system wouldn't allow it. So, I updated my description section where I redefined my ID with "Beautiful, Intelligent, Girl, North-Indian, Professional, Looking for Educated, Smart, Match. Hopefully this would clear up any ideas these perverts had about my ad. Worse of all, knowing how many perverts are out there was a chilling thought.

I came out of my bedroom to where Bobby was busy working on his laptop.

'You ok?' he looked up at me all concerned.

'Yes, just some weird emails that I had to deal with. I saw your father at the bank.' I reported to Bobby who stood up immediately.

'What!?'

'Yup, he was at the bank and I heard the manager telling him that the money had been moved. I think he must have put a trace on your account to know when the money was taken out. Maybe Jay Chand could easily put together the connection of his money leaving and my money coming in! Yup, he would figure it out and all this would be over and I would end up in jail!' I was babbling nonstop.

'Relax, nothing has happened yet, did he talk to you?'

'Yes, he just said something like hi or nice seeing you or something like that.'

'Okay, so to get him to stop wondering about the money, I need to go home today.'

Bobby pulled my hand closer to the laptop.

'Relax. Here is something to be excited about.' He signaled me to see what he had on his machine.

On the laptop was the bank account information of Sahara Solutions. Bobby and I were now the proud owners of our own business with a balance of half a million and another half coming soon.

Our plan had taken off to a good start. Sahara Solutions was going to be our new firm and would put Blossom Consulting out of business. I was listed as the President and CEO with one employee, me. My signatures on the check book would allow me to move money anywhere I wanted. I was holding the money to this new company. We had half a million in cash which seemed so far a pretty promising venture. This was just the beginning.

Despite the constant feeling of the cops bursting into my apartment from the door, windows, and roof, the anxiety attacks were worth the task at hand. Keeping Shrini, Asoke and Shoba in mind, the mission of our company was; as was said in A Few Good Men, Crystal Clear!

25

With Jay Chand seeing me at the Bank; both Bobby and I felt like he would immediately connect the dots. So, we decided to immediately come up with a plan to send Bobby home. We had to send Bobby back home so he could snoop around and stay connected with his father and their friends. His father had sent in many emails begging for the safe return of his son. Friday morning, as Jay Chand got into his car, he heard sounds coming from the trunk where he found Bobby tied up. Bobby had a few bruises to seem convincing. This time I had done the pleasure of boxing his eye and lip. I had never actually hit anyone and this was an opportunity to learn. Bobby stood in front of me like in the movie Sholay and I punched him in the face. Holy shit! My hand hurt like hell too.

Larry dropped him to the curb and Bobby, who had a spare key, easily got inside his home. He snuck inside his father's car and waited for dad to find him. Seeing his son all bruised up and bloody; Jay forgot about me. Bobby had convinced his father that it was someone from his gambling group who was behind his kidnapping. Since Jay owed lots of people money, he was easily convinced.

Bobby had setup a server in my apartment which had encrypted code to send secure messages. I was to never contact him directly. He was the one who would decide when to meet. If ever we needed to meet him in person, Larry would make that happen. Larry would visit Jay Chand every now and then and send home Bobby's favorite chocolate as a sign that we needed to communicate.

'Chocolate?' I liked the plan but why chocolate?

Larry had explained to me that when Bobby was a little boy, he would visit his father on campus. But his father being so busy would have Larry watch Bobby and that's how Larry and Bobby became close. Bobby loved the caramel chocolate from Ghirardelli so Larry always got some for him. Sending chocolate with Jay Chand would be a very common gesture and a great signal for us.

I love chocolate too but Larry never bought me any. But there was more serious stuff to worry about -the chocolate would have to wait. Now that the company was created, we needed work and we had to employ people. It was the chicken or the egg thing, which needed to happen first?

Thinking about all my friends, the one person who I knew had to be on my side was Anand. He was by far the most helpful, trustworthy and technical guy. But there was only one issue with him; if I went after him he would definitely think that I'm interested in him.

With a lot of introspection, I had no option but to go forward with it. I emailed Anand to meet me at my apartment for a cup of coffee in the evening. Within minutes he replied with a big yes. He wrote back saying he expected more than coffee, he wanted food. So, arranging for some pizza and coffee I met him. I had asked him to join me around 5pm, but at exactly 4:59pm the doorbell rang and sure enough it was him.

'Hey Anand. Come in.' He walked in with his black leather jacket, jeans, and a sweat shirt with FBI written all across. He entered my apartment and so did the smell. Before his arrival, I had made sure all my windows were open. With my apartment ventilated for the past few days, the smell was gone from my clothes; at least Bobby said that it had gone. Bobby promised me that all the smell had gone from my apartment, clothes and from me. When Anand's walked in, I could smell the same odor from his clothes that reeked of all sorts of masala smells. He made himself comfortable and soon we were talking about classes.

'Why is it so cold in your apartment?' Anand had taken his jacket off but now wore it back again.

'I am always hot so keep my windows open.' It was a dumb answer seeing that I too was wearing my winter jacket. But Anand was just so excited to be invited, he didn't notice.

'Anand, listen, I got some money from my dad and put that together to start a consulting company. We code all these programs for class projects. What if we did it for actual clients and made some money on the side? My company is called Sahara. Let me show you the website.' I pulled up the simple website I had created for the company. Being in my third year of Computer Science, I was decent in putting together a simple website.

'You did this? I like the name – good Desi touch?' Anand seemed surprised especially because he knew how bad I was in coding with HTML.

'Impressive! So what's your plan?' Anand talked casually despite my big news. He was more fixated on the Pizza.

'Well, it includes you. I need a person to do the project planning and actually coding for me. You interested?' Anand was still busy eating.

'Okay, I'll do it. But, only until I graduate. I need a real job after graduation with the whole H-1 thing.' I knew he was going to say that and I also knew that he had already invested with Jay Chand. So, for now, until I actually had clients, I just needed him partially.

'I know, but let's talk numbers. Right now your pay is zero until we actually get work.' Now I had Anand's attention.

'So, you will pay me once I actually get work?' He was looking at me like I was kidding around. I think he thought we would never get a client or actually make money. In a way, I too was thinking the same thing.

'Absolutely. Once we get clients and we make some money, I expect to pay you too. Something like that…still working out the details.' I didn't have a plan on how much I would pay him, but that could wait.

'Okay, I will help as much as I can. We should have more of these management meetings.' He seemed not so impressed with my company rather more excited about having coffee with me alone in my apartment. I knew he didn't take me seriously and just agreed to it knowing that there was no way I could actually get this company going. In a way, I too didn't think I could do it. But, at least we had our first employee. Anand was someone I could trust, someone with more knowledge about programming and someone who would do anything for me. Anand had six more months to graduate, so I had time to work out the details of his employment.

'What languages are you comfortable with?' I knew Anand had programmed in many languages and designed various programs that had won him a scholarship.

'I can do coding in C++, Java, SQL, also can do visual basic, pretty much all the ones in our courses and now started looking into SAP.'

'So, if I get a client, can you assess their needs and design software for them?' I asked him being careful to not sound too naïve. I had been given assignments in class, but to actually design something for a real client was intimidating.

'I actually have designed a few programs for Jay Chand already. He usually asks my help with some of his clients who need help. I worked with him a few times especially because it makes me look good and I know that's why he decided to help me.' Anand said confidently.

That annoyed me even more than Anand's smell. Jay was so good at deceiving these kids and to think that Anand was already doing some of his projects pissed me off.

'Tell you what; you will be the chief systems designer at my company. You get to design the lab and order what all you need BUT you immediately stop working for Jay Chand as of today. At least for the next six months. Deal?' I just wanted to put some distance between Jay and Anand. I felt protective of Anand despite his birthing hips.

Anand happily agreed and immediately gave me a list of servers, PCs, software needed to setup a mini lab in my apartment. He was so fast in making his list, like he had it already in his pocket for me. He also had requested additional software that I knew we didn't need but wanted it for his own interest. Initially, we only needed three PCs, a printer and software. Bobby had promised me that he would be the one getting me all the equipment. I emailed Bobby the list.

That evening Anand stayed longer then he needed to and I knew I was in trouble with him. I had to maintain a professional distance with him and with his smell. After he left, I lit a few candles and sprayed Bobby's cologne so that the smell would venture out of my apartment again. I didn't want to waste my poison perfume.

26

It was a matter of weeks when all the equipment arrived at my apartment. I called Anand to help setup a LAN network in my apartment and within minutes, he rushed over. He couldn't believe that I had actually purchased thousands of dollars' worth of equipment. His thought the concept of my company was a joke but at that moment, he was speechless. We had software servers, PCs and printers all brand new sitting in my apartment.

'Welcome to Sahara Solutions headquarters!' I was smiling ear to ear because in a way I too couldn't believe I had actually done this. Bobby had placed the order and I had been invoiced for my purchase and actually sent out my very first check of $15000. Even writing the check was challenging. I had never written so many zeros before on a check.

Once Anand saw all the new machines, software and printer in my apartment, he finally knew that I was serious about my Entrepreneurship. It didn't even take a day for Anand to tell everyone about Sahara and all twelve of my buddies were asking to be a part of this company.

'Rushmi, you really want to do this?' Anya looked into my eyes because she was taken aback with what she saw. Never had they imagined me doing something so big and to actually get the equipment surprised everyone. Just seeing that I actually had the money to purchase these servers, had the ability to setup a lab and showing them the website; everyone was now convinced that I wasn't just playing around. They all wanted a part of it. Now everyone was on board. This was the cheapest labor for me since I wouldn't pay them until we had actually acquired work.

Buying the machines was not the hard part. The hard part was getting work. While Sahara was ready for business, with zero clients, everyone used my machines to complete their assignments. Instead of staying up all night in the lab at school, everyone crashed at my place to complete their assignments. They also helped themselves to my food. Guess paying my employees with food was not so bad.

But having employees is only the first part of our plan. I needed work. From connecting with Bobby and Shrini, we knew a lot of the work that Blossom Consulting did was from software firms in Silicon Valley. Various small companies were getting their work done for cheap via Blossom. Blossom did a lot of QA, integration projects, creating simple websites for new startups, developing user friendly GUI for retail stores projects. But being a nobody, every call we made to these offices returned a "Sorry, but we haven't heard about your firm." It was obvious; we needed name recognition to even begin to make contacts at these new companies.

Anya had tried helping by taking my simple website and turning it into an amazing website for Sahara. She added great effects, made it very informative and used advanced imagery to create a facility picture of our firm. We created a company email address, with my previous experience with Bigniples, I stayed with the basic address of customercare@sahara.com. The website made us look like it was hosted in the rich part of Chicago. The contact phone number was my home phone for now, which unfortunately wasn't ringing.

Hersita had taken some sales classes in business school and used every means of creating flyers, business cards and brochures. We mailed out hundreds of these to pretty much every firm in the yellow pages. We had sent out flyers, called everyone we could find on the net, we even walked into some local business but were graciously escorted out. Every day after classes, we all would sit in my apartment disheartened about being rejected in every direction. My frustration level was so high that I actually had put on five pounds. Now, I was even more depressed about being a loser and fat CEO. Every day I would call people from our list of potential clients but no one would even allow us to talk over the phone. We needed help. Three weeks had passed and not even one interested party. I could see that the enthusiasm was dying. Something had to be done fast because in another four months Anand would be graduating. Without a real job, he would end up at Blossom.

Depressed, I logged into my matrimonial website to get my mind off. With my previous posting explaining Bigniples, the emails had dropped from 2000 to 3! I went through each response. One was DesiBoy17 who claimed to be tall, handsome, clean shaved Sikh looking for his Desigirl. Another was HandsomeHunk, he was looking for a good, Indian girl to make his life partner in the journey of life. I rejected him because anyone who calls himself HandsomeHunk is definitely insecure about his looks. But then again, I did call myself Bigniples; maybe I shouldn't reject him based on his ID. Then, there was Mahesh who was mature, which meant he is older and was looking for an understanding wife, which meant he had issues, possibly divorced. These ads are very tricky. You have to read between the lines.

Just going over these responses was challenging. How am I supposed to figure out which one of these guys is worthy and which one isn't? Glancing over the pictures of all these guys, I felt more depressed. I didn't see anything special in any of these guys. In fact, the perverted emails had better looking, sexy pictures of guys on motorcycles, of shirtless guys with great bodies. It's ironic, the good guys who are simple and sweet have boring pictures but the perverted guys had the hot pictures. It's too bad I couldn't get the best of both worlds. That's when it hit me! None of these good guys stood out, just like Sahara Consulting! We were just another consulting company lost amongst thousands of other consulting companies. We had to stand out. Even though our business is the same as the other companies, we had to do something totally off beat to get the attention that would make us a stand out. We had to create the best of both worlds in the brand called…Sahara.

I remembered the time in Zambia when the Indian community was putting together a fundraiser. We were getting little attention from the Zambian community in terms of attendance. We really wanted to come up with ideas that would encourage more people to come. Everyone was scratching their heads about how to get more people to participate and Shashi aunty was the only one to come up with the best idea. Dressed in a sexy red Saree, she had performed on the Chanay ke khet mein* song, making all the Madhuri moves. She had not only gotten the attention of every desi man but increased attendance by the local community. After her one performance, other aunties had joined in and we ended up raising a lot of money. Sex appeal does sell.

I had to come up with a dynamic marketing technique that would put the name of Sahara Solutions on everyone's mouth. Using the best mix of sex appeal, attention and totally out of the norm idea, I started working on my marketing plan. All day I had just been streaming information back and forth, looking at articles, newspapers, read the TIME of 100 most influential people. While wandering through all these readings; it came to me! I knew what my marketing gimmick was going to be. I had it. This would be the one thing that would make everyone talk about Sahara Solutions. It was a bit risky but it would do the job.

I called Rayani and Julie and the rest of the twelve troopers over. Going over the details of my plan, I convinced everyone that my plan would surely work. At first everyone was shocked to hear my plan. I think they all agreed to it just to see if I would actually do it. Kawal, Anand, Nikhil and Madhu would all stay at my apartment on Saturday and I would go with Rayani, Julie, Anya and Prashant to Cellular Field to watch the Chicago White Sox play against the Yankees. The baseball season was getting hot and now only two teams were left. The World Series was officially beginning with game one at Cellular Field. I had watched most of the games and with the Yankees making it to the World Series, the whole nation was watching. Larry had worked part time at the Field during summer breaks for extra work and knew how to get us in. There was a game tomorrow at noon.

'Are you insane Rushmi?' Madhu was shocked to hear what I was about to do.

'You know you could get in a lot of trouble right? She looked at everyone sitting in my apartment and the others just nodded their heads in agreement.

'I know it's a crazy idea guys but I have to try it. We have to think young and of new ways of getting our name out otherwise Sahara will die even before it takes off.' I was packing my backpack to take with me to the baseball field.

'If she wants to do it then let her do it.' Prashant smiled at the other guys and I knew he wasn't being supportive instead he just wanted to see me carry out my shocking plan. As long as everyone was helping out, I didn't care their reasons for helping. With no one to argue against my decision, the plan was set in motion.

Larry drove us to the baseball field the following day. This was my first live baseball game. Entering the Stadium, I saw thousands of people and their energy in the park was thrilling. Everyone was a maniac. Wearing Yankee and White Sox hats, holding large flags and banners, one of them said, "Marry me Jeter" – I wish I was holding that one. Larry got us into the park and the people working knew him well so we didn't have much trouble getting in. At first it pissed me off that Larry hadn't taken me to a game especially because he would have easily been able to get me in. But right now we had to focus on the task at hand. I would deal with him later.

We got four seats right in front of the dugout and that's where I spotted my baby. He was wearing his Yankee uniform, cap and he was stretching his arms and legs, my Derek Jeter. He looked so good in real life. His flawless face, his big bright grey with a hint of brown eyes, his normal size ears, his broad shoulders and his constant spitting of tobacco was everything I had ever imagined. I also saw Andy Pettitte, he was warming up in the pitching area. Alex Rodriguez was working on his swing. In person these guys looked like Greek Gods and for a moment I couldn't hear the 30,000 screaming fans. Everything went silent and I heard music as I enjoyed my view of the three most attractive men in my world.

This moment reminded me of the Hindi movie Disco Dancer. Just like in that movie, I imagined a moment where Derek had lost all hope of winning, it was the bottom of the ninth, the game tied, with the last pitch of the game remaining, I would scream from my seat to Derek. DO IT DEREK, DO IT FOR YOUR COUNTRY! With me screaming from the bleachers, he gets re-energized and makes the final ball count and getting the one home run the team needed to win. Then all the fans would hug him and cheer for him, but he would get past the fans and make it to where I was seated. He would take me in his arms and right there propose to me in front of everyone. If only Derek would turn around and look into my eyes maybe he would see my love for him.

But he was too busy warming up and never even looked at me. However, today he would notice me and if my marketing gig went as planned, I would be hugging Derek in the next hour.

None of the desi friends had any interest in baseball. Larry was a White Sox fan and hated the fact that he had taught me Baseball only to love the Yankees. When the game started, the screaming crowd, the large glasses of beer, the cheers from the stand all took my mind away from why we were even at the game. I was so into the game that almost had forgotten our entire mission. Bottom of the fifth, White Sox are up by one when Derek hits a home run tying the game. The crowd went crazy! I felt a burst of energy and thrilled, that's when I screamed out loud yelling on top of my voice,

'I LOVE YOU DEREK!!!!'

Rayani looked at me, held my hand and yelled, 'It's time!' She had no interest in Sahara Solutions but hearing about my marketing campaign, she had volunteered immediately. Anything to get attention was Rayani's motto.

Rayani, Julie, Anya and I took off our shirts, each wearing a black bra, our backs and belly painted with Sahara Solutions name and logo; we jumped out of our seats. We were on the field and made a run towards the players! We each had a flag of Sahara Solutions that we held up high. Anya made a run towards the nearest player, Alex. Julie went towards Andy, and Rayani ran towards Mariano, another amazing pitcher for the Yankees. But I had reserved my player. No one was supposed to go near Derek except me. I ran as fast as I could towards my man, Derek. He must have been scared off by the sight of a woman caring a large flag, in her bra, running towards him that he threw his bat and made a run for it. But, instead of running to the dugout, he ran onto the field giving me more time to chase him. So here I was running towards Derek and he's running away as fast as he could until I caught up and dove right on him.

The crowd had been going crazy! I remember seeing my face on the large screens until the security guys pulled me off Derek and dragged me out of the field. But the crowd had cheered for me the whole time. It was the best moment of my life. Just to have touched Derek, to have smelled his cologne, to have embraced him completely and to experience him talking to me, "get off of me you maniac", I think was all that he had said. But it had been the best moment for me and in years to come, no matter what he says, he will remember me too. When the cops yanked me off of Derek, the two officers dragged me away but my arms stretched out, I looked into his eyes and confessed my love for him. The moment the two cops were dragging me away, I had imagined a really sad Hindi song playing in the background as they separated two lovers.

'I have your underwear!' I kept screaming to him. Anya and Julie had also been dragged off the field. All throughout this ordeal, the crowd had cheered for us. I love this game! We were taken to an empty room and three of us were sitting in the empty room but we could hear the crowd. The game had continued. Listening to the second half of the game, the Yankees had lost because Derek had sprained his wrist and Mariano had hurt his back with our little incident. I guess little price to pay in love and war.

Prashant and Larry had come with us to bail us out. We were held in that room until the game was over and paid a fine for our stunt but to me, it was a small price to pay for so much advertising. I think Anand had desperately wanted to come just so he too could see us in our bras. One of the reasons I didn't want him to come.

What no marketing professor could ever teach you, we had done it. We made the front page of the Chicago Times, Tribune and made it on ESPN. The Times had a long article, first about fans going crazy, but I skipped over that to where they made references to our flags and logo and to Sahara Solutions. It also went into writing about new marketing ideas, described Sahara and had a picture of me on top of Derek. I framed that picture in my room; it comforts me.

My mother would have really gone berserk seeing my face in the paper again. First with the fish on my head and today, with me on top of Derek, but that was the best day of my life. A simple girl from Zambia had managed to make contact with Derek. I'd like to think that I did this for all the kids in Blossom even though I enjoyed it immensely.

The irony in doing a stunt like this was that my matrimonial prospects all vanished after that day except HandsomeHunk. These guys saw my face in the paper and the next day wrote back saying, 'NO THANKS.' I couldn't believe this! Mahesh wrote that I must be on drugs to pull a stunt like that. He wrote that any woman who would run the field in her bra was definitely not wife material. However, in college the guys in my classes all seemed to be interested in me. All of a sudden, guys who never paid any attention to me now wanted to be my friend; they thought I was an easy girl. Professor Pervert had me sign the picture and held a stupid grin because all this time he kept wondering my size but now, he knew exactly what my size was. He had posted my picture with Derek in his office.

Everyone was over at my apartment reading then rereading all the headlines we had made. Sahara had been officially launched. The guys had walked into my apartment but unlike the other times; they became very reserved in talking to me. It was like all of a sudden they realized that I was a woman. They behaved weird with me. Even though I was the one who had taken off the shirt, they behaved as though they had been exposed. Men are so goofy.

Anya and I knew that these guys were imagining us in our bras the whole time. Anya had made lunch and brought it to my place so we could all spend the day together and talk about our company. The phone would ring and customers would start calling to give us work. It had to work. It was our only hope. It must have been around 3pm when the phone did ring and we all looked at each other in complete surprise. Had it worked? Was this going to be the beginning of our company? Was someone really buying the marketing gimmick? Could this be the one? We were excited about receiving our first potential customer.

'Hello! Good morning, Sahara Solutions, how may I help you?' I was careful to use a good American accent. Everyone held their breath to ensure that no one made a sound. This was the most important phone call for us.

'Oh! Mom! Sorry, no nothing, not doing anything. It's nothing mom. Sahara is just a joke, you won't get it. Yes, fine, yes, no I didn't call him. No MOM, I am not ready. No, I do love you but, but, but, no, I can't mom, no, I do love you, I don't have a boyfriend, mom, please just give me more time. I know you had a very tough labor delivering me, okay, give dad my love.'

I took a depth breath in and hung up the phone extremely frustrated with her constant nagging about meeting Bittu darling. Totally sucked the air out of my excitement and she doesn't give it a rest, she has to call every week. Hanging up the phone, everyone around me was well aware of my dilemma. They giggled away at what now was a weekly phone call of many "no's", lots of "I do love you", and lots of" I'm not ready" conversations. Everyone in my apartment had a good laugh at my expense.

'How many hours of labor has she gone up to?' Anya giggled as she drank tea.

'It was fifteen last week, now we are up to thirty hours. She's budgeting for inflation.' We all laughed knowing that mothers are the same everywhere.

The phone rang again and that's when I just lost it. It was probably her again giving me Bittu's number once more. I was losing it with her.

'Hello?' I answered very irritatingly.

'Oh yes, I am sorry, this is Sahara Solutions. Yes, yes we do specialize in Java, Html. Yes, we also have visual basic programmers. Sure let me transfer you to one of our Sales Engineer to setup a meeting. Sure, please hold one moment please.' Covering the phone, I gestured a screaming face to the others. Everyone panicked trying to decide who was going to be our Sales Engineer? No one wanted to take the call. We were all freaking out and no one wanted to be the first one to screw up our very first deal. I gave a stern look at Nikhil and asked him to take the information. Nikhil was dragged close to the phone and finally he spoke to the caller. He wrote out who they were, contact information and I scribbled additional information he had to ask like, when to meet them, where and who would be at the meeting. Everyone wanted to be part of Sahara but when the opportunity came, we all ran away like mice. But Nikhil did a great job of sounding professional and had setup our first meeting with our first client.

Once the call was over, Anand looked at me and we all started screaming. Oh my God! Our first client! We had our first meeting with some start up in San Jose, California called Capik Software. They were looking for programmers to design a website to allow people to put up suggestions for good buys of stocks, post current buy/sell trends in the market and allows people to execute buys of Puts and Calls. This required the front end that would allow people to setup accounts, manage portfolios and the back end would have to connect to the trading websites like NASDAQ. It was the real deal. All of us had programmed for class projects, but this was way beyond our skill set. Unlike class projects, this involved real people. This dealt with real transactions and real money! I felt very anxious and excited at the same time.

I knew that this was just the beginning of good things to come. It reminded me of those Hindi movies where a person is on their dying bed and everyone in the family and neighborhood is shown praying to different Gods. They show images of people praying to Krishna, some to Allah and some to Jesus Christ. After the beautiful song is over, the sick person recovers and everyone rejoices. That's what this moment felt like.

After the call had ended, we all sat around talking about where to go from here. Anya had made dinner and she placed a large plate on the table which had two large grilled fish with some vegetables on the side. That site of fish in the plate made me chuckle and I just had to try it. I tightened my jaw, squinted my eyes and said,

"It's a Sicilian message. It means Luca Brasi sleeps with the fishes." I gave a big smile at everyone. But I got NOTHING! Not even a slight smile from all these FOBs. They had no idea who I was imitating. I needed some white friends.

Nikhil had done a fabulous job sounding professional and setting up the first meeting. Our meeting was going to be over the phone. We had a conference call the next morning and Anand would be the chief architect in designing the database. Anya would be working on the front end and Madhu, Lakshmi, Kawal and Prashant all would help Anand. This project would require all of us to work together. This was not an issue because everyone wanted to be part of our new venture. Whatever skills we had, we all brought them to the table to provide the best of Sahara Solutions.

'I need you to look into the connectivity with NASDAQ, I need you to have a look at Capik and study their business model. Find out what kind of similar sites are out there and what software is commonly used for projects like Capik.' Anand went into his role immediately delegating tasks, making lists of things we had to get into line before our conference call. He assigned each person a task to complete tonight so that Anand was ready to speak to our first client. He had to sound knowledgeable about the industry, had to show experience and had to show confidence. The only way to sound confident was by knowing everything about this client.

As we sat that night going over the client, their needs, I took in this moment to look around. Here were some really cool, smart, dedicated people putting their minds together. The joy at that moment for me was immense. Everyone was on a machine researching, taking notes and willing to put everything into making this a success. I had a vision of the famous Dimple Kapadia* putting milk on a Shiva Linga*. Why I don't know.

We searched on websites, did background research on our first client and educated ourselves as much as we could on stock trading. None of us knew anything about stocks. It was almost 2am when we shut down the mini lab and everyone went home. With a few hours of sleep, we all had to be back at my place by 9am to listen in on our conference call. Checking my email that night, Bobby had sent me a message. He found out that Vinod, Jay Chand and Shahil were all gamblers and regularly attended the sports bar on Lincoln Avenue. He also said that Jay Chand had seen my picture in the papers and my name had come up a few times. He told me to be careful and that he would write back soon.

With all the excitement of signing our first client, I had totally forgotten about being seen in the papers. Now, Jay Chand and his buddies all knew that I had something to do with Sahara Solutions. If they did their research well, they would now know that I had started my own company. What would their reaction be? How would they try to stop me? With that fear in my head, falling asleep that night was hard. I turned on the jewelry show and watching the women going on and on about the ugliest shoes on sale, I fell asleep.

The next morning, 8am sharp, Anand and Nikhil came knocking on my door. Still in my pajamas, I dragged myself to open the door. Seeing me in my tank top and SpongeBob pajamas, the boys were speechless. They froze as I opened the door. Why are boys so stupid? I show my bra once and they can never see me as a person again. I let the boys in the kitchen area and put on a robe just so that they could start letting blood flow back to their brains.

Before 9am the whole gang was in my apartment ready to listen in on the conference call. Larry and Mili also joined in because it was one of the most exciting days for all of us. Standing by the phone, we all heard the call from the Capik manager, Mr. Singh. He was from California. He was building a website that would allow users to create an id and log into MyCapik and allow users to view their accounts. This website would allow users to see what the market was thinking of doing, if the market felt a company was a good buy, they would put their bids to buy a stock at a certain price, using market demands he wanted to move the stocks. He must have spoken for over an hour but given that all of us were all techies, we didn't understand 90% of what he was explaining. At least I didn't. He went in detail about the kind of back end database he needed and how the front end would look, and the dates of our deliverables. Most of the information went over my head but Anand was able to make sense of some of it. He had a working idea of where to start. He engaged intelligently with Mr. Singh and then came the price negotiation part. No one had any clue about what to charge. Mr. Singh wanted to talk to the President of the company to discuss payment. So, Anand handed me the phone. The look on his face reminded me of Captain Hook pointing his sword at Peter Pan as Peter walked the plank. I had zero knowledge about what this thing should cost? If I priced it over market rate then we could lose the project. If I was underpriced, we might look like we don't know what we're doing.

'Mr. Singh, hello, I am Ms. Sharma, how are you?' I said, dreading this conversation. What was I going to do? Mr. Singh went into his expectations from us and ended with asking about the price.

'Well, we depend on good relationships with our clients and Sahara Solutions would like you to be our regular client. So, price depends on your budget.' I was having brain farts at this point. Everything I had seen in Godfather, Ocean's Eleven was streaming in my head and I was searching for the number to give Mr. Singh.

'Well, we have started this project with the intention of spending little in the beginning to see if this even goes anywhere. It is a prototype and we are not willing to spend any more than $50K.' Mr. Singh said and waited for my response. But before I could say anything, Mili started barking. Larry rushed to take Mili out but Mr. Singh had already heard her.

'Did I just hear a dog?' he asked me. I was cursing Larry for ruining our image at this point.

'Actually, that's my Golden retriever, Mili.' Anya held her head down and Anand walked away from the phone call. Who has a dog barking in the background while making a deal? We had blown it! What kind CEO has a dog barking while negotiating price?

'How long have you had her?' Mr. Singh asked, still interested in my dog.

'We have had Mili for the past three years, she is a cutie!' I didn't know what to say, why is he going on about the dog? What about the price? How am I going to save this deal?

'I love dogs! I just lost mine. He was by best friend for a long time.' Mr. Singh seemed more interested in Mili.

'I'm sorry for your loss.' What? Why are we talking about this? I thought at this point we were so off track our negotiation. For sure we had messed up.

'Ms. Sharma, we would like to work with your firm.' Mr. Singh discussed his expectations and agreed to pay for the prototype. He also said that if this project was a success, then he could assign us additional projects he had in the pipeline. After a lengthy call, I hung up.

'And?' Prashant stared at me while everyone waited quietly to hear the number.

'$75K!' I said the number and I was airborne. Everyone was dancing in my apartment. I gave Mili a big hug because Mr. Singh loved dogs and because of her, he seemed to calm down and more open to negotiating. He had talked to a few consulting firms and we all had sounded the same with the same kind of pricing. Mili had set as apart from the others. Something about her had made him take a chance with us.

Sahara Solutions was on its way! We were ready to put our brains to work. Anand took the lead on this project and went to work. He was ready to create a model that would best meet the client's needs. We were given a time line of two months to come up with the first prototype. After the prototype was approved, we would get $25K. Once the prototype was completed and approved, we had to start development, which would take another nine months.

27

Since all of us were new at designing an actual prototype, getting started took a long time. We all argued about how to setup the prototype. Anya had her opinions about what the front end should look like and what features took priorities. I took out various other models currently used in trading stock and tried to replicate some of those ideas.

We were such novices at all this that we didn't even think about getting Capik to sign any contracts. I never wrote anything down regarding payments and never even thought about how he was going to pay us. When I sent Bobby a message about our client, he sent me detail contracts that needed to be signed by both parties. He also sent me liability release forms and samples of project plans that I could use to handle Capik.

Each day I was learning something new. Bobby was feeding me with all the contracts, prototypes and providing me with all the emotional support I needed. This project was running our lives. With school in the day time then this client during nights, we hardly slept. The first deliverable was due in six weeks and we were so behind.

It was Monday morning and I was in my regular rut of making it to class. While I was walking down the corridor, I was stopped by Mr. Jay Chand.

'Rushmi, Hello.' He stood in front of me with a pretentious smile.

'Sir, good morning.' I said in a small voice. I felt like he was going to kidnap me or maybe the cops were around the corner to arrest me. My heart was sinking and there was no one around me to protect me from this man.

'So you are the owner of Sahara Consulting is it?'

'Sir?' My face must have been red because I was ice cold and I could hear my heart racing.

'I saw your lovely picture in the paper. Nikhil tells me you are starting your own consulting company. You actually have a client is it?' I had never told the others about keeping Sahara and its clients a secret. Nikhil had never told me that he had spilled the beans to this guy.

'It is nothing sir, just trying to get some experience that's all.' I was looking around for someone to rescue me from this monster, but no one was around.

'Well, good luck, just don't let your grades go down. You don't want to disappoint your parents do you?' He stopped smiling and stared at me. With a moment of awkwardness between us, he walked away. What did he mean? Was he okay with this? Was he upset? I couldn't tell. I rushed to the lab and sent Bobby an email. I told Bobby about everything that had just happened. Bobby wrote back saying that so far they just thought that I was being adventurous and were keeping a close eye on me.

After that lovely encounter, I sent everyone an email about company policy regarding privacy and secrecy. Everyone replied back with various symbols such as the middle finger, such as a boy peeing on the wall in response to my email. Anya sent me a picture of a Walrus on top of a girl she had photo shopped. With these professional responses from my team, I sent them all another email letting them know that if they revealed to anyone about our existing clients, our projects or anything about us, they would not be allowed in my apartment nor get any of my free food. After that email, no one had anymore smart-ass responses.

By the due date for the Capik project, we had a working prototype for Mr. Singh to see. Bobby had worked on this with us until it looked incredible. Our prototype worked and looked professional, it had the features we were asked to provide. For being college kids, we had outdone ourselves. Anand conferenced with the client and did his first demo. In front of an entire room full of people from Capik, Anand did his thing. With lots of questions and answers, the demo got approved. The audience was impressed with our delivery and wanted to do business with us. Our first income of $25K was deposited into Sahara's bank account. The look on Anand's face was the cutest. He had stuck his neck out in front of the client and he had delivered a great presentation. Now, we were ready to go into development.

With that one client on board, we marketed the hell out of our company using Capik as a reference. Capik also sent us more work and in a period of four months, we had acquired five accounts. Everyone was managing multiple accounts. My apartment was now looking like the lab. We had multiple computers, multiple phone lines and everyone was busy day and night completing projects in addition to their own classes. Each account being so different, we all needed additional skills. Anand took a finance class, Anya got into an advanced Visual Basic class, I enrolled myself in an accounting class. These classes helped us to keep up with the changing demands of Sahara Solutions. It was like the scene from Santa's factory. All us elves working day and night to make our little company grow.

I was handling the monies coming in and monies going out. My heart sank especially writing big checks to purchase servers and software. My head would hurt at the end of the day looking at numbers, and creating the company balance sheet and cash flow statements. I was so confused about what our assets were, all I saw was liabilities. I was writing checks left and right. I had deposited the remaining $500K but still couldn't balance my check book. But we were a real company operating out of apartment 3A.

With just the twelve desi kids, we were up to our necks with deliverables, and project plans. Sometimes we had no clue on how to answer some of our clients' questions. We would take our challenges into the classrooms and use them as case studies trying to get ideas from teachers and other students.

'Hypothetically speaking Professor, what is a model to bill clients on technical projects? How do you calculate time and material cost in software consulting projects?' As I asked these questions, the professors would go into detail explain all the ins and outs.

Bobby had managed to stay connected via email. He actually was the brain behind the company. Guiding us on every aspect, he taught me how to setup sales calls, how to develop project plans, and how to develop company specific contracts. After returning home, he was now guarded with bodyguards making it very difficult for him to meet us.

Once we had the experience of handling a few clients, Bobby wanted to move up his plan. He now wanted us to target Blossom clients. He wanted us to under price our services and provide them to their clients. He managed to get a list of Blossom Consulting clients and our job was to get as many clients over to our side. But the task at hand was getting larger and larger. We had to expand our firm and needed a senior designer on our team who had some knowledge of Blossom's clients. We needed someone who could help us attain some of Blossom's customers. I sent Bobby an email requesting for Shrini to join us. I waited for his response.

28

It had been six months; we had delivered various projects to clients and collected $80,000. But no one got paid anything until we could show enough assets that would qualify us for sponsoring H-1s. With Anand graduating in two months, he would be the first. Bobby had sent us the contact of a Mr. J. Singh, immigration lawyer, who would start this process. If all would go fine with Anand's paperwork, we had a sure chance of making this work.

Returning from my class, I entered my apartment to find Jay Chand and Anand, Nikhil and Nukul inside my apartment! I knew the guys would be there coding but seeing Jay Chand, I was in complete disbelief. He was walking around my living room looking at the computers.

'Oh, come in Ms. Rushmi. Good to see you again.' He walked closer and shook my hand. He seemed to be smiling, but I could tell he wasn't happy.

'I hear you are the person sponsoring Anand! That is quite an achievement.' Anand had been giving him the $1000 for sponsorship but ever since Sahara took off, Anand stopped paying Jay any money. Now, Jay Chand knew I was taking a potential victim away. He seemed irritated. His presence made me very uncomfortable.

'Anand, are you sure you want to base your future on her abilities? I mean look at her, one day she is running in her underwear and today she claims to get you a job. I thought you were smarter than that Anand.' He was demeaning and humiliating me in front of others.

'Sir, we actually have a chance of…' Before Anand said anything about our clients, I interrupted him. I didn't want Anand to tell him anything about our clients. I didn't want Jay Chand to know who we worked with, who our clients were or how we did it.

'Mr. Jay Chand, I think you should go.' I looked into his eyes and despite being scared to death, I maintained eye contact. It reminded me of the Soap Opera shows where every scene is exaggerated for a few seconds. First, my eye contact would be fixed on Jay and his would be fixed on mine for the next ten seconds until the next scene. Then, Jay Chand walked over to me and said,

'I hope you know what you are doing. The future of these kids is on your shoulders. When you fail, don't come begging to me for help.' He was so good at putting doubt in peoples' minds.

'I think better to fail than to be stuck at Blossom.' I wish I hadn't said that. The look on his face changed immediately. He knew that I knew more about his scam than he had thought. The color of his face changed and he marched out of my apartment. I shut the door behind him.

Looking around at the others, we all had fear on our faces. Anand was partially regretting his decision about working with me. Nukul looked flabbergasted and Nikhil was panicky. After all, in their mind, they had banked their future on my small company. They didn't know anything about Blossom nor did they want to piss off the most influential man in getting their first job. In their eyes they saw one girl doing this business. I hadn't even told them about Blossom. I had to show everyone that they were in good hands. I had to show them that I could get Anand his H-1.

'Blossom? What do you know about Blossom?' Anand asked me. I didn't want to tell him anything so I tried to walk away but he stopped me. He looked into my eyes. There was no escaping his question. If I dodged the question today, I could lose these guys and everything we had done so far would be ruined. So, I sat down and told the guys everything. I told them about Bobby, Asoke, Abas, Vinod and everything in between. The three of them listened with complete attention. They could not believe that the person they all worshipped; was the man I was describing. Anand was shaking his head. He was not buying my story and with Jay Chand already feeding him doubt, Anand was ready to run after Jay Chand. He wanted to ask Jay Chand for forgiveness.

'You played with our future Rushmi. You played with all of us. How could you do that?' Nikhil was upset. With everything I wanted to do for these kids, they were mad at me! I couldn't believe how fast these guys were blaming me. So quickly they had turned their backs on me and so easily believed Jay Chand.

'Guys! Listen, this is ridiculous! You think I would do all this for what? My own company? Think about it. I am doing this for all of you. Believe me!' But, no one was listening. They picked up their backpacks and left my apartment. That night, I kept emailing Bobby for help but he too was mad at me. Bobby was upset at me for telling the guys everything about Blossom. He felt like I had jeopardized the entire mission. Plus, I had told Jay Chand that I knew about Blossom Consulting which made things worse. Now, I had enemies all around me. Sitting in my bed completely feeling crappy, I began singing the old Hindi song from the movie- Mother India; Dunya mein hum aye hai*….it was the only song that kept me from crying.

Early next morning, the phone rang and I heard my mother crying. She seemed completely hysterical and unable to talk. She handed the phone to my father.

'Rushmi, we just received a phone call from the Dean of your college. He told us that you were running in public naked? He said that you are doing illegal things in America? What's going on?' Hearing my father tell me this felt so humiliating. I didn't know what to say. Jay Chand had called them. He had done what every villain does- sabotage. The one thing Indians are most scared about is parental emotions.

'Dad, listen, it is nothing like that.' Where do I even begin to explain myself?

'So, you were not running topless?' I heard him say that and I didn't have anything to contradict him. I just couldn't explain to him why I did what I did and being in the state that they were, I thought it better to stay quiet.

'I'm sorry dad. It's just very hard to explain what I did. But, I didn't do anything wrong.' That didn't sound convincing enough. Mom got on the phone and had me promise on her life that I was not going to get pregnant. She said that my time in America was only until my graduation. She would visit me at my graduation and also invite Bittu so we could meet and that was final. With her state of being so upset, I reluctantly said okay. Jay Chand not only alienated me from my friends, he also had my parents filled with fear and doubt.

Jay Chand had planned on ruining my life. He notified the University about the lab in my apartment. Apparently, he wanted me kicked out or the lab shut down because based on University policy, the dorms cannot be used for any other purposes. Starting a company in the dorms was definitely not allowed. He also claimed that I must have stolen the computers and software because there was no way I could have bought this equipment. So, exactly at 9am, the University police showed up at my apartment. They searched through my entire place and took all my computers and printers. They sent me a penalty notice and an evacuation note. I had to empty my place in the next two weeks. This was the shittiest day of my life. Everywhere I looked, things had gone to hell. My friends abandoned me, Bobby wasn't talking to me, my parents were upset, and now this mess. I was in hell. I tried to imagine a movie scene that would best fit this very moment, but couldn't come up with anything.

I got dressed and sent Bobby an email reporting to him about what his wonderful father had just done. Then, I went to the University to see the campus news department. Jay Chand had played his card, but now, I had to play mine. I had seen this on National Geography where the eagle watches from a distance and studies the movements of her prey. Instead of reacting, she acts. Jay Chand had put me in a situation of reaction but instead of reacting to his direction, I was going to act on my own. I met with the campus reporter and asked her to join me in a meeting with the University President. I also printed cases of successful start-ups that originated in garages, basements and Universities.

I entered my meeting with the University President, Chancellors and Heads of various departments including Jay Chand. With the reporter in the office, I went to work.

'Universities are in the business of educating students. With the hope that these students will go out in the real world and get good jobs, start new companies and in turn, make the University famous. So, here I am doing exactly that. Yes, I created a small company in my apartment. I bought machines and created Sahara. But, all that I have done had been the direct result of the good education provided at this University. Now, you want to shut me down? That is idiotic. If you don't want us here, we will move our base to another University. But, this will be known as the biggest mistake in the history of this University.' I presented my case to the committee with enough evidence that every argument against me seemed small. They argued about liabilities towards employees in my apartment and how the University could get in trouble for that. But, since I had not paid anyone, no one was officially an employee. At least not yet. They argued against stealing school property, to which, I showed them proper receipts for all the equipment in my apartment. The campus reporter was in this meeting too taking notes profusely. She was a young girl in her first semester in Journalism and this was the biggest story she had ever worked on.

After the committee met behind closed doors, the President, Vice President and his secretary came out of the office to tell me that they had agreed to allow me to keep Sahara Solutions. However, in order to satisfy University policies, they would allow me to use my apartment, but there was one condition. I had to allow other students to do their internships at Sahara and the University could use our name for marketing purposes.

These conditions were actually better for us, I agreed. By the evening, all my equipment would be returned to me. With their approval, I sat with the reporter, Cindy Cohen, and gave her an in depth interview about Sahara. Jay Chand had tried to shut us down but tomorrow in the paper, he would happily read about us in greater detail. The University had actually helped in setting up additional interviews with reporters and this meant free marketing for Sahara. Also, with interns starting at Sahara, my job was even easier in swaying new kids away from Blossom. This had actually worked out better than I had imagined.

Despite my small victory, I knew that without my team, I didn't have anything. I needed everyone to be on board again. I had to go and convince them that my mission was not a flake and Jay Chand was not what he seemed to be. On my way back, I stopped at Anya's apartment.

'Hey.' I stood by the door for her but she wasn't too thrilled to see me. Nikhil had told her everything and she seemed just as doubtful. Entering her place the others were also there talking about me. As I entered, everyone stopped talking. Standing between these friends that I had known for three years today seemed like the most awkward thing I had ever done. My friends had become so distant with me so fast, it was ridiculous.

'I know you all don't believe me but I still need you guys. I can't do this alone. I don't have proof of Blossom but I just need you to trust me.' I stood there surrounded by everyone. It was a scene from the movie, Pirates of the Caribbean. It felt like everyone would pull out their swords and slash my body parts. I looked around trying to explain to everyone how I fell into this situation and what I was trying to do. But no one said anything. Then, the bedroom door opened and Bobby walked in.

'What the hell are you doing here?' Bobby was in Anya's apartment. What was he doing here?

'I had to come because you messed everything up.' Bobby walked over and seeing the stress in my eyes he hugged me. Smiling, he gave me the tightest hug which was needed so badly. I had felt so lonely without my friends that when he hugged me, I started crying. I hated being alone especially with the responsibility of so many lives. I was carrying a lot of burden on my shoulders. Bobby had come back just to prove my story. He had told everyone about his real identity and came here just to make sure that Sahara was still in business. I was relieved but the tears just kept coming. Anand also gave me a hug because he had now believed me. But, I think he just wanted to take the chance to hug me.

'I hate you guys. You just left me and believed Jay Chand. You didn't even consider that maybe I was right.' I sat next to Bobby as everyone sat on the floor.

'Rushmi, you know, I can't play with my future. My parents are counting on my graduation and expecting me to send money home soon. I'm sorry, but when I heard Jay Chand point out that you were one girl, that I based my future on your abilities, I had so much doubt.' Anand sounded apologetic but I think he had just insulted me. He was graduating in a few weeks and I knew the pressure was on.

'You have my word Anand, your H-1 has been filed and you will have it soon. Rushmi has already met with the lawyer.' Bobby reassured Anand who was obviously tense. That night Bobby went over some of his ideas in moving forward. I think knowing that I was not the only brains behind Sahara was reassuring to everyone. In a way, I felt reassured too.

'I can't stay longer, but, I think you all need a day off. Rushmi, why don't you do something fun tonight? You all could use a break.' Bobby sneaked out of the apartment and disappeared somewhere. With the stress of work, Jay Chand, my parents and my friends, my head hurt. Bobby was right, I did need a break. I actually needed a "Chandni movie" moment of rose petals being dropped from the helicopter kind.

We needed a night out. It was about time we all took a break. With the riff raff between friends, we needed an ice breaker. I hadn't been to any clubs ever since the stripper show and tonight I just needed to get away from all the worries in the world. So, we all decided to go to a bar called Piers. Ladies could enter for free and the guys had to pay an entrance fee. The music was loud, the dance floors were full and drinks were everywhere. The guys had not bothered to change, but us girls were dressed in heels and miniskirts. I was in the mood to be free, especially worry free. I felt like I had just aged five years with all the stress. We danced all night, did karaoke until people asked us to stop, we played pool and finally we drank a lot. Returning to my apartment at 1am, I had the most brilliant idea. I rented the A-team movie and made everyone watch it. It just had to be done.

Getting the team to actually enjoy an evening out helped tremendously. I felt closer to my friends again and finally was able to open up to them. After our movie ended and with the help of alcohol, I had to tell the guys the truth.

'Guys, there is something I need to say. I know it might surprise all of you and if some of you get hurt, I apologize. But remember I'm saying this because I care-you all stink!' I raised my glass and sipped my drink giving everyone a chance to absorb what I was saying.

'Seriously, guys don't you smell that? You all are walking chicken curry and samber smell. Seriously, open your windows before you cook.' I saw the looks on everyone's face and twenty four eyes were exchanging looks. Just then, Anand picked up a pitcher of beer and poured the jug on my head. Leaving me sticky and smelly, we ended the night as friends again.

29

It was Thursday, 8am and I received an encrypted email from Bobby. He wanted to meet this afternoon. With his body guards, he asked to meet at the Starbucks by Shelton and Stevenson Blvd. He even asked me to bring a brown paper bag filled with some groceries. It seemed a bit strange but without much choice, I looked through my kitchen shelves and didn't find a thing. With students always in my apartment, all my food had disappeared. I went downstairs to Larry's apartment where he was still sleeping. I robbed him by taking cans of soup, pasta and tuna and filled my brown paper bag.

Making it to Starbucks, by catching two buses, I entered the coffee place. I saw few people chit chatting, saw two large guys standing at the entrance of the coffee place and figured they were Bobby's bodyguards. One guy looked like Mr. T and the other looked a lot like Sylvester Stallone. Dressed in nice suits they acted like they were guarding the President.

Bobby was sitting at the corner table reading a paper. I even noticed his brown paper bag by his feet. He signaled to take the chair on the table next to him. Putting the brown bag next to his, he got up and picked up my bag and left.

Gosh! It felt so cool to do this switch-a-roo just like in the movies. I had to come up with another clever movie line, maybe, *get this bag you must*, naaah, maybe, *"Frankly, my dear, I don't give a damn!"* nope, would have to work on a better line.

I took his bag, bought some coffee and took the bus home. By the time I returned, the team was already working. Nikhil, Nukul and Prashant were busy doing their thing. Anya was working on her project and simultaneously reading for her test in class, which was that evening. These people were so hard working, so dedicated and really awesome friends. I had to smile just watching these guys doing an amazing job.

'Mukul, did you compile the code yet?' Anya asked without even looking up. Wait, what did she call him?

'Who's Mukul?' I took a step back looking at Anya who was now looking at me. Her eyes looked like they had been looking at the computer for hours. I could tell she was tired.

'Who's Mukul?' I asked again. She pointed with her pen over to Nukul.

'What? Mukul I thought you were Nukul? In fact, I've called you Nukul for three years!' I was surprised. Anya burst out laughing then Prashant then Nukul. They kept laughing until Anand walked in and Anya hysterically told Anand about Mukul. Now, Anand too joined in their insane laughter.

They had tears rolling out of their eyes but no one could hold the laughter to tell me what was so funny. It must have been 15 minutes, finally the laughter came down. Anand and Prashant, who had rolled on the ground tried to get up, looked at me and what I thought was an explanation, ended up being another 15 minutes of laughing hysteria.

Well, it wasn't long until I found out that Mukul, who had a stammering problem, tried to introduce himself to me and unable to say it clearly, I heard Nukul. Since then, I have basically called him by the wrong name. No one EVER clarified it for me. This whole time they changed his name to Nukul.

'Ha ha, very funny.' I took a break from these maniacs and went over to my room shutting the door behind. I threw the brown bag over my bed and changed my shoes that had been killing me. My pinky toe was being squashed all morning in these new shoes. Stupid sale. Nukul, I laughed quietly, it was funny. This whole time they must have cracked up every time I called him Nukul. I put on my slippers and got up from the bed. Just then, I saw bundles of cash falling off my bed.

The brown bag was filled with bundles of cash. Dollars just falling like a water fall. At first, I was scared. Really scared! What did Bobby get me involved with? I quickly picked up every bundle and placed it back into the bag. Inside, there was an envelope. I opened the letter and it read;

Rushmi,

Here is the money that dad has been collecting from students for the past few years. I finally found his hiding place and there is a lot more than this. I am hoping you will find a way to return it to its rightful owners. I hope to bring all of it to you soon, so watch for my emails and we will switch bags until all the money has been transferred.

About getting a senior designer, Shrini cannot leave yet. She is the only eyes I have in the company but there is one guy I will be sending to you. I have already talked to him. He should be in contact with you soon. Get rid of this letter ASAP.
B.

These bundles of cash, the cash for which these students worked so hard belonged to them. Some of this was Anand's money too. None of this was going to be used in any other way. No matter what! I had to keep this separate. Putting the bag in my underwear basket, I ripped the letter in a million pieces and trashed it inside the garbage disposal. Wonder how much money this Jay Chand guy must have by now? Wonder if I should put it in the bank? How will I return it to those 300 kids? But more importantly, we would soon get our senior designer. We desperately needed someone with more skills to help us out. Just then Anya called from outside my bedroom.

'Rushmi! Phone call!' Wow, maybe that senior designer was calling me already.

'Hello? Oh, hi mom. Good, yes, and how is dad? No, I didn't call him mom. Not now! I am not ready right now. Come on, please…., no mom….. I haven't taken off my shirt after that day mom. I don't have a boyfriend mom….. I do love you. Yes…, yes…. but, please…., let me think about it. I am not lying….. I haven't taken off my blouse promise. Give my love to dad.'

I hung up the phone. By this time, everyone could predict my conversations with my mother. But ever since Jay Chand got into her head, she had become even more paranoid. I couldn't argue with Mom because Jay Chand had faxed a picture of me on top of Derek to my parents in Zambia. After seeing that, she had become so overpowering. But to think that soon my friends would meet Bittu was equal to the time I had encountered the snake in the tree – devastating.

I knew Anand hated these calls. He almost wished that he would pick up the phone so mom would ask him questions. I bet he wanted to talk to my mom so that he could introduce himself to her. But for me, I was totally not into either one of them. One was a Walrus the other was Birthing Hips.

Within two days, I received a call from the senior designer who Bobby had referred to me. We setup the meeting at the college cafeteria where dressed in a white shirt, navy blue pants, holding an old backpack I saw Asoke waiting for me. My Gandhi look-alike that I had met at Blossom was the senior designer that Bobby had referred to me. He seemed so out of place. Almost frightened to be here alone, he was waiting for me. But one look at me and he recognized me too.

'You are that agent.' Asoke said and he smiled almost glad to see a familiar face.

'Actually, not an agent. I am Rushmi.' I put my hand forward to shake his but he took his time shaking my hand. Shrini had told me that he was getting his green card soon and was thinking of staying with Blossom because he wasn't sure how he would get started finding another job.

'I don't understand, Shrini had told me to meet someone for an interview. Are you interviewing me?'

'I am the one you're here to meet. But the interview is done. You're hired! You come with great references.' I gave him a big smile.

'You will get paid 75% of what you bring. Agreed?' I sat up straight to exude confidence as my business class had taught me, after all this was my first official hire.

'Is this a joke? Are you making fun of me?' Seeing my young age, Asoke was almost about to leave. I had to think fast. I quickly did the math, $1000 per month for 24 months, he must have paid $24K to Jay Chand for is initial H-1; this cash I had. Before Asoke could leave, I blurted out,

'As a signing bonus, you get $10K right now and on top of this you get $1000 per month in cash for another 14 months! If you're interested?' He stopped in his tracks. He turned to me and returned to his seat.

'Are you serious?'

'You agree and I will have the money to you in one day.' Looking into his eyes, I could see the doubt of a man has who has been robbed blind for more than six years. But one thing about sales; always be closing.

'But you must sign the contract today and start tomorrow. And, you don't tell anyone where you're going.' With some hesitation, Asoke shook my hand

and signed the employment contract. I had reprinted the employment contract from a business text book. The contract said SAMPLE on the top, but Asoke wasn't looking, so I quickly covered that part with my hand.

Asoke had threatened to leave if he didn't get his money by tomorrow. Before I gave him any more information, I asked him to check out of his old employment and meet me at the cafeteria the next day by 8am. Walking away from the interview, Asoke seemed completely confused. He just couldn't believe that I would give him the money. Thanks to Bobby, I had exactly what Asoke needed – money. Walking back from the cafeteria, I received an email from Bobby, it read;

Just heard dad talking to Vinod about you. They know you hired Anand and also know that Asoke is meeting you. Dad said he was going to take care of you, not sure how. Be careful.

Crap! More trouble! Now what would Jay Chand do? I was very nervous dealing with him. Something about him made me so scared of him. I had two more semesters to graduate and my biggest fear was that he would somehow get me thrown out of college. I bet that's why Bobby turned gay. I called Julie to help me to spy on Jay Chand for me. I had to have some idea about his next move so that I wasn't caught off guard. By being more active than reactive, I had to come up with an idea that would take them off guard too. I marched into Larry's apartment.

'Need your help.' I marched into his apartment as Larry was watching another football game which he usually did in the afternoons.

'I need you to create some technical difficulty for Blossom. Anything to slow them down.' I wanted a distraction for Blossom, so instead of me, they became reactive.

'What do you have in mind?' Larry was very handy, he could do anything concerning homes and buildings, but coming up with ideas was not his specialty. So, I had to figure out what exactly we could do? Maybe shut off the power?.....that would last maybe a day. Possibly shut down their systems, but they did have backups. Maybe a fire?...that was taking it too far. It didn't need to be something really big, just big enough to get them frustrated. Larry suggested plumbing issues. Maybe Larry could bust their sewer pipe? This would flood their basement and force the agents out of their pigeon holes. I was thinking major damage but Larry said that he knew an easier way. He had a liquid that should never go down the toilet but if it did, it would solidify in the pipes and not allow anything to go through. It was a "dirty" idea, but would cause just the right amount of issues for Blossom. They wouldn't even suspect foul play over such an issue.

With that plan in mind, he drove to Blossom headquarters. This would give them something to smell for a few days. It reminded me of the movie Animal House – was a juvenile move but great ideas come in small packages, literally.

That evening, I sent an email to Bobby for Shrini to meet Larry in the parking lot. Hearing about my plan, Bobby cursed me, but agreed to it. Bobby had also found out about his father's plan for me. Jay Chand was going to get me expelled on cheating. He had someone from Blossom type a complex code and email that code to my email account. When I logged into my school account sure enough someone named Shanker had emailed me the code for my html project and the email read…

"Here is the code for your project, I have completed it, please send payment ASAP"

This would definitely get me expelled. If Jay Chand showed the administrator this email, they would have to believe that I was paying someone to do my work. Since Sahara was already my company, everyone would easily believe that I had one of my employees do my work. Suddenly, the thought of my parents finding out and believing this would make them immediately pull me out. I would have no choice but to return to Zambia then be married to Bittu and eventually kill myself. There was no way I would let that happen. Now what? Even if I deleted this email, the server would have it and it would be easy for Jay Chand to pull it again as evidence. No, I had to outsmart him.

I emailed Bobby to have Shrini send out the same email to everyone at the University of Chicago. It was the only way. We had to infect the entire school system with the same email then no one could point a finger on me. It was like in the movie Jurassic Park when those dinosaurs moved in herds; we had to move as a herd so no one could spot me. Jay Chand was the fat guy selling dinosaur eggs and eventually he would be eaten by a Brachylophosaurus.

Awaiting the commotion, I arrived to school early anticipating the worst. Sure enough, I was called into the Head of the Computer Science Department office and there were the two professors involved with Jay Chand, there was Penguin, Pervert, Waldo and the University President. My code was on their table and a print out of the email from Shanker all ready for my execution. That moment reminded me of the Hindi movie Bhagat

Singh*, when all the white people are standing by, waiting to hang Bhagat. The only difference was that I was no Bhagat Singh. I was their worst nightmare.

'Ms. Sharma, we seem to have a problem.' The President, who had once supported my business venture, and whose name I could never pronounce, Gusteshapher, spoke in an upset manner. I could tell he was disappointed.

'What seems to be the problem sir?' I saw Jay Chand with his idiotic smile as he looked at me.

'I believe you have been buying your school assignments. We discovered this in your email. What do you have to say Ms. Sharma? You do know this is grounds for expelling you?' He continued to show me the evidence.

'Mr. James, this email is a mistake. I have never bought any code from anyone. Why should I? I actually am in the business of creating code; why would I need to buy it.'

'Then explain yourself.'

'Well, may I show you something?' I walked towards the computer on his desk and asked him to log into his account. He logged in and sure enough he had the same email in his account. Surprised he looked around and then asked Jay Chand to log into his account. Seeing the same email in his account too, everyone started checking into their email. Jay Chand was sweating as everyone started looking at him.

'What is this?' They all asked Jay Chand but Jay had nothing to say. He was lost too.

'Sir, it is actually a virus. It has infected the entire school network and when my team looked into it, we found the source of it to be coming from Blossom Consulting.' I hadn't finished my sentence when Jay Chand, Sunil and Mr. Jain started panicking. Hearing the name of Blossom in front of the other school admins made them freak out. They thought I would send the cops over at Blossom and then everyone would know about the concentration camps. The President made a few notes on a paper and had his secretary notify the FBI of the security breach at the University. He spelled out Blossom to her making sure the FBI had the name on file.

After making my move, I went back to my classes, leaving the three professors to clean up their mess. Yes, this time victory was mine. I could really use those rose petals at that very moment. With crisis diverted, I hurried to the cafeteria where I knew Asoke was waiting for me.

Anxiously waiting for me, I met Asoke. He was wearing the same shirt with brown pants sitting in the cafeteria. He was holding an old suitcase which was definitely made in India. He had resigned his old job, had $500 in his account and was the owner of one suitcase. It was a very sad moment to see a smart, educated and good guy like Asoke to be made into a homeless looking guy by those vultures. He really needed an ego boost. I knew he was horrified with what I was asking him to do. But, with Shrini's convincing and his hunger for the 10K, I had seduced him into joining Sahara.

I took him to an apartment complex not far from campus. I showed him one bedroom and two bedrooms apartments.

'Why am I looking at these places?'

'Well, you need a place to stay don't you? So let's find you a place. You can pick one room or share it by getting a two bedroom, pick?' I handed him an envelope, which he opened and found his $10K in cash.

'As promised!' I gave him a big smile. I was happier than he was. He was out of that concentration camp and into his own place. But Asoke didn't smile. He held the money in his hand, stared at it for a few minutes and then walked over to the window and cried. He cried and cried. He was staring out of the window of the apartment and he kept crying.

I could see in him the agony of what he had been through. What they all were going through. I could see how much he had struggled to make it in America and I could see how disappointed he had been with life. He had held his tears for so long, but today, they just came rushing out.

Giving him time to gather himself, I left him alone in the apartment and waited downstairs. He met me outside the apartment and thanked me. He seemed like he needed to be alone to just take all of this in. I was so happy that I had been there at that moment. The experience of giving someone hope and being the one to hold up the light, to someone living in the dark, was one of my most precious moments. It was a Swades* moment when SRK* finally brought light in the village.

'I want a one bedroom apartment. I don't want to share my space with anyone, please.'

'Absolutely! Let's get you set up.'

We signed all the lease documents and Asoke got his very first apartment key. I had already called Larry to pick up the finest furniture from his storage and helped Asoke move into his very first place. He wanted a few days before starting work again, so we agreed for him to start in two days. He wanted time to undo what Blossom had done to him and he also believed that whenever starting a new venture, always start on a Thursday. He had told me that last time he hadn't waited for Thursday but this time, he didn't want to take a chance.

Asoke had a lovely one bedroom apartment with a cute little kitchen and living room. Larry had found him a sofa set, dining table and a few utensils. But, I had promised Asoke, if all went well, he would be shopping for new furniture soon. I left Asoke alone and left his apartment. Walking downstairs to the parking lot, I saw him standing by the window looking into the far distant and for the first time I saw a smile on his face. He did look like Gandhi.

With Asoke working for us, we had a senior designer who would be able to design large databases, assist in complex projects and guide us in newer technology. Asoke was extremely aware of user friendly front end work; he would be guiding all of us reducing the time we spent figuring things out to half. He was so experienced and familiar with Blossom clients that with his help, I could move faster than we currently were today.

Returning to my apartment, I told everyone about our new hire. Bobby had sent an urgent message, which I had failed to read because of Asoke, but now that I looked at it, I couldn't believe my own eyes. Blossom consultants were all moved out into a motel until their bathrooms were fixed. It would take a few days to undo what ever Larry had done. This was brilliant. No one was coding at Blossom for the next few days. Bobby wanted me to use this opportunity to convince Blossom clients to switch over. With no one managing the phones, Blossom clients would definitely be looking for them. If I played my cards correctly we could easily do some real damage.

With the list in hand, we all started making our phone calls, "Mr. So and So, I think you should know that we at Sahara offer a better product for a fraction of the cost. Actually, if you are experiencing delays in your existing projects, we hope you will consider Sahara. We highly recommend you contact Blossom Consulting because most clients we have talked to, say that they are having lots of technical issues at their center." Every one of us was repeating this script with every Blossom client.

We had three days of Blossom shut down and three days to create panic in their clients. To top it all, Asoke was a big help! With him on board, we were able to make our existing clients happier. It took us less time to figure out what was once a challenging project. He even spoke to his old clients convincing them to try Sahara.

Asoke's presence amongst our group was thrilling. We all appreciated him. But for Asoke, he had not worked in a fun, casual environment before. Watching all of us monkeying around and having fun while working, was very foreign to him. For all of us, he was a brilliant coder; his skill set was remarkable and his talent was an inspiration to all of us novice programmers. Knowing where Asoke was coming from, we all boosted his ego as much as we could. Asoke brought with him thirteen new clients!

One thing I made sure during our initial hire was that Asoke was to work for us for only eight hours. Even when he wanted to stay longer, I insisted he leave. I just could not allow him to leave one prison and enter another. Even though we really needed him, everyone agreed after hearing his story that he just had to go home. We all were so happy for him.

After the three days of bathroom issues at Blossom, the revelation of losing thirteen clients to Sahara had pissed them off. Plus, with the FBI investigating the virus on Blossom, things had gone very wrong for them. To top it all off, they had to keep all 300 agents in a motel which cost them even more money.

30

With the thirteen new clients and existing twelve, we were running out of room to work. Every room in my apartment was packed and I was left with zero privacy. After Asoke's move to Sahara, getting more kids from Blossom was becoming more attractive. Bobby and Larry had found a bargain on a warehouse close to campus. Once used to store manure, Sahara Solutions headquarters was now being relocated. We needed more room and with the money coming in, we could afford it.

It was a thrilling adventure to clean this barn, setup tables in the open hall, with phones on each table, large monitors everywhere, a server room, one large office and a coffee area. It was one of the most wonderful feelings to have been part of such a venture. Everyone was in a state of awe and disbelief. We had actually pulled it off! Coming from my little apartment to this 5000 square feet barn, Sahara had definitely grown. It wasn't much to look at yet, and we couldn't bring clients to our site just yet but it was the most fabulous working environment. Asoke had taken the lead on our projects. He was directing everyone on each task and hearing about his success, we were able to get additional senior Blossom employees. With the attraction of the signing bonus and the testimony of Asoke, we were getting requests from so many kids at Blossom. We currently had sixteen H-1 transfers in the pipeline. It was a small number, but at least we had a path laid out for them.

It took us three weeks to clean out the barn and setup Sahara but the smell stayed in the barn. I figured the smell from all these desi kids would mix with the smell in the barn and eventually all of us would pass out. Once the barn was ready, we decided to make opening day the same day as Anand's

Graduation Day. Anand had graduated from college, received his H-1 from Sahara and now was about to leave for his sister's wedding.

We were in the office when Anand came in to talk to me. He was beaming with excitement and I was getting a weird vibe from him.

'Anand, here, I bought this for your sister's wedding. My best wishes.' I handed Anand some clothes and perfumes I had bought for his sister. He was a wonderful person, real asset to Sahara and I was glad he had been rescued from the tentacles of Blossom.

'Rushmi, I need to ask you something, before I leave for India, there is something I need to do.' He was hesitating to speak. I kind of had this weird feeling he wanted to talk about us, crap! I didn't want him to do anything like this. Saying no to him would mean our friendship might even end. Please, Anand don't say it.

'Anand, can't it wait?' I pretended to work looking at documents on my table.

'Actually, I wanted to ask something and I thought I better do it before I go.'

'Let's just get everything you need for the wedding.' I was speaking fast and heading towards the door.

'Actually, Rushmi, wait!' I took a deep breath and turned around. Guess it was time. He was going to ask me and I had to let him down easily.

'I am thinking about proposing to Anya!' He was very shy when he said the word Anya. I, on the other hand, was puzzled. Anya? Are you kidding me? Was he serious? Did he say the wrong name? Anya? Really? All this time he had this crush on me and now he's proposing to Anya! At first, I was extremely irritated. I mean, four years of being friends, of him practically drooling over me, and now he's proposing to Anya. He never even noticed Anya. This has to be a mistake. In my head, he's supposed to propose to me and I have to let him down gently. I always had my speech practiced. It's not you, it's me, we are great friends, I have never felt like this about you, and on and on, then me consoling him.

'Rushmi? Are you okay?' Anand was standing in front of me and a little taken aback by my unhappy face.

'Grreaaat!!, Wow! Anya right? Wow, I never knew you two were like this.' I said trying to keep my smile.

'Well, she and I have always been really close, but now I think I'm ready. What do you think? How should I ask her?' He pulled out a beautiful gold ring.

'I saw it a few months ago and bought it. I think I want to give it to her.' He was bursting with happiness. I felt so happy for him. He deserved a wonderful girl like Anya and he probably stopped chasing me because he knew I would have said no. Yeah, that's probably what happened.

'What are you waiting for dummy, go give it to her?' I held his hand and walked with him towards the door, but then, I had a great idea. I took him to the center of the project area, we had white boards all posted with clients lists, project plans, staffing lists and we also had a microphone we used to announce new clients to the whole team.

'Your attention please, we have an announcement of a major staffing change. Please, your attention please.' I handed Anand the microphone. He was sweating now. He had never imagined I would put him on the spot like this. But, I always believed in romance and if I was Anya, I would want it this way.

'Hello, Everyone' Anand's voice was shaking and his shyness was adorable.

'I have one thing to ask,…. Anya…. will you marry me?' The whole warehouse screamed and cheered. Everyone was clapping for the two of them. With all eyes on Anya, who was looking for a place to hide, she was airborne with five guys carrying her towards Anand. She looked like she would have melted away if she could. Once in front of Anand, he went down on one knee and held out the ring. With a smile and tears, she giggled and held out her finger. Anand placed the golden ring on her finger and they held hands as everyone whistled, screamed and cheered for them.

'Party! Party! Party!' Everyone was yelling.

'Throw a Party, you must.' I proudly announced on the mic. But, once again, got nothing back. Everyone was looking at me like "what's her problem?" These FOBs were no fun. It had been agreed, Anand was going to throw everyone a party tonight before he left for India the next day. That night at Piers, there was a great feeling among all of us. Watching Anya and Anand together, I was so happy to see them happy. Anand had also managed to get through tough times and was beginning to create a life for himself. But each time I felt like celebrating, I remembered people like Shrini who were still stuck in that insane place. They deserved to live, they deserved so much more than what those people were doing to them. I would be happiest when Blossom was closed for good.

31

It was Saturday morning and I had felt like staying in bed. With my apartment back to normal, I enjoyed the peace and quiet. But 6am and someone was knocking on my door. Dragging myself out of bed, I finally opened the door. There she was, Shrini, standing at my door step looking extremely distort.

'What happened to you?!' She looked like she had walked from downtown all the way to my apartment.

'Vinod found out that I had sent those emails to the University network. He threw me out and told me that he was going to get me deported.' Shrini was sitting on my sofa having a panic attack. I quickly got her something warm to wrap around and made her some tea. But she was inconsolable. She would have to leave the country in 30 days. With her visa cancelled by Blossom, even I couldn't help her.

'Don't worry, we'll figure something out.' I got on my computer and emailed Bobby. He was always the one with better ideas than me. Sitting in my apartment, Shrini talked so much about how hard her parents had worked in getting her to the US. How much she had tried to please Vinod and his buddies and she only had another year to go before getting her Green Card. Shrini held her head in her hands and cried. She reminded me of those Hindi movie scenes when the actress finds out that she is pregnant before marriage and is considering killing herself.

Giving her room to calm down, I got on the phone with the lawyer trying to find out if there was anything that we could do. It must have been 10am when another knock and another surprise. Bobby came to see Shrini. Bobby had never wanted to be seen in my apartment because he always thought that someone was watching me from Blossom. But today, he didn't care. Seeing

Bobby made me so relieved and I think Shrini too felt so much better once Bobby was here.

'Shrini, I knew something like this would happen. Did he catch you videotaping the facility?' Bobby was holding Shrini's hand.

'What videotape?' I asked butting in their conversation. I had never heard of any video tapes.

'I had asked Shrini to tape as much of Blossom Consulting just in case we needed something to black mail them with.' Bobby explained.

'I think that's what got me in trouble. They found the tapes in my room and that's when they looked in my computer and found out that I had sent out the emails too. They think I am spying for Sahara.' Shrini was still tearful. She had done nothing wrong, she was just helping.

I had tried all day in figuring out what we could do to save Shrini from being deported. But the lawyers all agreed that she would need to leave the country. There really was nothing much we could do.

'There is one way. You need to get married to a US citizen.' Bobby was hugging Shrini and doing a great job of comforting her. He was right. Now, the only thing that could help her was getting married to a citizen. But, wait, was he thinking that he would do this for her? Would he marry Shrini? Wasn't he gay? He couldn't just change himself could he? What about Shrini? She had the right to know that Bobby was gay. She needed to know what she was getting into. I felt torn between what Bobby was trying to do to help her yet he was also hurting her.

'Rushmi, we need to plan for this wedding. Not a small wedding, but a large, media focused wedding. I need your help.'

'Bobby, I know Shrini needs to get married, but don't you think she ought to know the truth? I thought maybe we should discuss this for a little while; tell her the truth about SOME things before making such a big move?' I didn't want to be the one to tell Shrini that the man she was marrying was gay. I thought maybe Bobby ought to tell her. I was taken aback about how Bobby was making such a big decision without being upfront with her.

'She is marrying me, what more is there for us to discuss?' Bobby held Shrini's hand and they both looked into each other's eyes.

'What?' I was a bit confused about how Bobby could so easily marry this woman, what about Roshan?

Bobby was looking at Shrini and they both were holding hands. After seeing my confused face, Bobby turned to me and said;

'Rushmi, I'm not gay!' Bobby held Shrini's hand and kissed her hand. My ears could not believe what I had just heard. What was he saying – all this time he was not gay? Did I convert him?

'What? What are you saying? What about Roshan?'

Bobby walked over to me and sat me on the chair. He said;

'Roshan and I were just friends. Dad had seen Roshan in the study, but he never saw Roshan leaving and Shrini walking in. All he saw was me kissing someone wearing Roshan's black jacket. Shrini had borrowed his jacket and that's when dad thought I was kissing Roshan. But, had it not been that moment, I would never have found out about Blossom Consulting. All this would never have been revealed to me. My only regret is that Roshan had to pay the price.'

'But wait, when you moved into my apartment, you said you were.' I stared at him trying to remember everything I had done during the days that he had lived with me. All the bathroom jokes, all the pillow fights I thought I was having with my girlfriend were fake? I had become so comfortable with him around only because I thought he was gay.

'Sorry, but you wouldn't have let me stay with you otherwise. So, I had to say I was.' Bobby held my hand to console me but I was mad. All this time he had pretended? But how could he have planned the heart pajamas, the Heff robe and his soft hands? What about all those lotions and colognes? Straight guys stink but Bobby always smelled good. I was lost. Was he gay and lying to Shrini? Or was he lying to me?

For sure, he had to be gay first because had he been straight all this time, he would have fallen in love with me. Impossible, he must be gay but just doesn't know it. I was convinced that I converted him.

'So, you are not gay anymore?' I asked Bobby again.

'Rushmi, I was gay before but after living with you, I decided to change my mind.' Bobby said that as he looked into my eyes. I couldn't tell whether he was mocking me or being serious. But, at this point, I bought his explanation. I think it was the time when we had our pillow fight. I knew we had a special moment and I bet that's when he had a change of heart.

'Rushmi, the Force is with you, "Help us, you Must".' Bobby said. I looked at him and smiled. That was the best Star Wars line I had heard from another person in these four years. I agreed to help them with their wedding plans.

'This wedding has to be done in the most extravagant manner. It must be with Media presence and we must invite every Professor on campus. Dad has to see this in front of everyone.' Bobby had a plan, which meant, we all had to get to work.

'Okay. So, we are sure about this wedding?' I asked both of them just to reconfirm if anyone was gay.

'Sure.' Bobby replied.

'Sure.' Shrini replied.

They both seem to have thought about this, but I had so many questions. If Shrini wants to go through her life with a gay husband then more power to her. There is no way Bobby isn't gay. He is lying to himself and to her. But, I wasn't going to say anything.

It was all agreed on. I called the local TV station, local newspaper and radio stations and the college media. Larry had spoken to the college administrator and reserved the gymnasium for this wedding in two days. Nikhil was assigned to get the cards printed. Every professor on campus was invited to attend and the entire Sahara Solutions staff was invited. With over two hundred people attending, we were busy planning this gay wedding -as I called it.

The entire wedding was being planned. We had to be ready in two days! Flowers had been ordered, food was being catered and enough decorations had been ordered to make the gymnasium look like a Reception Hall. In such short notice, we found a software engineer, who was also a Hindu Priest. The only reason he agreed was because I promised him an interview at Sahara Solutions.

That night, Shrini and Bobby spent the hours discussing all the legalities of the mighty Green Card. They were so involved in saving Shrini from being deported, focused on how Jay Chand and his buddies would react to finding out that Shrini had been helping Sahara. But, I felt like we were overlooking a very important moment. After all, we were about to have a wedding. Given, it was not an ideal wedding with the gay issue and all, but after all a wedding. So, I called the desi gang over, ordered desi food and forced a game of Antakshari. After all it was a special moment for Shrini and we needed to make it special for her.

Nikhil sang a song, then Mukul, and we went around in a circle singing. I saw Anand and Anya singing love songs and then Bobby and Shrini singing; these moments reminded me of moments when my parents would sing to each other. Grossed me out. The room was filled with happiness, doubt, frustration and fear. Bobby was taking a big step in saving Shrini and he was about to do it in a very big way. He wanted enough witnesses at the wedding just so that Jay Chand and his gang would not dare to harm Shrini. With the media talking about this wedding, Jay Chand would get all the attention he had been avoiding. One word from Shrini to the media, and the entire empire could go down. But, what Blossom didn't know was that we didn't want to shut them down, not just yet, we wanted to save the other kids.

The next day, I went to the Desi hub in Chicago, Devon Street, looking for clothes for the bride and groom. Both, Bobby and Shrini couldn't leave my apartment. So, using my camera, I took pictures of outfits that were ideal for the couple. After showing the pictures to the new couple, I went back and bought the happy couple a lovely red Saree for Shrini and a white grooms' outfit for Bobby. I also picked up a special wedding gift, the entire set of Dada Khondke movies.

That evening, when the entire gang was at my place, I was so excited to show them my gift.

'Guys, a little gift from me.' I placed the box on Shrini's lap. When she opened the box and showed everyone the movies, the whole place was happy and cheerful.

'Let's all watch it Bobby.' Nikhil said as he was putting the movie on. Shrini had a shy look on her face and the guys were giggling away.

Once the movie got started, the look on my face changed from a smile to utter embarrassment. Dada Kondke movies were full of double entendres, mostly sexual. He was so obscene and perverted. Watching that movie in a room full of men was so humiliating. This was no religion movie. This movie was full of perverted, sexual jokes that would make anyone blush. We must have watched twenty minutes of the movie, when I had to stop it. I couldn't take it anymore. The new couple couldn't hold it any longer and they burst out laughing. With their infectious laughter, everyone started laughing too. The look on my face must have said it all because everyone was looking at my expression. It was like the moment when a person first learns about sex. You can't believe that that thing goes where kind of moment. I couldn't make eye contact at first but then I burst out laughing too. This time, I was laughing with them. I finally understood their jokes.

32

The Hindu priest was on stage and the holy fire was burning. The event had started. Bobby and Shrini were sitting in the limo. They both were dressed as bride and groom waiting for the right time. Inside, the guests started arriving. Everyone was asked to come at 3pm, but the invitation cards sent to Blossom Management and Jay Chand said to come at 4pm. These cards didn't indicate a wedding, rather it read- Intel Corporate Relations Gala. This way, we were sure they wouldn't sabotage the event. But, Jay Chand had found out that Bobby was getting married and sent the body guards looking for him. However, the last place they thought to look was my apartment.

Just to ensure their safety, Bobby and Shrini had been hiding in a Limo and waited until the Media was present before they stepped out. Once the cameras were on, no one would dare stop the wedding.

Promptly, at 3pm Bobby and Shrini entered the gym. Bobby wore a white and maroon desi wedding outfit and next to him dressed in a gorgeous red Saree was Shrini. She looked so beautiful. She was wearing Bobby's mothers gold necklace, big pretty bindi and white flowers in her hair. She looked like Aishwarya in one of her movies. The two of them made a lovely couple, even though Bobby was gay. I was still convinced that he was faking it.

The ceremony was adorable. With every verse the priest recited, they both recited – To love and honor, in health or sickness. My favorite verse was:

Now you have walked with me around this scared fire. I will love you and you alone my wife. I will fill your heart with strength and courage. This is my commitment and my pledge to you.

Each verse was completed by the two of them walking around the scared fire as they held hands. It was beautiful. They smiled at each other. Shrini and Bobby took their vows in front of 150 people, and news reporters. Their wedding had made waves because Bobby was from a rich family and Shrini was from a poor family in India. Being the son of someone like Jay Chand, the reporters had rushed to see this event because Bobby had told them that he was handing over his entire estate to Shrini.

Sitting in the crowd, I spotted Jay Chand! He was sitting at the very last seat. He was observing his son's wedding from a distance. He didn't seem angry. Rather he looked hurt. I guess, Bobby being the only child, here he was getting married without his father's blessing. I guess, he could still feel.

When the wedding was over, Vinod and his gang arrived. They were carrying flowers. I think they still were expecting the Intel Gala. When they walked in and saw the new couple, Vinod and his wife stood speechless.

Bobby and Shrini walked closer to Jay Chand and touched his feet. With everyone watching, Jay Chand said,

'How could you?' Speaking softly to avoid any media attention.

'No, dad, how could you?' Bobby whispered as he hugged his father.

With that statement, the wedding had taken place on TV and in front of the entire University of Chicago. Bobby had tied the knot with Jay Chand's prisoner. Saving Shrini was not the only purpose, rather standing up to his father, who had loved him dearly but never understood him at all.

With the entire University present, Jay Chand was being congratulated by all his peers. In front of everyone present, he had to accept his new daughter in-law. He hugged Shrini, which was the most awkward hug I have ever seen. With reporters waiting for an interview, the entire Chand clan sat down to answer questions. Bobby was answering questions about how he and Shrini fell in love, what their back grounds were and then came the harder questions.

'My father has decided to retire and spend more time with his family.' Bobby explained to the media. Jay Chand was speechless. He couldn't argue at all. I think finding out that his own son was sabotaging Blossom Consulting; Jay Chand realized that his hands were tied.

Bobby announced to the media that he was the COO of Sahara Solutions. This news was the biggest shock of all to the entire Vinod clan. Their reaction to hearing this news was complete disbelief. Actually, it was news to me too! We had never discussed his position and today he made himself COO? However, with him COO, Jay Chand would get the message. He wouldn't go against his own son. They were done.

After that lovely event, everyone left. Left behind was a room full of Sahara employees, Jay Chand and the Vinod gang. There they stood, all exposed. Asoke stood their looking at people who had robbed him for the past six years. Everyone stared at these people who had taken away so many dreams. Today, united, we were taking back what was ours. We didn't need our father figure anymore, we wanted them gone.

Bobby talked to his father and their clan. With little to say, they agreed to all of Bobby's demands because they didn't want to go to jail. At this point, I would have loved to send them to jail but saving the other kids was more important.

Bobby had done it. He had played his last card.

33

Within one year of getting our new COO, Sahara grew from a one person company to over 300 employees.

It took eight months of constant oversight to get each and every employee transferred, but at the end, each one was worth it.

With my last year over, Graduation day was here! My parents were supposed to have been here before graduation. But, with the expected delays, they had just landed at O'Hare international Airport on the day of my Ceremony. They were going to take a cab and Larry would meet them at my apartment. Later, he would bring them to the Gymnasium. The ceremony was being held at the Gymnasium where four hundred and twenty three kids were graduating.

I got ready for my big day. Wearing my navy blue skirt and white collar shirt, I looked like I worked at American Airlines. I tied my hair in a bun and wore tiny pearl earrings, with matching navy heels, I was ready. My heart was pounding loudly for so many reasons. Graduation, seeing my parents after four years, not meeting Bittu but the notion of introducing him to my friends was making me go into cardiac arrest. Besides, as the CEO of Sahara Solutions, all 310 employees were here to see me graduate.

Entering the gym, I saw students had started gathering in the lobby area. Chairs had been setup in the main hall for the invited guests. There were so many parents with their proud graduates. I saw moms fixing their childrens' hair, some pinning the crappy graduating hats on their child's head with fifty pins.

I saw dads standing with their chests out with sheer pride of watching their sons becoming men today. I saw graduates beaming with happiness for completing such a big part of their lives. It was a wonderful moment. I was actually thrilled to have my parents here too.

The Master of Ceremony was getting ready and other invited guests were taking their spots. The main invited guest was Mr. Bobby Chand. He had been cordially invited because he was an alumnus and had hired so many graduates from this University. He had also developed the internship program and the success rate of graduates getting into great jobs had tripled. With his new found success, he was the perfect MC.

Parents were being escorted to the bleachers and we were asked to get in line. My whole gang had come to see me graduate. Anand and Anya had already set the date for the wedding and soon they both would get married in India. Nukul was back to being Mukul again.

Bobby was seated with his Shrini and they both seemed very happy even though he was gay.

The ceremony went under way. Bobby had some inspiring words about taking risks, about looking out for each other. He also mentioned that someone special had taken a big risk for him and in the end had saved hundreds of lives. Then we heard encouraging words from other invited guests too. Finally, our names began being called and I eagerly looked for my parents. I wished they were here so they could hear my name.

It was a beautiful ceremony. We threw our caps in the air and cheered for the class of 2002. It was going to be the most memorable years of my life for sure.

'Rushmi!' I saw my mother and father running towards me. Larry had been able to get my parents to the ceremony just in time. My mother, who I think wanted to modernize herself, wore a pretty Kurta with my dad's pants. She looked like an old hooker. They both hugged me for eternity. It felt so great to see them again. Four years had gone by and they seemed older and very tired. They had been so worried about me this whole time. Even to begin to explain to them what all I had been through was a daunting task.

'It was beautiful ceremony. We are very proud of you.' Dad was patting my back like I was his son. Mom was sobbing about having missed me, but quickly, she went into her mode of, you need to lose weight otherwise you won't find a suitable husband.

'Did you start the Monday fast as I told you?' She had already started her harassment.

'Congratulations.' Standing patiently was a tall, clean shaven, military cut, and well-built, good looking guy. He looked like a better version of my Walrus. I couldn't believe my eyes. It was like someone had pulled him and stretched him out thin. Wow! He looked so different. Could this be Bittu? He had lost maybe 200 pounds, grown six inches and lost the glasses. He looked better than anyone I had seen in a long time.

'Remember me? I'm Bittu.' He handed me a box of chocolates and flowers. He had really cleaned up nicely. This was a really great surprise. He was wearing blue jeans, white T-shirt and a lovely blazer. But the only thing that got my attention was his Yankee cap. He was a Yankee fan! I think I was staring at him. One thought in my head was the scene from the Godfather where Michael is hit by the thunderbolt when he sees Apollonia. I was just hit by the thunderbolt. Bittu was really cute. I was staring into his eyes when the rest of the crowd came towards us.

With everything I had tried to get rid of Bittu, he was just the one I was looking for.

'Auntie, we have heard so much about you. It's like we already know you.' Anya took my mom and Anand walked with my dad. Everyone was making their way towards my apartment giving me and Bittu enough time to catch up.

I walked with my Bittu darling, catching up on old times. He had graduated from the NDA which I didn't know meant National Defense Academy. He was on vacation for the next month. No wonder he had lost all that weight. Returning to India, he would start his training at the Air Force Academy. He wanted to be an Air Force pilot. The more he talked, the more I liked. But even more importantly, I had to ask him one question,

'Do you know what the A-team is?'

'Sure, the program with Mr. T.'

'How about Star Wars?'

'That's a classic, of course.' When I heard him say that, I knew he was the one for me. On our way back to my apartment, I found out his favorite movie was The Godfather. He enjoyed baseball but was more of a football man.

We walked into my apartment and the gang had setup food and drinks for my graduation party. Everyone had come to be part of my happiness. Today, I had so many people in my life that cared for me. The whole building was filled with people drinking and eating and just living the life they had once imagined.

I introduced Bittu to everyone. Amongst all my friends, Bittu stood out as the most handsome looking guy. I wasn't hiding him from others. In fact, I was showing him off to everyone.

He looked stunning. Once the party started, I had to do one very important thing. I had to play Antakshari. I needed to hear Bittu sing his romantic song but this time, I wanted to be in those dreams. When it was time for Bittu to sing, he sang a Krishna Bhajan. Not what I had expected. Maybe he was being careful because the last time he had sung a romantic song, I had entered his dreams and beaten him up. I promised myself I would be nicer to him this time around.

My mother was thrilled to see me get along so well with him. I hated to say it, but she was right again. Bittu was perfect for me. But, I still wanted to take my time with marriage. I wanted to complete my Master's program and not even think about marriage until Bittu and I had dated for a year or so. When mom heard this, she started with her guilt trips again.

'No one dates in our family. I never dated your father and we turned out okay. You have become too Americanized. Look at the length of your skirt. Had I known after thirty seven hours of labor you would turn out like this I would never have sent you to America.' She went on and on and on. Some things don't change. She was adorable. She had been right all along. So, I decided to drop all charges against her.

ABOUT THE AUTHOR

Yukti Singh lives in California and runs her own business. She has worked for Silicon Valley startups as an operations manager. Yukti holds degrees in Psychology, Finance and Information Systems. She has co-authored articles in the Journal of Psychology and has self-published a novel "Two Possibilities, a Journey we travelled alone" in 2009.

Learn more about the author at www.yuktisingh.com
Send your feedback at yukti@yuktisingh.com

CPSIA information can be obtained
at www.ICGtesting.com
Printed in the USA
BVOW06s0120160217
476315BV00014B/137/P